House
of
Silence

WITHDRAWN

SARAH
BARTHEL

KENSINGTON BOOKS
www.kensingtonbooks.com

KENSINGTON BOOKS are published by

Kensington Publishing Corp.
119 West 40th Street
New York, NY 10018

All Kensington titles, imprints, and distributed lines are available at special quantity discounts for bulk purchases for sales promotion, premiums, fund-raising, educational, or institutional use.

Special book excerpts or customized printings can also be created to fit specific needs. For details, write or phone the office of the Kensington Sales Manager: Kensington Publishing Corp., 119 West 40th Street, New York, NY 10018. Attn. Sales Department. Phone: 1-800-221-2647.

Kensington and the K logo Reg. U.S. Pat. & TM Off.

eISBN-13: 978-1-4967-0609-6
eISBN-10: 1-4967-0609-9
First Kensington Electronic Edition: January 2017

ISBN-13: 978-1-4967-0608-9
ISBN-10: 1-4967-0608-0
First Kensington Trade Paperback Printing: January 2017

10 9 8 7 6 5 4 3 2 1

Printed in the United States of America

For
Mom and Dad

$\mathscr{P}$ROLOGUE

May 1875
Bellevue Sanitarium, Batavia, Illinois

The shadows from my flickering candle shifted against the rose wallpaper so rhythmically that I began to question if I actually belonged in this sanitarium. No matter how grand they became, I resolutely ignored the reflections. To acknowledge them would cost me more than I was prepared to pay.

As I did every evening, I sat on my bed with a copy of *Jane Eyre*. In vain I hoped to find answers through Jane's and Bertha's unfortunate fates, but no revelations came. They were the product of unfortunate circumstances . . . perhaps I was no better.

A slight shift in the room's color made me look up. My breath caught in my throat.

My neighbor stood in the doorway. Her silence added to the stillness until it felt as if I'd implode. Her loose, dark gray hair was stark against her pale pink nightgown. Without her hoop and mounds of skirts, she looked slight, like half a woman. Yet, her presence grasped for my attention as if she were the president himself.

Her eyes met mine and they pierced me with sympathy. I shifted my gaze to the hallway. Surely at any moment, Nurse Penny would appear to return this intruder to her room.

But no one came.

Her nightgown shifted in the slight breeze. Every few moments she twisted her head and regarded me from a different angle. The silence grated on me as much as her presence frightened me.

Perhaps I should have demonstrated my insanity by screaming and pulling on my hair, but I was so tired of pretending. Besides, something about this woman told me that my act wouldn't fool her.

After what felt like ages, she stepped over the threshold and into my room. Her stride was careful and deliberate. Her movements showed her age more than the gray in her hair did. She was old beyond her years.

"Speak to me, child," she commanded.

I clutched the book to my chest as if it could shield me from my troubles. Even though she'd already attacked me once, I wanted her to like me.

"We all have our reasons for silence. Yours will end." Her words made my heart race.

She didn't know why I was here or why I remained mute, but she showed more empathy than Dr. Patterson had. Despite this, her kindness chilled me. I couldn't allow myself to trust anyone. Trusting Gregory was how I got into this predicament. I refused to make the same mistake twice.

"If you need anything, you come see me. Dr. Patterson told me to watch out for you, and I intend to do my best. Understand?"

Unable to respond any other way, I nodded.

She tilted her head and read the title of my book. A smile

pulled at her mouth. *"Jane Eyre.* There ought to be more heroines like her. She shaped her own destiny and let no man decide for her." She smoothed a wrinkle out of my bedspread.

My mouth dropped open at her declaration. So many friends didn't understand my attraction to Jane's character. This woman, older than my mother, was a true kindred spirit. A bit of my determination crumbled.

She must have noticed my warming to her for she demanded, "Make room," and sat beside me. I pulled my legs to my chest.

She took the book from my hand and flipped back to the beginning and read aloud, "'There was no possibility of taking a walk that day. We had been wandering, indeed. . . .'"

Thus my friendship with Mary Lincoln began.

CHAPTER I

March 1875
Oak Park, Illinois

It wasn't fair that before my engagement party began, I was faced with choosing between my fiancé and my best friend. As I stood looking down at the crowd forming in the Town Hall's entryway, my stomach rolled uneasily. At that very moment, Lucy, my best friend, was secretly marrying her love. Her logic made sense: With everyone celebrating at my party, she and Patrick would have no trouble sneaking a few towns over and pledging their lives to one another. Patrick was leaving for Montana in a few days, and they needed to be sure Lucy couldn't be married off by her parents while he was gone. Which was wise, as Lucy's mother was busy mingling with a variety of eligible gentlemen. The moment Patrick was out of the picture, she was prepared to pounce.

We were both being wise to secure the lives we wanted. My Gregory was the man I had always imagined marrying: charismatic, smart, and handsome. We would create a wonderful life together. I had put a lot of thought into my decision. Lucy had too, only her thoughts were more of love than practicalities. For example, how would her secret wedding impact our friendship? Gregory wanted to pursue politics, which was the main reason I accepted his proposal, but having close friends who eloped could ruin his chances for a nomination, let alone victory.

But, I could no sooner give up Lucy than I could give up air. It didn't matter what crazy thing she decided to do. I'd support her through it just as she would me. Through a slit in the balcony's curtain I examined the crowd and located her parents. Mrs. D'Havland wore a blue satin gown cut to the peak of fashion. However stubborn the D'Havlands were, they had impeccable taste. As I spied on her, she gestured toward the entrance and invited someone to join them. I waited for their guest to emerge into the crowd and sharply inhaled. Those bouncing blond ringlets gave her away before I saw her face. Lucy! What was she doing here?

I dropped the curtain and began pacing the small room. What had gone wrong? Lucy should be saying her vows, not celebrating my engagement! It was at such moments I missed Papa. The emptiness his death created left me breathless. Mother had fretted over our year of mourning, as I was without suitors when Father passed. No matter her argument, I refused to shorten my grief. If I had, I wouldn't be standing here celebrating my engagement to Gregory. I smiled. Father would've liked my choice in husband. Had the fever not taken him, he'd have probably found a way for Lucy's family to accept Patrick as well. The lining of my gloves scratched against my fingertips. I yanked them off.

Behind me the door opened, flooding light into the room. Mother glided toward me, her gown skimming the floor. I had never mastered her gracefulness. She stopped when she saw my gloves.

"They're about to announce you. Why aren't you ready?"

Leave it to Mother to turn what could've been a meaningful moment into one of ridicule. Of course, it must be some huge personal flaw that left me without gloves.

I pulled them back on and buttoned them closed at the wrist. "I'm ready," I insisted.

Whether I was or not, the curtain pulled open and I stood before everyone. My dark purple gown had been selected not only because it highlighted my brown hair and eyes, but because it popped against the light green curtains and cream walls. Mother also insisted that purple would convey a regal tone to all who saw Gregory and me. Personally, I was happy with the gown more so because the alternative was an amber monstrosity. Thank goodness for small favors.

"May I present Oak Park's own Isabelle Larkin and her fiancé, Gregory Gallagher." Uncle Walter's announcement made me catch my breath. The importance of this moment overwhelmed me. I was claiming Gregory as my own, forever. I'd never been shy, but I'd never made this kind of commitment before. I was stuck in place.

Gregory appeared beside me as if from nowhere. Taking my arm in his, he escorted me down the stairs as if it were the most natural thing in the world. To him, no doubt, it was. His blond hair put me in mind of a greased turkey, but I didn't let it show upon my face. He was the one who asked Mother for advice on men's hairstyles. As he met my eyes, his mustache twitched as he struggled to avoid a smile. True to form, he held to propriety and said nothing, but looked out over our guests. I followed his lead.

The moment we touched the marble floor, he led me to the center of the dance floor and grasped me in his arms. His hand was firm against my back as he prepared to lead me. The confidence in his grasp put butterflies in my stomach. We were the couple of the moment and he would make us shine. I lifted my skirt with my left hand as the band took their cue and began a waltz.

All worry for Lucy evaporated from my mind as he whispered in my ear, "Let us make all lovers jealous with this dance."

Before I could reply we were twirling around the ballroom. Never before had such a smart-looking couple danced so gracefully. Ours would be a profitable marriage, for he had good instincts and I followed him well.

The music gave a final swell and then faded out. I pulled my eyes from Gregory's and glanced around at the circle of friends that had formed around us. Their applause roared in my ears. In the front, mere steps from us, Senator Quincy's wife whispered something to her husband as she gestured toward us. Mother stood beside them and gave me a pointed look.

"Kiss me," I insisted.

Gregory grinned down at me. His breath tickled my ear as he whispered, "That may take the point a bit far. Your mother is already eyeing us." I smiled despite myself. I knew these people better than he and tonight I'd draw the line of decorum.

"You have won my affection. Now it is time we capture the hearts of everyone else. Kiss me."

His lips pressed against mine so quickly I didn't have to mimic my surprise. I gasped as he pulled me close to him and purposefully melted my body against his. No doubt, to our guests we seemed ardent in our mutual affection, but I was too focused on appearing blissful to actually feel anything.

Gregory pulled away as quickly as he began. "She is a vision of beauty. I couldn't help myself," he announced as everyone clapped.

I had demanded his embrace, and still my face felt warm with embarrassment. Mother's friends were surely taken up in Gregory's desire of me and the romance of it all. Every family in town courted Gregory when he arrived and yet he chose me, a girl of twenty who was still mourning the loss of her father. Not only did he ignore other women, but he waited to call upon us until the mourning year had passed. I know those who lost men in the war noted his patience and would remember it. Slowly, we were gaining respect and status. I glimpsed at Mrs. Quincy's wet eyes and broad smile and knew my trick had paid off.

Mother strode to our side, hushing the crowd. "I know your father would've joined me in wishing you every happiness, Isabelle." It should've been Papa who spoke. For a moment, I thought I saw the same loss cross over her face, for she flushed and looked around as if he might appear and speak. Composing herself, she opened her mouth to continue, but was interrupted.

"Darling niece," Uncle Walter declared. "May your loveliness shine joy upon you both for years to come."

"As I've no living family to speak for me, I humbly thank you for welcoming me into your community and allowing me to meet this beautiful creature." Gregory pulled me to his side.

"Isabelle, you are a woman of class and integrity. I only hope that one day I can claim to honestly deserve you. Until then, I shall do all I can to make you happy."

Gregory's cheeks flushed as he kissed my hand. Ladies around us sighed, but for once, I didn't observe whose heart he'd inspired. I was too moved by the flutter of emotion inside myself to bother.

The orchestra struck up a new song and the floor around us quickly filled with couples and well-wishers.

"There are several gentlemen I'd like you to meet, Gregory," Uncle Walter said, glancing toward a group of men across the room, including the president of our bank, our local congressman, and several others. Gregory's eyes lit up. I was not so naïve as to ignore the influence Uncle Walter's connections would have upon Gregory. Having a family member who was already in Washington would make our ambitions much easier to achieve.

"That is the point of this gathering." Then, turning to me, he added, "Besides celebrating our engagement."

Someone jostled my back. "Of course. Uncle Walter, take care of him."

The two men laughed at my words.

"Join us?" Gregory tugged my arm gently.

Tempting as listening to Uncle Walter's friends was, there were other people with whom I needed to visit.

Glancing around the room, I spied Lucy standing alone beside the tall stained glass window. "I think I'll let you go uncover the secrets of Washington society. Lucy is waiting for me."

Uncle Walter nodded. "Mr. Melton has some horse-breeding questions."

Gregory laughed. "I'll answer what I can. You know my folks died before I was old enough to learn much of the business, but any Kentuckian worth his salt has some horse-breeding knowledge. I think we are born with it."

"No one would ask for more than that." Uncle Walter clapped Gregory on the back and turned him toward the waiting circle of gentlemen.

Letting himself be led, Gregory glanced over his shoulder and promised, "I'll find you soon."

Once he was gone, I hurried across the dance floor to where I last saw Lucy. A few of the couples paused to wish me well, but I merely nodded. Lucy waited for me beside the rose garland and I refused to be waylaid.

Up close I could see the disappointment radiating off her. Doubtless no one else noticed how her handkerchief wasn't exactly folded in her hand or that her smile pinched her cheeks.

"I didn't think you'd be here," I blurted out as I took her hands in mine.

Lucy raised her finger to her lips, urging me to be quiet. "Patrick's mother is ill and he needed to leave immediately to be with her." She turned toward the window, where no one could watch us speak. "Now, I've nothing to prevent Mother from marrying me off." Tears brimmed in her eyes. "She's already invited Mr. Stewart over for dinner next week."

"Surely Patrick will return soon and you will wed. He'd not part with you for a moment longer than necessary." I squeezed her hand.

"You don't understand, Isabelle. Your mother loves Gregory. If you didn't marry him, she'd probably do so herself. But Patrick is tainted by his father's treason. So long as he remains here, that act will taint his life." She paused, then met my eyes and continued. "Once he has a home and land, I plan to follow him west."

"What?! No!" The words flew out of my mouth without caution. "I cannot imagine setting up house or raising children without you next door. Do you even know what you speak of? There are savages in the west who would sooner skin you than look at you. You can't be serious."

"I will not survive without him." Lucy's voice was soft, but firm. "You chose Gregory because his dreams match your own. Never have you mentioned love. I accept that is your choice. Now, please accept mine. I love Patrick and will make whatever sacrifice I must to maintain that love."

Her shoulders squared as if she braced for some kind of impact, but I couldn't yell at her. She had what everyone wishes for—the love of a good man. I'd not make her feel guilty for it.

"I hope Patrick knows how lucky he is to have you." I pulled her into a hug.

"Oh, Izzy! Thank you. I was so worried you'd be angry. This is such a relief."

Behind us, the orchestra struck a new tune. In the corner of my eye, couples switched partners and prepared for the polka.

"Lucy, I could never stay mad at you." I paused, struggling with how much honesty I owed her. "You are my best friend.

The last thing I want is for you to leave, but I can respect your choice."

If she was going to elope, their move to Montana might actually prove to be positive. With so much distance between Lucy and me, Gregory would have no reason to prevent our friendship. That realization calmed my heart, even as it shamed my pride. Could I really let propriety dictate who our friends were?

Half listening to Lucy's designs for her future house, I searched the crowd for Gregory. Locating Uncle Walter's tall and wide physique was easy, but Gregory no longer stood with that group of men. I frowned and kept looking through the couples, wondering what had caught my fiancé's attention over such influential gentlemen. Just as I was scowling at Mother's flirtation with a stranger, I spied him. By the side door, he glanced back and forth as if looking for someone. I rose to my tiptoes and waved to him, hoping he'd find me quickly through the crowd. Instead, his unfocused eyes drifted over me, and before I could make another movement, he slipped out the door and onto the veranda.

Lucy stepped close beside me and clucked her tongue. "What on earth did he leave the party for? You can still feel the rain's chill in the air. Surely no one is visiting outside tonight." As she so often did, Lucy had voiced my thoughts perfectly.

"Perhaps he's ill." I bit my lip anxiously. "I have to make sure something isn't wrong."

Lucy nodded. "Of course you do. We'll talk later."

Skirting the edge of the dance floor, I made my way past the dancing couples and to the side door without anyone stopping me. The windows were fogged with the unusually cold weather. I pulled the door open, shuddered against the wet wind, and slipped outside.

The veranda was drenched from the afternoon's rain, but it was deserted. Gregory was not there. Folding my arms around myself, I searched the wraparound porch, but still couldn't find him. I was about to give him up for lost when I heard voices from behind the tall evergreen bushes. The wind blew and my eye was drawn to the hem of an ivory skirt billowing below the bushes.

"Gregory?" I called out. I'd no desire to intrude on a couple's private moment if it wasn't him. "Where are you?"

The voices halted. The skirt moved back toward the entrance to the gardens. As she stepped out I was surprised to see it was a woman in servant's attire. Her hair was tied back in a low braid and her arms were covered with linen to protect her sleeves from stains. She was a washer girl. She bobbed her head to me, grasped her skirt, and rushed back toward the servants' entrance.

A moment later another crunch of footsteps gained my attention. I turned my head back toward the lane and saw Gregory adjusting his cuff links as he gaily climbed the steps.

"Isabelle, what on earth are you doing outside?" He smiled up at me.

"I could ask you the same question." I frowned. "Who was that girl?"

He glanced at the servants' door and then shrugged at me. "She asked me for a private word. I didn't see the harm in it. I was worried there was a problem and hoped to solve it without distracting you or your mother. But, alas, she thought I was someone she knew. It was a mistake. I'm so sorry I troubled you."

Inhaling sharply, I asked, "Are you sure that was all it was? A . . . misunderstanding?" If it was that simple, why were they hiding in the garden? I wanted to question him harder, but the look on his face stole my confidence.

Gregory stepped back and glared at me. "Whatever else could it be? We must be missed. Let's go back inside." He took my hand, ignoring my obvious distaste of his attitude. When I didn't move fast enough he gripped me harder and pulled me toward the door. "Let's not make a scene. No one will think it strange we wanted a moment alone at our engagement party. Nevertheless, it is time to return."

When we entered, the orchestra struck up a waltz and I glided in Gregory's arms the rest of the night. Together, nothing could stop us.

CHAPTER 2

With the engagement properly announced, Mother wasted no time planning the wedding. She probably had these appointments arranged for at least a month. The morning after the engagement party I had hoped to spend resting, but instead Mother dragged me from appointment to appointment until I was sure I'd smelled every flower in Illinois. It would have been fun if any of my opinions had been taken into consideration. I held my complaints, for we'd yet to undertake the most important task: the creation of the bridal gown. I could handle having roses instead of lilies and hiring a string quartet instead of a single violinist for the church, but the gown would be my taste.

After standing on the pedestal at the dressmaker's for nearly two hours, I could hardly remember what design I wanted. Discarded fabric bolts lay in a pile, rejected. Miss Margaret, our seamstress, was pinning the beaded ivory fabric we had chosen for my shift. I tried to remain still, but it was taking so long the excitement was wearing thin. Even so, I did my best to watch Mother, who continually pointed out details to Abigail, our maid. Poor Abigail had been brought along to collect our packages and take them home before we had lunch with the ladies. It wasn't a part of her duties, but Mother insisted that having her with us would turn people's heads. In my opinion, we looked pompous, but I could only fight with Mother so often.

"I dare not lace her any tighter or I'll crack a rib," Miss Margaret explained while keeping a protective hand on my back.

Mother frowned and tapped her finger on her lips. She paced back and forth in front of me and clucked her tongue. "People must remember this wedding. It needs to be the social event of the year. For that to happen, Isabelle must be breathtaking."

"But, Mother," I said between the shallow breaths the lacing permitted. "Need I be breathless in order to be breathtaking? Or perhaps you wish my guests to remember this wedding due to the bride fainting."

"Impertinence is not an enjoyable quality," Mother declared. "And it is certainly not a quality that Gregory will put up with."

I glared at her as Miss Margaret filled her mouth with pins for another adjustment. I knew that neither Senator Quincy nor Uncle Walter would be interested in Gregory's career if he weren't joining our family. Despite that, Mother's words set off a warning alarm. Marriage would not gain me independence, but a husband I would be sworn to "love, honor, and obey."

I made eye contact with Abigail in the mirror, imploring her to say something. Someone had to be on my side. After a moment she stepped forward and cleared her throat.

Abigail glanced from Mother to me, and the weight of what I was asking fell upon my shoulders. She couldn't speak against Mother, not without consequences. Even so, Abigail walked to the far side of the room and flipped through a catalog on the side table.

"Pardon me, Miss Isabelle," Abigail said, holding up the book. "But didn't you ask me to remind you of a design you saw in Godey's?"

"Oh my, yes. Thank you, Abigail. I nearly forgot!" Ignoring

Miss Margaret, I stepped off the platform and rushed for the book in Abigail's hand. She'd opened it to the fashion plate in the beginning, and her finger pointed to the center girl. The skirt had countless layers in varying lengths, each finished with a ruffled hem. The effect made the waist look smaller without seeming garish.

"See, Mother?" I handed her the book. "I thought, perhaps, this kind of skirt would look wonderful. See how the layers give the illusion of a tiny waist?"

Abigail took a bolt of fabric from Mother's grasp and placed it back on the rack. Adjusting the book in her hands, Mother examined the gown. Her tongue clicked again and she tilted her head.

"Very well," she relented. "However, the bodice on this is all wrong. This high cut is too matronly. Perhaps if we lowered it to here?" She pointed to just above my bosom. "And then layer lace over it to give her the propriety needed."

Miss Margaret grabbed a sketchbook and let her hand fly as she drew out the design.

"Like this?" she asked, holding out the book for us to see.

I gasped. Without knowing it, I had guided us to my dream gown. The tiered skirt and fitted bodice would be perfect on my frame, and the lower neckline would highlight my femininity without shocking the world.

Miss Margaret pulled out her measuring tape and went to work taking all new instructions for the dress. I stood with my arms out and blandly stared into the mirror. Abigail stepped to the side and met my eyes. The smile on her face was genuine. She had helped and I was grateful. I'd have to find a way to show it.

Later, Mother and I left Miss Margaret's shop and walked down Main Street while Abigail trailed behind weighed down with our packages of jewelry, hats, and other trinkets Mother insisted on purchasing. I tried to avoid the puddles and horse droppings as gracefully as possible, but knew I failed by the edging of dirt that congealed at the bottom of my skirt. Mother strode smoothly through it all while twittering on about how lovely the engagement party was and what a success Gregory had been with all the ladies. It was as if I hadn't been there at all. I hid my disappointment with a smile and pretended to agree with her observations.

Through the Town Hall windows, I could see men sweeping the floor and pulling down the flower arrangements from my party. I paused for a moment. Abigail stopped beside me.

In a loud voice she declared, "Miss Isabelle, shall we look for your glove?"

Mother turned to face us. "Your glove?" she asked me.

I stared at Abigail, unsure of what she referred to, but her big eyes implored me to play along. After her help at the dress shop, I couldn't embarrass her.

"Yes," I concurred. "My glove."

Abigail relaxed and filled in the details. "I couldn't find it after the party. Perhaps one of the girls found it here as they cleaned."

Mother, now bored, looked on toward Hotel Horizon with impatience. I knew she was longing for a bowl of their wonderful chowder.

"Why don't you go on ahead, Mother?" I suggested. "Abigail and I will inquire after my glove and meet you promptly."

"Don't be too long, dear," she insisted. "You don't want to miss lunch." Before waiting for a reply, she rushed off down the street.

Once she was out of earshot, I turned to Abigail. "What was all that about?"

Abigail motioned for me to follow. "I know this is highly improper, Miss Isabelle, but I promised someone an audience with you."

Balancing her load in one arm, she ushered me through the side door. In the bright light of midmorning, the hall wasn't nearly so grand. Instead of glistening with promise, now the flowers wilted and hung oddly from the banister, while huge boxes lay on the floor waiting to be packed up with the serving ware.

"This way," Abigail said, walking toward a back room. I followed, wondering whom I was about to meet.

Abigail pulled another door open, and we entered a small room lined with wooden shelves, where a girl sat at a table shining a tarnished silver platter. The girl's blond hair was braided down her back over a blue uniform and white apron. She looked up as the floor creaked.

"Miss Isabelle!" The girl jumped to her feet. "Abigail, how did you manage—never mind, thank you."

Abigail gripped the door, obviously uncomfortable. "This is Katerina," she explained to me. Then to Katerina she said, "I'll make sure you aren't disturbed. Don't be too long. Isabelle's mother is expecting us for lunch." She gave me an inscrutable look before she left and then closed the door behind us.

Katerina put down her polish and stared at me as if trying to find words. Her dark blond hair glistened in the light from a small window behind her.

"You wanted to speak with me?" I asked, hoping to move things along.

Katerina took a deep breath. "Yes. I apologize for disturbing your day, but I am desperate."

"Oh?" I squirmed. *Desperate.* The word made me want to run.

"I knew Gregory as a boy and I need him to hear me out."

"You knew Gregory as a boy?" I repeated.

She nodded. "It would be improper of me to say anything further." She paused and sighed. "I tried at your gala, but he wouldn't listen. I mean no harm, but I truly need his help."

"If he doesn't wish to see you, there is little I can do." I shifted my stance. The further we went in politics, the more often we'd deal with such requests. I supposed this was good practice for the future. "What is it you need?"

Katerina flushed. "I'd rather not bring another into my affairs. Could you just try to have him meet me at this address?" She handed me a folded piece of paper.

I took it, but paused. This felt wrong. "I can give him your message, but I think it would sound better if I could explain why you wanted to see him."

Katerina stiffened. "My mother helped take care of him when he lived in Joliet. She's gone now and I am alone. Please . . ." She reached forward and took my hand, but I pulled away.

"Joliet, Illinois?" I clarified.

"Yes, my mother worked for his family for near two decades."

"I'm so sorry, but you are mistaken. My Gregory grew up in Kentucky, not Joliet." I tried to contain my relief. "You sought out the wrong man."

"But . . ." Katerina's voice drifted off. "Of course, how silly of me. I haven't seen him since we were young. I'm so sorry to have troubled you."

Placing her note back on the table, I offered, "It is a common name. I'm so sorry you wasted your time."

Again, Katerina replied, "Yes, so silly of me." She refused to look at me.

I backed out of the room and left her with her disappointment.

True to her word, Abigail remained right outside. Before she could say anything, I pulled the door closed swiftly behind me.

Hotel Horizon was filled with small tables of women, their heads bent together in conversation. The restaurant was a sea of pastel hats and gowns as everyone showed off their afternoon best. I pursed my lips at my own choice in gown, an olive green day dress. Despite the flattering color, I wished I'd chosen a lighter shade. I felt like a weed in their garden of finery.

"Isabelle." Mother stood to gain my attention. "I hope your errand went well." Sitting at her table were Mrs. Quincy and Mrs. Abrams. I would hear about my delay this evening.

"Yes, thank you," I replied and took a seat. I prayed Mother hadn't mentioned the missing glove story. Such carelessness was something only tolerated in young children.

The women returned to their discussion of the latest style of boot as I demurely sipped from my teacup. Perhaps my presence was good for future connections, but footwear was something to be worn, not discussed.

Despite Katerina's misidentifying Gregory, the girl's plight weighed on my mind. I didn't doubt her need, nor the fact that she was mistaken. And yet, she and Gregory had been in the middle of a heated argument when I discovered them. Shouldn't it have been resolved then? I added two sugar cubes to my tea, nodded to Mother about the impropriety of loosely laced boots, and tried to decipher my dilemma.

As if answering my thoughts, Gregory walked into the restaurant. He handed his hat to the waiter and scanned the room for someone he knew. When his eyes met mine, a smile lit up his face, and after saying a few words to the maître d', he walked over to our table.

"Isabelle, you look radiant," Gregory said, leaning over and kissing my hand. "The color of that gown makes your eyes a deep mystery I'd like to unravel." He wiggled his eyebrows, making me laugh.

"Please join us, Gregory," Mother said, gesturing to the empty chair in between us.

Instantly Mrs. Quincy and Mrs. Abrams gushed greetings to him. After kissing their hands, he took the seat beside me. His cologne filled my senses and my heart sped faster. He was in his element and more attractive because of it. Mother took Gregory's arrival as a chance to steer the conversation to us and began an elaborate description of the wedding flowers.

I leaned over and whispered to Gregory, "Is everything all right?"

"Why shouldn't it be?" He lifted an eyebrow.

I put my teacup down and turned toward him. Keeping my voice low, I explained, "That girl you argued with at the party, Katerina. She sought me out."

Gregory's face paled. He took a sip of tea. "What could she want from you?"

"She thought you were someone she knew growing up, but was mistaken." I paused to examine Gregory's face, but it didn't betray any emotion. "I feel bad for her. She seemed truly distraught."

"She does seem to be in some trouble. I tried to explain I wasn't who she thought I was, but she was insistent." He shook his head. "She shouldn't have brought you into her troubles."

I shrugged. "It's in the past."

"How did you uncover her mistake?"

"Oh, she said she knew you from Joliet and I knew she had the wrong Gallagher."

Mrs. Quincy interrupted us. "Oh, to be so young and have such secrets. I don't know when I've seen a more handsome couple." She stirred her tea and smiled at us.

Gregory tipped his head in her direction. "Come now, don't be modest! I saw you and Senator Quincy dancing about the hall like newlyweds yourselves. Yours is a beauty to treasure."

"You flatter me, Mr. Gallagher," Mrs. Quincy scolded, but her pink cheeks told a different story.

Our waiter arrived with a tray of desserts and placed them on the table. Mother glanced at the lot and then sighed. Before she could say anything, I took a bite-sized lemon torte and took a bite. Mother insisted on watching our figures for the wedding, but I refused to give up all sweets.

Mother was expressionless, but I knew she was annoyed. "I believe the time has come for Isabelle and me to return home," she said, folding her napkin and placing it on the table. "Thank you for a lovely luncheon, ladies. It was a pleasure seeing you, Gregory."

Gregory took my hand and pressed his lips to it again. He lingered a moment too long. Behind me, the ladies swooned. He nodded his head to Mother and returned to his seat, offering the tray of sweets to Mrs. Abrams.

Sitting in the carriage, I glanced back to our group through the restaurant's window. Gregory used large gestures to explain something while the two women sat in silence, captivated by every word. Mrs. Abrams didn't even notice her hat was slightly crooked.

"That is how you make connections. Gregory can now stay the rest of the afternoon and impress those women until he's had enough," said Mother.

I watched as Gregory tilted his head back in a large chuckle, and I felt my stomach flutter. Whatever concerns I had flitted away. Gregory was a good man.

The following afternoon, I took my sketch pad out to the front yard. The first tulips had sprouted and I hoped to draw them. My efforts never amounted to much, but it gave me an excuse to sit outside for hours without Mother chastising me. I know she hoped I'd produce something wonderful, but my sketches were too obvious to excite any real interest.

The tulip petals were just blossoming and the light cast a rosy complexion to the garden. The charcoal in my hand flew over the page as I examined the lines in front of me.

"Another flower?"

I jumped and looked over my shoulder.

"Lucy!" I climbed to my feet. "I didn't know you were visiting."

"Well, I didn't really tell anyone. Mother and Father have

gone to the city for the day and I can't stay in that house all alone."

I led her to our porch swing. Before sitting down, she unpinned her hat and placed it on a small table. In unison, we kicked off and swung in silence for a few moments.

"Have you heard from Patrick?" I asked.

Lucy shrugged. "He has written, but he's so worried about my reputation. I have to read through his words to understand what he really wants to say. It is exhausting."

"I'd gladly have his letters come here, but Mother reads all the mail."

"And she'd surely tell my mother." Lucy sighed. "He's such a good man, Isabelle. Better than most. I wish people could see that."

"I know." I looked down our street. Many of our neighbors had secrets in their past and yet had been forgiven. But Patrick would forever carry the guilt of his father's actions. It didn't seem fair. His father had died in prison before the war even ended.

Lucy clucked her tongue. "Enough about me. How are you?"

I smiled.

"I know that smile. What happened?" Lucy's eyes lit up with delight.

"Nothing has happened, not like you think." I met her gaze. "It's just—the more I see Gregory in society, the more I realize how lucky I am."

Lucy smiled and kicked our swing higher. "He is a good man, Isabelle."

"I never hoped to have both an advantageous marriage and an affectionate one. It has taken me a bit by surprise."

Lucy squeezed my hand. "You deserve no less."

"And you. Are you certain your parents will not change their minds about Patrick?"

Lucy silenced me with a look.

"Mr. Stewart is coming for dinner tonight. He works at the bank with Daddy. He's kind and respectful. Some even find him handsome. I should be excited, if not grateful." Lucy's voice was thick. "He just isn't Patrick."

My friend's head fell to my shoulder and we swung as she cried the tears she dare not shed at home.

CHAPTER 3

Abigail had the third Tuesday of each month off. She often spent it at her mother's house on the outskirts of town, visiting with her family since Mother didn't approve of them coming to our home. It had been a few days since the dress fitting and I still needed to thank her properly. That morning I filled a basket with fruit, assorted muffins, and tea. It was a small gesture, but it would do.

The front porch steps of Abigail's family's house tilted unsteadily to the left, and the small white home seemed to lean with them. I shook the road dirt from my skirt and adjusted my lavender gloves before knocking on the door.

Shuffling sounds filled the air as Abigail shouted, "A moment!"

I smiled at what Mother might say if I shouted through our door.

"Miss Isabelle," Abigail exclaimed, and pulled the door tight against her back. Her sage gown and brown apron were covered with flour. "What are you doing here?" Her eyes darted down the street. "Is something the matter?"

I held the basket out to her. "I wanted to thank you for your help with Mother at the dress shop."

"I didn't do anything but give your mother an image to work from. She only wants your happiness." Abigail flushed.

I pressed the basket into her hands. "Without your influence, I'd be getting married in a dress I hate." Wind blew over the yard, scattering a few stray leaves.

Abigail released her grip on the door and took the basket's handle with both hands. "I appreciate your thoughtfulness, Miss Isabelle." She glanced back into the house. For a moment, I wondered if she would invite me inside.

I spoke quickly to save Abigail any embarrassment for the state of her home. "I don't have much time, and must be on my way. I just wanted to thank you."

Abigail's cheeks flushed, clearly seeing through my ruse. "Thank you, Isabelle. I'll bring the basket back with me this evening." She slipped back inside and shut the door behind her.

I sighed and glanced around the neighborhood whose homes all looked as if one good storm would topple them.

A crow cawed over me as I turned down an unfamiliar street and made my way toward the center of town. The spring breeze felt crisp as it pulled small pieces of my hair free. I was tempted to unpin my hat and let the wind do its bidding, but knew I'd never hear the end of it from Mother. Instead, I kicked a pebble down a side street just to prove I still had my own will. I watched it bounce the length of nearly five houses before it landed in the garden of a small brick home with dusty windows and no porch. It seemed silly, but I wanted to keep the memento of my small defiance. I turned down the road and went to retrieve the stone.

As I knelt to pick it up from the moist dirt, familiar raised voices filled the air. I bolted upright and turned to look for Gregory. But I was alone on the street. Rubbing the smooth pebble with my thumb, I shook the notion from my mind. Gregory had no business here; I must have been mistaken. I was turning into those silly women Lucy and I deplored. Those who could only think of their beloved and saw him everywhere. I laughed at myself and turned to leave.

"Gregory, please! Mother said you'd be able to help." My mouth went dry. Hearing his name, I could no longer deny it was him.

The front curtains were thin. Not wanting to be seen, I crept toward the side of the house, hoping to hear more. On the side of the house was a row of bushes just tall enough to conceal me. I hid myself and listened for more. He must have known Katerina previously. He wouldn't have come here if he hadn't.

"Your mother is a liar, Katerina," Gregory exclaimed, his tone raw with anger. "I will not let you make a fool of me! What else has she told you?"

I reclined against the house and closed my eyes. Why would Gregory lie about knowing that girl? Such behavior didn't fit with the respectable man I agreed to marry. I opened my eyes as a breeze caressed me. Had I deceived myself about who Gregory was? Did I know him well enough to make any assumption?

A scream pierced the air and shattered my racing thoughts. Gregory murmured something low, and the scream was cut short.

Without thinking, I jumped from my hiding spot and lunged toward the front door, ripping my skirt on the brambly bushes. I pushed against the front door, but it wouldn't budge. Something crashed inside. I pushed harder against the door, hoping they were all right, but it didn't move. In fact, all my efforts barely made a sound. I put my ear to the wood, hoping to hear something. Had they been attacked? Had she hurt Gregory? Perhaps one of them had become ill and fallen. I wanted to run for help, but who to fetch? When something else thudded to the floor, I'd had enough.

I stepped back from the door, looking for a window or hole. The front windows were too dirty to see through, but the side ones were covered inside only with a sheer spring curtain. Another thud came from inside the house. I pushed through the bushes and, grasping the window ledge, peered in.

At first I couldn't see anything, but as my eyes became used to the dim light, I could make out the furnishings of the room. Pillows were strewn across the floor, and a kettle on the stove steamed. I squinted, looking for Gregory or Katerina, but couldn't find them. Then, I shifted my gaze and spotted two figures on the floor, one on top of the other. My head spun. Were they lovers?

No, if that were true, her cries for help didn't make sense. I forced myself to look again.

Gregory was on his knees, his hands on Katerina's throat. As I made sense of what I saw, he pressed down harder against Katerina. Her hands clawed against his coat sleeves and her legs struggled to move away from him. Nothing she did made any difference. Gregory didn't move.

My fiancé, the man I was to spend my life with, couldn't be capable of something so horrific. Yet, the truth was directly before my eyes. There had to be an explanation. I willed myself to be calm and swallowed the tears threatening to overwhelm me. Katerina didn't have time for me to be hysterical. I had to stop this!

Lifting the top layer of my skirt, I wrapped it around my fist, forming a layer of protection. As I prepared to break the window, the scene inside changed. Katerina's arms slowed and slid to the floor and her legs stopped kicking. I was too late.

Gregory sat back on his heels beside Katerina's still body, raking his shaking fingers through his hair. Even through the curtain, I could see the terror on his face as he took in what he'd done. The redder his face became, the less brave I felt. Attempting to stop him in the moment was one thing, but walking in just as he realized he'd killed someone was something I wasn't prepared to handle.

Gregory knelt over Katerina's body and felt her neck. He shook his head. I could just make out his low voice muttering to himself.

"Damn it!" He balled up his fists and shook his arms in the air. Then he jumped up, adjusted his coat, and looked around the room. I ducked, trusting he hadn't seen me, while I willed breath to enter and exit my lungs. Slinking down the side of the house, I let the bushes shield me from view, their thorns piercing my face and arms.

My fiancé was a murderer.

The front door burst open followed by the sound of Gregory's footsteps walking down the steps. I couldn't see him, nor did I try. Instead, I pulled my knees to my chest and held my skirts as close as possible, hoping he'd not look around the house for witnesses. I didn't know how long I sat there, counting my heartbeats and praying to God to make me invisible, but when I reopened my eyes, dusk had settled.

The smooth pebble was still in my hand, and I tossed it onto the stone path around the front of the house. Knowing I had to finish things, I swallowed my fear. I had to see her body and know that she was dead. If she lived, I needed to help her. Slowly, I rose to my feet and crept toward the front door. Gregory hadn't taken the time to lock it, and it swung open at my touch. Katerina's feet were mere inches from mine as I stepped into the house and closed the door behind me.

Immediately, I stepped back. Katerina's vacant eyes stared at nothing, and her face was discolored from strangulation. There was no doubt. Katerina was dead, yet I kept expecting her to move. I stepped backward until the wall supported me. Her eyes seemed to follow me. As I tried to muster the courage to move, a scuffling from outside the front door nearly made me jump out of my skin. My heart pounded in my ears, but I couldn't move an inch until I heard the visitor fall against the front step. The small room held few pieces of furniture and even fewer hiding places. Thinking fast, I flew across the room and crawled beneath the bed, pulling the quilt down low to conceal myself.

A moment later the front door creaked open, and Gregory reentered. I recoiled from him and curled up tighter under the bed. His footsteps were heavy and his breath was loud and uneven. If I hadn't known better, I'd have thought he was drunk, but Gregory had refused every drink I'd ever seen offered to him. I slithered as close to the wall as possible and held my breath. Gregory knelt beside Katerina and lifted her lifeless hand to his chest.

"I didn't mean it," he whispered hoarsely. "I'm so sorry. I didn't mean it." His voice cracked.

I slid forward slightly so I could see better, careful not to make a sound. His brown suit was wrinkled, and his mustache needed to be combed.

Rocking back and forth, he hugged himself and shook his head as if in a fit. Then he snorted and regained his composure. His face was splotchy, but his mouth was set in a stubborn line. I knew that expression well—he had come to a decision.

Carefully, he placed his hands under her neck and knees. As he stared into her bluish face, his cheeks flushed again.

"I can make this right," he insisted. "You will not have died in vain."

Then, he lifted her corpse into his arms and walked slowly out of the house. The front door closed with a slap as if Katerina herself were angry with me. I let that monster carry her away, and for what? To make it right—what did that mean? The only person he could make it right for was himself; she was dead.

I swallowed the bile that rose in my throat. He had brazenly walked out of the house without any kind of cover upon her. The first person who spied them would know she was dead. But Gregory was too smart to allow that. He was going to dispose of her body, I was sure of it. Quick as I could, I crawled out of my hiding place and ran from the house, not even worrying about the dirt and dust that was surely stuck in my hair. He would not get away with this, not if I could stop him.

Once I was out of the house, Gregory was nowhere to be found. How had he moved so fast while carrying her? I gulped and lunged into a run. I had to find the sheriff.

I turned down the street that led straight into town. These roads weren't as well cared for as the ones I was used to and after only two steps, my foot slid into a hole, twisting my ankle.

"Blast," I exclaimed as I fell to the ground. My ankle was already swelling. I'd never make it back to town alone. There was only one path left to take. Summoning my strength, I hobbled down the road back to Abigail's house. As I approached, I saw her in the front yard unpinning laundry that had been drying in the sun.

"Abigail," I called out to her, wincing as I put weight on my injured foot.

She looked up, startled, as if she didn't recognize me. My breath, already uneven, sped up in fear.

"It's me, Isabelle," I called out, now only two houses away. The stays of my corset felt as if they were tightening, and I had to stop walking to catch my breath. Yet, even standing still, the world turned and the full weight of what I witnessed fell upon me.

"Isabelle?" Abigail reached me and put a hand on my shoulder.

"He did it," I wheezed, trying desperately to breathe. "He killed her."

"What?" Abigail asked.

I grabbed her hand and clawed at the back of my gown, trying to loosen my corset, but it was too late.

I slid into darkness.

CHAPTER 4

Voices surrounded me, all clamoring to be heard, but the darkness refused to let me go. The familiar scent of vanilla and orange soothed my confusion and the soft quilt I gripped told me I was in my own bed. Safe.

Something cool and wet was pressed against my forehead, and I finally pulled myself fully into consciousness. Light beat against my eyes, but I refused to open them and rolled my head away from it. There was a rustling as Abigail leaned over and whispered, "Do not awaken yet." I clenched my eyes to show that I heard her, and she returned to dabbing my forehead with the cool compress.

Finally the commotion calmed enough for me to differentiate the voices.

"What do you mean 'attacked'?" Mother's demanded. Her voice was shrill.

"Mrs. Larkin, look at her. Her gown is shredded and her arms and legs bruised and scarred. Her corset was loosened at some point and her ankle is swollen." The man's deep voice was familiar. Searching my mind I realized it was Dr. Carson.

"When she wakes up we'll probably have more answers, but you should steel yourself to the possibility that someone did your daughter harm."

"All this to bring you a basket? I hope you're happy, Abigail." Leave it to Mother to blame a servant.

"She was fine when she visited me. It was when she returned that something was wrong, ma'am." Abigail rinsed the washcloth and reapplied it to my forehead. Water droplets trickled down my cheeks, but I resisted the urge to wipe them, for I wanted to hear Mother's response. "I don't know what happened, but I am sorry she was harmed."

Hadn't I explained to Abigail what happened? My head pounded, and I couldn't remember what I'd said or not before I fainted. Abigail pressed her hand hard against my forehead, preventing any movement.

"I believe the noise is distressing Isabelle," Abigail whispered, her voice thick with concern.

"Of course," Mother replied. "We'll leave." The door creaked as she pulled it closed behind them. I could hear their muffled voices from the hall. "Shall I call for tea, Dr. Carson?" How could Mother think of tea when I was injured?

"Yes, thank you." Their voices faded as they walked down the hall.

Once I heard our top stair creak, I opened my eyes and tried to sit up. Dizziness slapped against me and I lowered myself back onto the pillows. "What happened? Why is Dr. Carson here?"

Abigail raised a finger to her mouth before pressing her hand against the door to make sure it was closed. Once satisfied, she returned to my side and took my hand in hers.

"If I am right, you will thank me. If not, no harm's been done by the deception."

My head spun. "What do you mean?"

Abigail silenced me with a look of true pity. "Before you fainted you said 'He killed her.' Do you remember?"

Her words brought those last moments back to the forefront of my mind. I nodded and tried not to look away from her. Despite my desire to bring out the truth, I was ashamed. I could've—should've—stopped Gregory. "Yes," I whispered. "I remember."

Abigail sat beside me as she demanded, "Who? Who killed whom?"

My mouth went dry. I looked down at the diamond ring I wore as a symbol of Gregory's devotion, and dread flushed my face.

Before I could answer, Abigail whispered, "Was it Gregory?"

I inhaled so quickly that I coughed. Abigail jumped from my bed and paced the floor. "Forgive me, Isabelle. I don't mean to offend. It's just I'd gone to fetch Dr. Carson for you when I came upon Gregory carrying Katerina's body to town, and your words wouldn't let me think otherwise."

I raised my hand to stop her. "No . . . you are right." I paused, took a deep breath, and pushed the words out. "It was Gregory. I saw him . . . saw him kill Katerina." On the last word my voice cracked, and a lump swelled in my throat.

Abigail knelt beside my bed and pushed the hair from my face. "I thought as much. Isabelle, you must listen to me. Gregory brought her body to Dr. Carson's office claiming he found her disheveled, as if attacked, and gasping for air near our side of town. He claimed he tried to revive her once she went unconscious, but couldn't and so he rushed her to Dr. Carson, hoping she'd live. Dr. Carson was so moved that he's hailed Gregory as a hero for trying to rescue a poor servant." She paused and gripped my hand.

I sat up, but was again overcome with a wave of nausea.

"Isabelle, Dr. Carson believes you were attacked by the same man who killed Katerina, since you were in the same part of town visiting me. Nothing I've said has corrected his impression. He believes a man took advantage of you and left you to die before finding his next victim."

My mind reeled with this news, but I couldn't let it deter me from my path. It would be hard, but Gregory's tale must be discounted. My stomach rolled at the thought of him, but I steeled myself to my task. I was safe. In Dr. Carson's eyes, my words carried more weight than Abigail's. Before I could open my mouth, Abigail patted my hand.

"I'll get them for you. See for yourself what they believe."

"Thank you, Abigail," I said. "For your protection and your trust."

Abigail paused. "Before you speak with them, may I say one more thing?" I nodded. "Gregory killed Katerina. We don't know why. Don't give him another target." She slipped from the room.

My hand shook as I reached up to dry my eyes. Abigail pointed to the very thing I had tried to avoid. This was more than a horrific attack. This was my Gregory. My smart, handsome, and charismatic fiancé, whom I'd trusted my future to . . . and now that future was gone. The tears spilled over and down my face. Abigail was right. Forget about trusting him. If he knew I was witness to this, he'd surely kill me as well. I'd seen the fear in his eyes. Whatever happened between them went deeper than I understood.

The tears subsided to a burning threat and I dried my face with the edge of my nightgown. I struggled to elevate myself on the mountain of pillows around me.

Just as I managed to settle against the cushions, I heard Mother's distinct clip-clop stride approach my room. She flung the door open and entered, her dramatic lily scent accompanying her.

"Isabelle, you're awake!" she exclaimed. She flew across the room and perched on the edge of my bed. "We've been so worried, my darling."

I matched my smile to hers, wondering what she'd say if we were alone. With Dr. Carson following at her heels, propriety was above all else. Knowing that would be on Mother's mind, I reached my hand out and gripped hers, showing our solidarity. Such an image might give me credibility with the good doctor. He took my other hand and pressed his fingers to my wrist.

"Hmmmm," he grumbled and rubbed his bald patch. "You seem a bit excited, but that's to be expected. How do you feel?" He laid the back of his hand upon my forehead gently as if I were a porcelain doll.

I shook him off. The idea of any man touching me sent shivers throughout my body. "As well as to be expected, thank you." I allowed him a small smile. Then, sitting as tall as I could muster with my pounding head, I said, "But I must explain. I went to see Abigail. But after, I heard voices and they were shouting and . . . I mean, I saw . . . I saw Gregory with Katerina in her home this afternoon."

The two looked down at me with blank expressions. Then Dr. Carson cleared his voice and turned away from me.

"Confusion is a symptom of such attacks," Dr. Carson explained to Mother. Then to me, he clarified, "You saw him discover her, you mean?"

"No." I struggled to find the words. "I saw him . . . I saw him . . ." Words failed me as the tears clogged my throat. "H-he strangled her."

Mother dropped my hand and backed away, the look on her face horrible enough to silence anyone. "What is the meaning of this? Isabelle, do you realize what you are saying?"

Dr. Carson busied himself with his bag of bottles.

"Yes, Mother." Of course I knew what I was saying. "I saw Gregory kill that servant girl, as you call her. I know it sounds impossible, but I *saw* it happen. I stood beside her and looked into her dead eyes. We must call the sheriff. I need to tell him what I remember before I forget any detail."

Mother was silent for a moment, staring at me as if I were a confusing stain she wanted bleached away. "No. You are wrong, child. Gregory is the one who brought her to the doctor. Why would someone do that if they were guilty?"

I shook my head. "I don't know." So that was what Gregory was after by taking Katerina from the house.

Slowly Gregory's words made sense. Katerina did not die in vain, for he had turned his horror into an advantage for himself. He'd gain countless connections for trying to save someone so beneath his station. My stomach churned.

I cleared my voice. "Don't you see what he's done? By bringing her to town himself he's blinded you to the truth. He wants you to believe that he is the hero when he is really the villain. It's a brilliant lie." My head pounded and I had to stop talking.

Dr. Carson cleared his throat. "He was, and remains, very distraught over the girl's death. His suit was not disheveled, nor were there any scratches on his cheeks or hands. You are mistaken." His voice softened. "Wanting to forget what happened is understandable. You clearly went through an ordeal yourself, but that is no reason to continue with this falsehood."

Both looked at me as if I should burst into tears and apologize for my sinful accusations. Instead, I met Dr. Carson's eyes and repeated, "It was him. I scraped my skirt and legs on the rosebushes outside her house, twisted my ankle running from her house, and loosed my stays when I couldn't catch my breath. But, I know what I saw. It was him. Gregory killed her." My voice strengthened as I spoke.

I waited for Dr. Carson to pale and for Mother to exhale and crumple with the weight of my insistence, promising me we'd find a way out of this together. Isn't that what mothers are supposed to do, protect and love their children? Instead she gestured to Dr. Carson and said, "Could I have a moment alone with my daughter, Doctor?"

"Of course," he replied, shutting his bag and slipping from the room.

Mother waited until the door clicked shut before turning her red face to me. "Perhaps this falsehood is easier to believe than the truth, but no good will come from lying to yourself. Tell me what happened, and I'll do my best to see your attacker punished."

I fixed my eyes on her. "You think I concocted this whole story? What could be worse than believing my fiancé a murderer?"

"Oh, my dear. You have been robbed of so many things. You're afraid this man stole your honor? Perhaps some would turn their backs on a woman after such an attack, but not Gregory. I assure you, Gregory will love you no matter what you tell us. He wants to build a life with you. Don't let your fear of rejection make you a liar." Mother rubbed her forehead as she sat beside me. "If this is about your wedding night, I assure you, it will be fine, perhaps even enjoyable. . . ."

"Mother!" My voice cracked in shock. How could she be so ridiculous? As if I cared about sex at a time like this. "I saw him kill her. His hands pressed against her throat until she turned blue and died."

"I don't believe you." Mother's voice was flat. "Gregory is not capable of doing such an awful thing. You are mistaken."

Afternoon sunlight cascaded through my bedroom window, reflecting off my bedspread, and forced a cheeriness into the room. Yet, Mother stood still as a cat, waiting for me to admit I'd been lying.

"Mother, I am quite certain of what I saw. I will not yield." I spoke with a voice that was stronger than I felt. The soft pile of pillows on which I rested threatened to engulf me.

"Isabelle, this is nonsense. What possible reason could he have had to do that girl harm?" She didn't wait for an answer before she shook her head. "No, you are mistaken. A man of Gregory Gallagher's character wouldn't stoop to even associate with such a girl, let alone have reason to kill her."

The throbbing of my ankle radiated up my leg. "You raised

me. If you truly believe that I am capable of such a lie, then you are a fool." With my good leg I adjusted myself in such a way that I sat straight and glared at her as she so often did me. "Fetch the sheriff. Perhaps he will be able to find proof of what I saw."

Mother's face pinched with rage. "And have you destroy your reputation by accusing your fiancé of such an atrocity? I think not. Gregory Gallagher is the best match you'll ever make, and I'll not stand by and let you ruin it due to some servant's unfortunate death."

"No, you'd have me marry a man I believe a murderer!" My hands shook. I forced myself to gain control. I would not cry and show Mother any weakness. That was not the way to gain her trust.

"I'd have you marry the best man for you. I'd have you marry the man you've pledged yourself to by accepting his hand. No one pushed you into this match, Isabelle, and I won't have you ruining it because your brain is addled. You'll stay in this room until you've recovered yourself."

No sooner had the words left her mouth than she walked out the door, shutting it without a sound behind her.

CHAPTER 5

Abigail brushed through a rough net of snarls in my hair. She yanked so hard that I nearly fell off my chair, but I held firm. From the strange and frightening nightmares I had, I knew I'd been drugged after my conversation with Mother and Dr. Carson. Not only that, but my drug-induced slumber hadn't been restful. I felt as if I'd walked to Chicago and back.

"It isn't right," I spat. Abigail paused her brushing for a moment while I fidgeted, then she resumed her work.

Cocking her head to one side and meeting my eyes in the mirror, she said, "Perhaps if you tried to see it from their perspective?"

I rubbed my forehead and sighed. "Abigail . . . never mind." My voice felt limp. Never before had I ever felt so alone. Did Mother really not believe me at all? Could she reject me so carelessly?

Abigail did not get a chance to reply, for at that moment Mother burst into the room, a large box with a card attached in her hands. She placed the box on my bed and opened the card. Holding it high in the air as if posing for a portrait, she read,

"'My dear Isabelle. Please enjoy the roses this morning, and feel better knowing my affection is with you. Love, Gregory.'"

I flinched as Mother read his name. When I said nothing, Mother held the card out to me. "Darling, is there another such man in the world?"

Abigail yanked the brush harder through my hair as a small, astonished cry escaped my lips. "You can't be serious, Mother," I exclaimed. "You expect me to rejoice in this gift? He is not the man we thought he was!"

Mother came behind me and snatched the brush from Abigail's hand. "Not this nonsense again. I thought we'd finished with that yesterday. Your own attack has confused your mind."

"What attack? I have already explained that no one did me harm." Abigail backed away from us and began making my bed. It seemed that she was determined to stay in the room but out of the conversation. Still, her presence gave me hope. "I know what I saw."

Mother raked the brush through my hair over and over until the strands shown with clarity and my scalp burned in pain. "I want no more of this foolishness, Isabelle. If you cannot control your mind, then say nothing at all. I will not drag that man through the coals. I won't do it. You will come to your senses soon and thank me. I am sure of that."

"I'll never thank you for this," I insisted and grabbed the brush from her before she could attack my hair again.

Mother, attempting to ignore me, picked up the roses and turned toward the door, then stopped. "Gregory is the man *you* chose, Isabelle. You will marry him and I shall dance at your wedding." She slipped out the door and pulled it closed behind her.

Abigail plucked the brush out of my hands, stepped behind me, and asked, "Shall we braid your hair today, or simply tie it back?"

"Braid," I whispered and then let her turn me into a proper lady.

* * *

I waited until Mother left to pay calls to her acquaintances before slipping out of my room. My boots clomped against the hard floor, the sound echoing off the walls. With every step I took, I was sure I'd be discovered, but no one came. The clock in the hall chimed ten o'clock, and I exhaled in relief. There was no one here. It was Tuesday. Our cook would be running errands and Abigail most likely was walking the wash down to the laundrywoman.

Despite my swollen ankle, I was determined to see the sheriff. Perhaps he would believe me enough to investigate my story. My hand was on the front door handle when someone cleared her throat behind me. I turned.

"Good morning, Abigail," I said, trying to sound nonchalant.

"I can't let you leave, Miss Isabelle."

"Pardon?" Had I really heard her right?

"Your mother charged me with keeping you home. The windows and doors are all locked. Dr. Carson warned the sheriff of your condition already, so talking to him won't have any effect."

Instead of replying, I turned back to the door and started to unlock the lock. Immediately, Abigail grasped my wrist and spun me so that I was pressed against the wall. Losing that control sped my heart into such fear that I nearly passed out again.

"Abigail?" I asked softly.

"I'm sorry, Isabelle. I care for you and your situation, but I need this job."

A long moment passed before I wrenched myself out of her grasp and limped down the hallway. There was nothing left to say. If I couldn't leave, I could at least rest my ankle so that when I was free I had two legs to stand on. My stomach growled.

"Isabelle," Abigail called behind me.

I raised my hand without looking behind me. "I'm going to find a meal. I hope you are all right with that."

She didn't reply and I didn't look to see if she followed.

The kitchen table was covered in a pale pink tablecloth and devoid of any breakfast remnants. My stomach growled in disapproval. Mother had only permitted me plain toast and broth since the incident. I scanned the counters and shelves, but found only fruit. I sighed and resigned myself to an apple when I noticed that the door to the pantry was cracked open. Nudging it open further, I was met with the most delicious smell of cinnamon scones and strawberry jam.

With a full plate, I left the kitchen and walked down the hallway and into the front room. Mother would have a fit if she knew I had food in her precious parlor, but for once I didn't care. I placed my meal on a side table beside Papa's bookshelf. Claiming they were an assault to the eyes, Mother had gotten rid of all the books in the house except for these. Secretly, I thought it was because she'd been jealous over how much time he spent reading on topics in which she had no interest. However, she knew if I were to make a good marital connection, we'd have to appear to be well read. So Papa's collection had remained where it was after he died. I was grateful for that, for each time I opened one of his books, I felt him beside me, reading as he'd done when I was a young child.

I knelt to the floor, reached to the back corner of the bottom shelf, and pulled my old friend *Jane Eyre* out of her hiding place. Papa had bought the novel for me a few months before he became ill. Despite it being a woman's novel, he had read it on one of his travels and admired Jane's spirit. He handed it to me and said, "She's a plucky one. Read it and learn from her." I needed her spirit now more than ever.

Settling back onto the pink sofa, which neatly matched the rose patterned rug and Grecian wall tableau, I took a bite of the scone and reentered Jane's world. A few crumbs fell onto my blouse, and I brushed them away. As a young child, Jane was trapped as I was by misinformation. I felt her situation more keenly than ever before.

Enthralled in her world as I was, I didn't see Abigail enter the room.

"Miss Isabelle!" She put a tall vase of roses on the center table. "You should not be eating in here. What would your mother say?"

"I truly don't care," I replied.

Abigail looked at me with a pained expression before placing a card on the receiving plate beside the vase and walking out of the room. I tried to return to my novel, but the flowers continued to distract me. The ones Gregory had sent earlier were red, and these were pink, probably chosen to match the parlor. Mother was annoying like that. And yet, if Mother had ordered them, she would've ordered tulips, for their shape better highlighted the curvature of the furniture. Mother would never have chosen roses for this room.

Stuffing the rest of the scone into my mouth, I dusted myself off, not caring where the crumbs lay, and walked to the table. Upon closer inspection, I noticed how the tips of the roses were a darker pink than the insides. Someone had put a lot of thought into this. I snatched the card from the plate, pulled the envelope open, and read the inscription:

To my darling Isabelle. May these flowers illustrate the complexity of my love for you. Recover quickly. I miss your smile, for it brightens the darkest parts of my soul.
Eternally yours,
Gregory

My lips twitched. He sent *more* flowers!? What on earth was he after?

Just standing in the same air as the flowers made me feel . . . dirty. Rage swept through every limb of my body until I had to expel it in some way or burst. Instinctively, I grabbed a flower from the vase, ripped the petals off it, and flung them across the room. The action felt so good I grabbed another and another and another. The stem's thorns pricked my fingers and palm, but even that felt better than letting them reside in my home.

Before I knew it, I was out of breath, and there was only one rose left in the vase. Gregory's bouquet was destroyed. I had expected to feel better, but only felt empty. My situation had not changed, and now I had a mess to clean up. Flower petals and leaves lay over nearly every surface in the room, but it wasn't enough. The petals mocked me still. Gritting my teeth, I dug my heel into a petal, twisting it back and forth until it was imbedded in the carpet. It looked broken and shredded, and satisfaction welled in me. Over the next few moments I mangled the rest of the petals, letting my feet say to Gregory what I couldn't.

That was how Mother found me. I hadn't even heard the door creak open, but there she was, standing in the center of the doorway with her mouth open like a codfish. Calmly, I cleaned the bottom of my shoe off and turned toward her. I tilted my head slightly to the right, questioning the look of horror she gave me. Her cheeks were flushed and her lips pursed in a tight, thin line. For a moment I tried to view the scene through her eyes and realized what I must look like: crazy. The thought sparked more anger in me. I met her eyes, lifted my foot, and ground another petal into the carpet. *I dare you, Mother,* I thought. *I dare you to call me crazy.*

Slowly, she reached up and unpinned her hat and set it on the rocking chair. As she unbuttoned her overcoat, her eyes darted about the room and widened when she discovered the crumbs and plate of jam. After what felt like a very long time, she cleared her throat. "Well, this is a mess. Abigail will have to clean it up before Lucy and her mother come for dinner this evening."

She'd achieved her goal. By pointing out the added work I'd created for Abigail, she'd made my fit seem childish. There was nothing I could say to undo the mess so I knelt to the floor and began collecting the remnants of the flowers into a pile. The shredded petals left little marks on the carpet. I traced them with my finger.

Mother returned the vase to its place in the center of the table and sighed. "He really loves you, Isabelle. You must remember that. Men like Gregory Gallagher don't come into your life more than once. I know you are struggling, but try to remember."

I looked up at her, searching for some revelation. All I found was anger. Hot tears burned my eyes as Mother fingered the card he'd left. I didn't think, just grabbed the vase from the table and hurled it against the wall, sending shards of glass to the floor.

Mother gasped, but remained motionless. Slipping the card into the bosom of her gown, she left the room whispering, "You'll remember. You must remember."

No. You must understand, I thought as I collected the larger shards of the vase. But Mother had given me one small hope to cling to: Lucy was coming to visit. If anyone could help, she would.

CHAPTER 6

I secluded myself for the remainder of the day in my room, trying to find some way out of this impossible nightmare. Yet, every plan I came up with was ruined by the fact that Dr. Carson and Mother would refute my claims. Even the sheriff, who had listened to their suspicions, agreed that I'd been attacked and was befuddled as a result. As I hadn't done since Papa died, I curled up in the corner of my room with my knees held to my chest.

Everyone who could help me viewed me as a fragile doll. How was I to survive if no one gave my mind any credit?

Lucy and her mother arrived promptly at seven, dressed in elegant silk gowns, fans hanging from their wrists. I watched in darkness from the second story landing as they entered and made their way through the main hallway. Mrs. D'Havland and Mother walked side by side into the living room, their heads bowed together so I couldn't hear what they said.

Right before they entered the room, Mrs. D'Havland turned around and snapped her fingers at Lucy. "Shoulders back, dear. No one likes a slumpy dumpy." Once Lucy corrected her posture, Mrs. D'Havland followed Mother into the front parlor.

The moment they were gone, Lucy lifted her head, and her eyes met mine as if she had known I'd been spying in the shadows the whole time. Still dressed in my afternoon gown, I stepped into the light as Lucy rolled her shoulders into a more natural position. Without a word, we met at the middle of the staircase.

"Izzy," Lucy gasped and took my hands, giving me support as we walked. "Are you all right? I can't imagine! Attacked by a murderer? What would've happened if Gregory hadn't appeared?" Her eyes were wide.

Her questions sent a cold chill through me. Clearly there were stories already circulating. It went without saying that none would contain the truth.

"What?" I was flabbergasted. "What have you heard?"

Something in my tone made her look up at me. Ignoring the fear on her face, I clutched her arm and led us to the main floor.

Lucy sat on the bottom step of the stairs and pulled me down beside her. "Mother heard that the man who killed that poor servant girl attacked you. They say if Gregory hadn't carried you back to town, you'd be dead now. Is it true?"

Had Gregory's story grown to have him rescuing me as well? Anger welled up in my throat, but I forced it away. "No," I began calmly. "Gregory carried Katerina to town, not me. She was already dead when—"

"But Mother told me!" Lucy's brow wrinkled, and she shook her head. "She said you'd be dead were it not for him. It's very romantic."

"Romantic?" I gasped in shock. "Far from it."

Lucy patted my knee. "Well, Mother painted it as such. I'm sure reality is never so colorful."

If Mrs. D'Havland was repeating the story, the truth would never be known. A shiver slid up my neck. Gregory was intelligent. If he realized I'd been to Abigail's at the same time he was with Katerina he might suspect I knew more than I should. Such a realization could put me in real danger.

Mother would say anything to smooth Gregory's concerns. He needed our connections to fulfill his aspirations, so I knew he'd forgive much. But I couldn't let those soft hands touch me again. They were now tainted with Katerina's death. The thought made my heart race and my stomach lurch.

"You look pale, Izzy. Did I say something wrong?"

Lucy couldn't know the truth. I'd not put anyone in the path of danger until I figured out what to do next. "My ankle hurts," I explained. "Have you heard from Patrick?"

Lucy sighed. "I got a letter today. His mother died. He was thankful he arrived in time to see her before she passed. He's going to work in his brother's business in Montana. Hopefully by the end of the year he'll have saved enough for my parents to accept him. Yet, I fear Mother will marry me off to Mr. Stewart by then."

Biting my bottom lip, I tried to find some comforting words for her. We both knew her fears were valid. "You always have a say. The choice may not be nice, but it is available."

"No," Lucy insisted, shaking her head. "You know Mother. Once she finds a suitable man, she'll pounce." Lucy rubbed her hands upon her skirt.

Perhaps she couldn't stop Mrs. D'Havland, but she could prevent a gentleman from pursuing her. A woman's reputation was her greatest ally, or so Mother always told me. "She may push you, but you can always change the man's mind."

Lucy looked at me, her eyes showing that she knew I had a plan. "How?"

I cleared my throat. "Patrick will marry you no matter what, correct?"

A dark expression spread over my friend's face. "Of course. No matter what." She paused. "You're scaring me, Izzy."

My tongue felt swollen in my mouth as I thought of how distasteful Lucy would find this. "To avoid whomever your mother brings home, if the normal dismissals don't work, you can have him running for the hills with a simple lie." I paused, unsure if Lucy would see my solution as plausible, as I did. "Tell him you have had intimate relations with a man. No gentleman would marry an impure woman."

Immediately, all color drained from her face, and she pulled away from me. Shaking her head, she whispered, "No. I could never make such a declaration. I'd be ruined!"

I flinched at her reaction, but grasped her hand as I insisted, "Patrick loves you and would marry you no matter what. You deserve the future you want. We have so little control over our lives. It isn't the best course of action, but it would certainly set you free."

"What's come over you, Isabelle?" Lucy exclaimed. "This isn't you. You know how important a woman's reputation is."

Her words made me pause. Lucy was right; this was unlike me. Had Katerina's death altered me so deeply? "I guess I think you and Patrick belong together. Our parents' opinions shouldn't matter. It's our lives."

Lucy flushed. "Oh, Izzy. At least one person is on my side."

"I guess recent events have made me realize that what you and Patrick share is special."

Lucy's eyes clouded over. "Oh, Izzy. I'm so glad you finally recognized your love for Gregory."

As Lucy pulled me close, her chiffon sleeve caressed my cheek. I swallowed my disappointment in my friend.

As usual, dinner was one elaborate dish after another. I picked at my food as Mother and Mrs. D'Havland dissected the usual gossip. After they both gave me a startled look, neither commented on the fact I'd not changed for dinner, but I didn't know how to take their neglect. Did they think I was past help or behaving childishly and thus unworthy of comment? For myself, it mattered little. I was preoccupied with bigger issues.

Dragging a potato wedge across my plate with my fork, I

wondered about my advice to Lucy. If one's reputation was the only card a woman held, how could I use mine against Gregory? My virtue was already in question since Dr. Carson warned Mother my attack might have been sexual in nature. If I decided to give in and claim that, they would make the necessary explanations, and Gregory would, no doubt, marry me. I was his ticket to Washington and politics. No, if I were to get out of this union, I'd need to find something even more despicable.

Lucy nudged me with her elbow. When I looked up toward her, she twitched her head toward her mother.

"Well, Isabelle?" Mrs. D'Havland placed her fork on her plate. "What did you think of the opera?"

My hand froze, and I glanced around the table. What opera? It had been months since Mother and I had gone to the theater. Glancing at Lucy was no help, for she was focused on her plate.

Swallowing, I met Mrs. D'Havland's eyes and said, "The soprano was a bit lacking."

"Exactly!" She turned back to Mother with a smug smile. "That is just what I said, but Mr. D'Havland insisted on attending the party in her honor."

Lucy nudged my foot and rolled her eyes. I sensed I should've known more about this dispute, but couldn't place it in my mind. Luckily, Mother artfully steered the conversation in another direction.

"You should see the flowers Isabelle chose for her bouquet. They highlight each other perfectly. I won't ruin the effect by giving you the details, but—"

"Mother!" I hissed. "Please?" Why would Mother bring up the wedding knowing how I felt?

Placing her water glass down, she blinked innocently. "I'm not divulging details."

"No. I don't want to discuss the wedding at all." My cheeks burned in indignation.

"Why? Come now." Mrs. D'Havland patted my hand. "You only get married once."

"Mother knows why." I grimaced. Hot anger flooded my face. Did I dare tell Mrs. D'Havland? She would be a powerful ally, but telling her she'd been spreading an incorrect story was never wise. Mother paled. "Darling . . ." she began.

"Oh, stop," I insisted and dropped my fork against the china plate. "You don't care one snit about me. If you did, we'd not be here now having this conversation."

"Isabelle—" Lucy gripped her napkin, about to go on, when shouting erupted down the hall.

A muffled voice echoed through the house. "I have to know she's all right."

Gregory stalked into the dining room a moment before Abigail. His hat was in his hands and his coat was slung over his arm.

"There she is, Mr. Gallagher." Abigail gestured toward me with her hands. "Just as I said, she is recovering and eating with friends."

Gregory's eyes glistened as he stared at me, his face full of worry. Yet for all his care, all I saw was the frantic twitch of his eyebrow and the anger brimming beneath the surface. Anger directed at me or something else, I wasn't sure. I pulled my gaze from him and forced a bit of lamb into my mouth. Appearing as inconsequential as possible seemed best. Lucy noticed my discomfort immediately and scooted her chair closer to mine.

"Izzy," she whispered. "What's wrong?" She glanced at me and then followed my gaze to Gregory.

Mother stood and walked around the table to embrace Gregory. "Dearest Gregory, how good of you to check on Isabelle." They separated, and she led him to the head of the table. "See how her cheeks are regaining their rosy hue. I suspect she'll be quite well again soon."

"You do look pale, Isabelle. Are you in much pain?" Gregory asked.

The closer he got to me the more I felt his anger. My hands were shaking so much now that I tried to clasp them together under the table, but that only made my legs shake as well. I needed him gone. Katerina's dead stare sat frozen in my mind. She accused me as if I could do anything.

Gregory took a step around the table toward me. All of my shuddering halted. Did he know what I'd seen? And if he didn't, what did he want? I stood up so fast that my chair fell over. Lucy gasped and grabbed for my hand, but I yanked it away from her. "Please go away. Stop. I can't see you anymore. Leave!" My words spilled over one another before I could think them through.

"Isabelle," Lucy soothed. She came by my side.

"I can't—" My voice caught.

I wanted to say more, but couldn't. Seeing him in person, he was too powerful, and Lucy didn't understand. I couldn't beg her for help. I had to find a way out myself.

"Please, just leave." I backed up until my back was against the wall. Lucy remained by my side, my only shield against him.

Gregory took another step toward me, his hands raised as if he were approaching a mad dog. "Isabelle, what happened?" He glanced from Mother to me.

"Stop this, Isabelle, immediately." Mother snapped her fingers as if trying to end some trance. "She gets fear into her very soul and can't control it. I'm so sorry, Gregory. Come now, Isabelle, end this foolishness."

Surrounded by disbelieving eyes, I thought I'd lose all fight, but instead strength welled up in me. I turned a cold eye to Mother and demanded, "No, Mother. *You* end this foolishness."

Not waiting for her reaction, I stalked out of the room, hiding my limp as best I could, and rushed up the stairs to my room. I paused on the landing so I could hear what they said in my absence.

"I apologize for her behavior," Mother said. "You are the first man she's seen since the incident, aside from the doctor, and I'm sure she's trying to sort her emotions out. What an ordeal! Perhaps, if you give her a day or two she'll have recovered."

"I agree. A day or two and she'll be the girl we know again," Mrs. D'Havland insisted.

"Yes, a few days." Mother sounded tired. "She's just shocked by the attack."

"Of course, I'm sure the attack distressed her," Gregory said smoothly. "Such things change people. When she is calm, please convey to her my concern. She must fear that the fate of the servant girl would be hers as well. That is a great fear to live with, no matter your station. Luckily, she has you to protect her here at home."

Mother simpered at his compliment, but I heard the veiled threat in his words. Did he know I was a witness to his crime? Was he warning me to fear for my life? I'd be a fool to underestimate Gregory again.

At the top of the stairs, I glanced over the banister and caught Gregory peering out of the dining room up at me. He gave me a forlorn look and smiled before turning back to Mother. "I'm so sorry I wasn't able to help her. Surely if I hadn't come upon that servant girl first, I might have prevented Isabelle this pain."

"No one can predict such things. What you did was heroic, no matter what else happened that day. Isabelle will be herself again in a day or two," Mother promised. "Please join us for dinner, Gregory." Pushing my bedroom door closed behind me, I clenched my fists. If there was one thing I knew now, it was that I would not do as Mother predicted.

Mother opened the door so fast that it slammed against the wall, the knob leaving a deep, angry mark.

"What on earth is the matter with you?" She gripped my arm

and stood me in front of her. "That display downstairs earlier was entirely inappropriate."

I yanked my arm out of her grasp and stepped clear of her dominance. "No, Mother. It was the only way to make my point. I am done with Gregory Gallagher. I don't care how many flowers he sends or how many times he arrives to gallantly check on my injuries. I am done with him. He is a murderer, and I'll not have him in my life. I know I can't put him behind bars without your support, but I can—and fully intend to—dissolve the engagement."

"You'll do no such thing." Mother walked over to the window, looking down on the departing carriages. "He asked you to spend your life with him, and you accepted. You are not going to set idle tongues wagging over a story you fabricated to make your attack easier to deal with. I'm your mother, and I'll not let you ruin our lives! If you continue down this path no decent person will so much as look at us. I can't let you give up your life for a story."

"You are my *mother*. Why can't you protect *me* instead of my reputation, for once?"

"I am protecting you," Mother hissed. She stepped toward me. "You have no idea what will become of you if you accuse that innocent gentleman. Not only will you ruin your marriage, but your entire life as well. Your friends will shun you socially. Young men will not ever look at you. Your wealth and connections will mean little. Not only that, my friends and confidants will despise me as well. Merchants will no longer take our credit, theaters will close their doors to us, even our Uncle Walter may disown us. You seem to believe I am only concerned for your future with Gregory, but I am actually worried about your life. Because of that, we are done with this nonsense. You will say nothing more on the topic. When in public, if you wish for heated words, I demand you stay silent. I'll hear not another word against Gregory or of that dead serving girl. I'd rather live in silence than discuss this again. Do I make myself clear?"

As she spoke, I stepped back from her, practically falling onto my window seat. I adjusted myself so I sat with dignity, but her words tore tiny holes in my determination. Would my friends really turn their backs on me? Would Uncle Walter? I couldn't imagine such a future.

Mother raised an eyebrow at me and I nodded in response. I understood what she said.

"Very good. Good night, Isabelle." Her skirts swept the floor as she left me alone. One candle remained lit on the bed-side table. Its flame flickered in the evening darkness, wavering along with my resolve.

If I was going to avoid marriage to Gregory I'd have to do something drastic. Mother had to believe she'd broken me. That she'd pushed me too far.

CHAPTER 7

Setting my easel up on the front lawn, I laid out my paints on the side table and took my seat. With great show to Mother, who was sitting on the porch drinking lemonade, I unbuttoned the top three buttons of my blouse and raised my skirt so my ankles were exposed to the sunlight. Despite it all, she didn't even flinch. I grimaced, but pulled out the painting of a tree I'd started long ago and grabbed a paintbrush.

All week Mother left me to my own devices and seemed not to notice my behavior. She told everyone of my vicious attack and thus all my evening commitments were excused.

The tree I had been working on for months was nearly done. Its leaves were multiple shades of green, the grass illuminated its shadow, and the cobblestone street only needed more outlining. The image reflected a world that I couldn't see anymore. I glanced at Mother and gritted my teeth. Perhaps she could ignore me, but she wouldn't let me make a spectacle on our lawn. Swallowing my pride, I dipped the brush in red paint.

Finally, Mother could stand it no longer. She rose from her rocking chair and crossed the yard to me. Clasping my shoulder, she demanded, "Isabelle! What on earth are you doing?"

Not flinching at her grip, I continued to add red to the tree so that it appeared as if it were bleeding over our lawn instead of basking in the sun. The more I dabbed, the tighter her grasp became, but I was determined to continue.

"I was going to hang this in the parlor and now look at it." She released her grip and knelt beside me. "Please, Isabelle. Stop this. Don't make me do something we'll both regret." Her voice was soft, but I continued to paint.

As I mixed a darker shade of red to add to my painting, a large blue carriage turned the corner and came down the lane. The two brown horses pulled to a stop in front of our house.

A smile spread across my face. I recognized the footman instantly as Lucy's. She had come to visit. It felt like forever since I'd seen her despite only being a few days. I'd been foolish not to tell her the whole story. Lucy would believe me. But, even as I thought that, I realized I couldn't speak to her, not in front of Mother at any rate. Dropping my paintbrush in the water jug, I took a deep breath. I approached the coach, but froze when the door swung open, revealing a disheveled Mrs. D'Havland instead of Lucy. Her hat pin was loose and her brooch fastened on the wrong side. But that wasn't what concerned me. Her eyes were rimmed in red, and she continuously wrung her hands as if disturbed.

Stepping out of the carriage, she scanned the yard until her eyes landed on Mother and me. Mother stepped forward to greet her friend, but Mrs. D'Havland bounded past her until she was face to face with me.

"You!" she exclaimed. "This is all your fault! If you hadn't given my Lucy that horrible idea, none of this would be happening."

Mother looked at me with narrowed eyes. "What has happened?"

"Your daughter has ruined my Lucia," Mrs. D'Havland sniffed. "Mr. Stewart asked permission to court Lucy and, after we consented, he came by twice this week. His earnestness and extravagant gifts left little doubt to his intentions. I was planning to announce their engagement within the month. But at his visit this very morning, my daughter stood before us all and declared that she could marry no one but that Patrick boy, for she no longer possessed her virtue."

Only the threat of engagement to that horrible Mr. Stewart could force Lucy to act on my foolish idea. Sweet Lucy was ruined permanently. Mrs. D'Havland was right, it was my fault. I hated that Lucy was put in such a spot, and yet a strange pride trickled through me. Lucy had taken control of her life. I'd never cared for her more. Mother stepped between me and Mrs. D'Havland. "Not sweet Lucy!"

Putting up a hand, Mrs. D'Havland continued. "After everyone had left and Lucia was properly punished, she finally explained where she came up with the horrible idea to make up such a lie."

Following Mrs. D'Havland's gaze, Mother looked at me. "Isabelle?" she whispered. "It isn't possible. Isabelle would sooner set herself aflame than hurt Lucy."

"Nevertheless, that is where the lie began." Mrs. D'Havland pulled herself to stand her proper height and glared down at me. "You are never to speak to Lucy again. We are sending her away tomorrow to visit family in New York. Perhaps Mr. Stewart will forgive her, but if he doesn't, she'll find a match out East and settle down there. Either way, I'll have no more of your meddling; I don't care what happened to you. You are to stay away from my family."

I knew she spoke the truth. They would keep Lucy either locked up or fully engaged from now until her move so that I'd never be able to see her again, neither for a farewell hug nor to apologize for the horrible fate my advice pushed upon her. Lucy and I were nothing more than pawns in our families' quest for societal power. It was silly for us to think we were anything more than that or had any ability to make our own moves. My stupidity had cost me and Lucy everything. It was more than I could bear.

Mother stepped between the two of us and put a hand on Mrs. D'Havland's arm. "I'm sure Isabelle meant no harm. Don't all girls have such thoughts from time to time?"

If Mrs. D'Havland's eyes had been cold before, they were nothing compared to the gaze she bestowed upon Mother now. "The apple doesn't fall far from the tree, does it, Fanny? If you are going to defend your daughter's terrible thoughts, then you are little better than she. I'll be glad to be rid of your social company as well."

Mrs. D'Havland climbed back into her coach and instructed her footman to leave. Once the carriage was no longer audible, Mother put her hands on my shoulders and guided me toward the house. I made it as far as the front parlor before I yanked myself free. Frustration for my friend radiated through me. Mother refrained from reaching for me again.

"Isabelle, pull yourself together." Her voice betrayed her tears. She brushed the hair off my face and grabbed my cheeks. Instead of soothing me, her touch pushed further sorrow upon me. The pain of her betrayal shook my core. Hatred over Gregory's actions made my face burn. But Lucy's fate sent me into near convulsions. The tears were so strong I could hardly catch a breath.

After a period of time, I know not how long, Mother called for Abigail to fetch the doctor and for our hired man to come carry me to bed.

Once my sobs quieted and I lay calmly in my bed, Dr. Carson examined me. When he was done, Mother left my side and met him in the hall. I could hear their low voices through the partially open door.

"Well?" Mother insisted.

Dr. Carson shook his head. "I can see nothing wrong with her physically. I suspect she has simply encountered too much shock in too short a period of time."

"But how do I help her? I can't undo what happened."

"No, no one can do that. Perhaps she needs solitude for a period of time." Dr. Carson's medical bag locks clicked.

Mother sighed. "Is there no more aggressive treatment? We just announced her engagement. There are parties and fittings every week for the next month or so. If I start canceling, people will talk. It could damage her future."

"My only other recommendation is to send her to a sanitarium. Just until she's better. It is possible she'll recover faster away from the familiar. I can't be sure, of course."

I could imagine Mother wringing her hands and shaking her head. "Dr. Carson! How can you think of such things! She'll be ruined!" Mother's voice quivered.

"Then give her time and rest to overcome this. I have not seen shock linger long when treated right."

"Rest. Yes, that will bring my girl back." Mother's voice became muffled as they walked down the hall and down the stairs.

The implications of a sanitarium were too great for her to imagine: social ruin and ostracism for both of us. Once word got out where I was, no respectable man would marry me.

No man would marry me.

The thought stuck in my mind.

CHAPTER 8

Unless Mrs. D'Havland was lying, I had only one chance to
see Lucy before she was sent east. Once Mother had retired for
the night, I slipped out of the house and ran to our childhood
meeting spot. If she was able to get away, I knew she'd go there.

When we were still in school, we found an old abandoned
cottage in the woods. It was shabby and sort of tilted backward, but it was ours. A place to play house when we were
young and then to tell secrets as we got older.

The weeds were high in Mr. Garvouch's garden, but I pushed
through. My ankle had almost healed, but it was tight as I made
my way through the brush. I tried not to think of the noctur-
nal vermin that might be underfoot and invisible in the spring
moonlight.

By the time I reached the cottage, I was heaving for breath.
It had been ages since Lucy and I had met here and it showed.
Even in the dark, I could see the slant was more pronounced
and the wooden slats more precarious. We could very well be
risking our lives to meet here. If the wind blew the wrong way
the whole building could collapse. I pulled on the door and the

whole house shook so that I jumped back for fear I'd toppled it over.

A small slip of paper stuck between two of the slats of wood fluttered to the ground. I knelt down and retrieved it; it wasn't wet like the grass, nor stiff with age. It was new. Surely a message for me. I unfolded the note and lifted my lantern so I could read it.

It wasn't signed, but it was Lucy's handwriting:

I will be at the creek tonight waiting. This is not safe.

I was too late. My heart raced. What wasn't safe—the building or something more? A twig snapped and I jumped to my feet, glancing about me.

"Someone there?" I stuttered in as loud a voice as I could muster. My small voice felt like a shout in the stillness.

No response.

The creek had to be the one behind her house. Close enough for her to see me signal, but far enough away that no one would see us without the lantern's light. I ran down the streets until her massive home was in view. A slight trickle of rain started to fall, making the grass even slicker. I slid once, but managed to remain upright.

As I got closer to the creek, I noticed a figure sitting on the bench. Lucy turned toward me and sighed in relief.

"I wasn't sure you'd come. Everything has gone so terribly wrong." She took my hands in hers.

"I know. I'm so sorry!" We sat on the bench. "I don't know what I was thinking."

Lucy held up her hand, silencing me. "It's done. Mr. Stewart is done with me and all things considered, traveling east doesn't sound so horrible. Although it will take longer for Patrick's letters to reach me."

"Only you could see the good in this situation." I shook my head. "But that message. If you are at peace, what danger scared you?"

"Surely I'm being silly. Even now I feel foolish mentioning it."

"What?" Goosebumps prickled my skin.

"Gregory came to visit me."

For a moment I heard nothing. In all of our courtship, Gregory had never sought Lucy out. He seemed to find her vapid, though he couldn't have been more wrong.

"Oh?" I managed to squeak out.

"Yes, I found it strange as well. Since the dinner party, Mother and he have spoken a few times. He found me reading on the veranda after one of their meetings and asked if there was any special place you might go to think or to confide in a friend. It was strange. All his words were correct, but he sounded unlike himself."

"Oh," I repeated. Why would Gregory want to know if there was a special spot I frequented? My palms began to sweat. He was planning on coming after me. He'd seen me at Katerina's.

"I didn't tell him. I figured if you hadn't confided the information then it wasn't for me to say. But I came here instead just in case."

I nodded. My voice felt locked in my throat. The outside was too exposed. Anyone could be watching us. Anyone could be following us. I shuddered.

"Is everything smoothing out for you? Should I be worried?" Lucy still held my hand, but I couldn't sit another moment. I jumped to my feet and paced beside the creek.

How I wanted to tell her everything. She deserved to know what was happening, but it was all too possible that Gregory was listening at that very moment. The very fact that he had been trying to sniff out information about me was suspicious. Even Lucy saw that he wasn't behaving like himself. I couldn't vocalize what I saw and risk him knowing everything.

I looked at my friend and her kind eyes and I finally realized the truth of the situation. I couldn't stay here. Not beside the creek, nor even in Oak Park. Gregory wouldn't stop until he knew exactly what happened to me and when he found out . . . I couldn't think about that. Dr. Carson, without meaning to, had given me an escape. A sanitarium. The title of insane.

Mother and I hadn't spoken a word since the dinner party. Silence wasn't enough, but it was a start.

"I have to go," I declared. Lucy winced as if hurt, but I couldn't solve that problem too.

No longer could I behave like myself. I'd make it up to her, I promised myself. "Be sure to write. I will miss you." I put my lantern in her hand.

Lucy stood and waved a hand in farewell. I waved back and took off in a run. The tie in my hair loosened and it bounced behind me in the night wind. I stopped to grab a pile of leaves from the ground and rubbed it against my scalp, face, and hands. The more disheveled my appearance the better. I had to give Mother no other option but to admit me to a sanitarium. If I knew her, silent and disheveled combined with all that had happened would be enough.

I burst through the kitchen door and stomped through the hallway. It was the dead of night, so everyone was asleep. The vase still sat on the center table of the front room. I paused, then walked into the room and lunged against the table. The vase fell with a thud upon the floor. It didn't break as I hoped, but the sound sparked movement upstairs.

"Isabelle?" Mother called out.

How should I behave? I wondered. I couldn't behave too wildly or Dr. Carson would send me to an asylum, where the truly insane resided, as opposed to a sanitarium. This was a game of balances and I had to be sure to win.

All right, Mother, I thought to myself. *If you don't want me to speak, I won't. Not one word until you agree to believe me. We'll see how quickly you fold.*

Lying on the floor, I stared at the ceiling and shook my head over and over while pounding my fists beside me.

Mother's slippers padded down the stairs. "Is someone there?" she called out.

The moonlight was bright, making the room just light enough to see faint objects. Mother walked into the room and stopped. She righted the table and her breath became jagged as if afraid.

"Isabelle?" she said more softly. A moment passed and then she inhaled with such force I knew she'd seen me. "Isabelle, darling! What's the matter?"

I continued to shake my head.

Mother grasped my neck and pulled me into a sitting position. My eyes remained unfocused and I pounded the floor next to me. Mother tried to take my hands, but she couldn't get a grip to stop me.

"Isabelle. Stop this now." Her voice lacked its strong nature. It shook with emotion. "Please, Isabelle. Please?"

When I didn't respond to her pleas she lowered me back to the floor and shouted, "Abigail! Abigail, get up. We have to fetch Dr. Carson."

The tightening of my stomach subsided. My head stopped shaking and my fists stopped pounding. I lay still as Mother made her plans for Dr. Carson. No matter what happened now, I had scared her. She wouldn't let me stay home to recover my sanity. I had won.

CHAPTER 9

Jostling back and forth in Aunt Clara's carriage, I tried unsuccessfully to find a comfortable position. In a matter of moments, I would see my new home, the place that would both set me free and condemn me to a life of mockery. I wished Mother had let us take the train, but she insisted that no one know where I'd gone, and that meant having Aunt Clara fetch us. They told our friends that they were taking me on a trip to the country for peace and relaxation. Gregory even dropped off a new fan for me to use while traveling. After she explained our trip to him, it was clear she still hoped to marry me off to Gregory. The thought sent chills through me. I hadn't come this far to fail. If Bellevue Sanitarium was what it took to obtain my freedom from that murderer, I'd make sure I was admitted.

"I'm still not convinced that this is the right move," Mother fretted.

Aunt Clara patted her hand and replied, "Once Isabelle is situated you'll see this decision is right. She will recover."

The two swayed slightly with the carriage and stared at me. I didn't even pretend to think about replying. I had worked too hard to show even the slightest chink in my resolve. And now, we were trotting down the streets of Batavia to declare me insane. The thought left my mouth dry and jaw clenched, but I was left with no other option.

"This is not how I planned on spending the summer, living with Clara and visiting you in a sanitarium." Mother snapped her fingers in my face, making me blink and glance up at her. "You'd better work hard and heal yourself. I want none of this fiddle-faddle come fall."

Aunt Clara put a hand on Mother's knee, pulling her anger away from me. "Fanny, don't be so hard on the girl. She is young to deal with such grief."

Mother raised her eyebrows and turned to her sister. "Grief? You think she is grieving? Clara, she didn't know the girl. That girl was a *servant* and new in town. She's created this whole story around a stranger. It is ridiculous!"

"Oh, Fanny," Aunt Clara said, sighing. "Grief, perhaps not for the dead, but for herself. Whether you believe her story or not, something happened to her, and she has to find a way to come to terms with it."

As Aunt Clara continued to speak, my heart hammered in my ears. She understood how what I had seen weighed on me. For that small allowance alone, a small weight left my shoulders.

A short time later the carriage pulled to a stop, and both Mother and Aunt Clara took visibly deep breaths. We had arrived at Bellevue.

I drew one of the curtains back and stared up at the square, tan brick building that was now my home. It didn't look like a place for the condemned. In fact, it looked relatively normal except for the wire covering the second story windows. White lace curtains outlined the windows, neat flower beds and trees surrounded the property, while a gazebo rested peacefully on the far side of the lawn. If I hadn't known what this place was, I'd have called it charming.

Our driver quickly untied and unpacked my luggage from

the back of the carriage as I looked up at my new home. I could practically smell the flowers in the crisp spring air. Mother stood a few steps away, gazing up at the windows.

"No, Clara. This is simply not right. No daughter of mine belongs here." Mother shook her head and turned toward me. "You don't have to live here. Just say one word, and I'll take back everything I said, and we can go home."

Did Mother really mean that? Take back all the promises she made about keeping my engagement to Gregory? No matter how nice this place seemed, I knew I'd miss my own room before the day was out. Her offer was tempting. I licked my lips, wondering if I could trust my own mother. I met her eyes and saw how hope radiated from her. My gaze didn't unfocus as I weighed my choices and I saw her grasp onto my moment of weakness.

"Just one word, Isabelle, and you can return to your life, get married, and move on from this harrowing chapter." Despite it all, she still held on to Gregory. There was no doubt where her love truly lay.

I glared at her for one long moment before lifting the side of my skirt, walking over the gravel and up the front porch of Bellevue Sanitarium. Behind me Mother sighed, but didn't try to stop me.

Whatever I had expected to feel when I entered the sanitarium was forgotten when an old housekeeper with dark gray hair and a wide, round face met us at the door. Without a word she took my handbag from my hands and motioned for me to follow her. I did as she demanded, and a creeping sense of dread filled me. The hallway was dark; the doors were all shut so the only light came from the open front door. This was not the soothing rest home I'd imagined. This place was hard. The ramifications of my choice were becoming clearer and I didn't like what I saw. Nevertheless, it was still the better option.

I sighed and tried to smile as the housekeeper opened a tall wooden door and pushed us into an office.

The far wall was lined with bookshelves overflowing with titles I'd never seen, which is saying something as I'd spent hours reading books from Papa's library. A lone window let in the warm colors of sunset and filled the room with shadows. Jars with frogs floating in yellow liquid sat on the doctor's desk. The remaining walls were covered with large charts of human anatomy.

"Dr. Patterson will be here soon," the housekeeper said and shut the door, leaving Aunt Clara, Mother, and me standing alone in the small room.

"Let's sit down, Isabelle," Mother said. I could hear the resignation in her voice.

I sat in a straight-backed chair and tried to look comfortable. Mother and Aunt Clara perched on the edges of their chairs with well-practiced expressions of contentment. The sight took my breath away. If I didn't maintain my stance I'd end up just like them: pretending to be content for the rest of my life.

There was a knock on the door, and a tall man with graying hair and a black suit entered the room carrying a file and a mug of coffee. "Mrs. Larkin, I presume?" His voice was smooth and deep. Mother's tight expression loosened slightly in his presence.

"I am Mrs. Larkin," Mother said as she stood and shook his hand.

She returned to her seat, and Dr. Patterson crossed the room and sat in the tall leather chair behind the desk. He had a long, square beard, which made reading his face difficult. "And this must be Isabelle," he said, gesturing to me. Our eyes met. "Why don't you tell me what's been happening with you, child?"

Immediately, Mother and Aunt Clara exchanged a glance. I could guess what they were wondering: *Do we let her stew in silence for a spell, or just let the truth out?*

Instead of answering, Mother simply turned her gaze to me and waited. After a moment Aunt Clara did the same, though she, at least, seemed more worried than angry. Yet, I could feel the strength of their expectation pulling the answer out of me. Biting my bottom lip, I stared at my hands. The nails were already destroyed from my nervously biting them. There was nothing left for me to do but wait them out.

Coldness passed over my heart as I watched Mother eventually turn away and betray me with silence of her own.

Aunt Clara was the one who finally answered. "Isabelle has been having fits of . . . I don't know exactly what. She won't reply. The girl stopped speaking nearly two weeks ago."

"What do you mean stopped speaking?" Dr. Patterson asked the question of me again, but I looked down at the paisley rug, avoiding his gaze.

Mother glared at me. "She claims to have witnessed the death of a local servant, and somehow has convinced herself that her fiancé is the murderer. Our family doctor thinks she may have been attacked herself. After it happened, she turned mute. I don't know how else to help her."

I stared down at my hands and picked at a hangnail. There was no depth to how she defined me. When had Mother and I grown so far apart?

I could feel Dr. Patterson's eyes on me, studying my reaction, but I refused to look up. If he were to admit me, I had to seem troubled, but not beyond help. I didn't want him to turn me away and send me to an asylum. I couldn't imagine living beside truly insane people. The thought made me tear up. Were tears good or bad here? I wasn't sure how to behave. He cleared his throat and drummed his fingers on his desk. Still, I looked down.

A pad of paper and pen were placed in my lap. Lifting my eyes, I met Dr. Patterson's gaze and raised an eyebrow.

"I'd like you to explain what's troubling you." He spoke as if it were a simple task.

This wouldn't do. I couldn't communicate with them in any way. I had to behave in a manner that would ensure my admittance. I picked up the pen, unscrewed the top, and poured the ink all over the paper, and my skirt, although, since it was black, the stains were nearly invisible.

"Isabelle Larkin, what are you doing?" Mother screeched, scooting her chair away from me.

When the paper had absorbed all the ink, I handed it back to Dr. Patterson.

He quickly dropped the ruined pages in a small wastebasket. Grabbing a second pen from his desk, he said, "Let's try that again, shall we?"

Blast. He wasn't falling for my act. I'd have to do something else to get his attention. Taking the pen from his hand, I again unscrewed it, and this time I poured its contents into my mouth.

Dr. Patterson's eyes widened in surprise just as Mother jumped to her feet, exclaiming, "Isabelle! Ink is poisonous!"

Aunt Clara jumped to her feet. "Do you have an emetic? Ipecac perhaps?"

Dr. Patterson rummaged in the small cabinet mounted on the wall. Multiple bottles fell out as he looked. When he didn't immediately locate the correct emetic, Mother grasped my shoulders and shook me. By then, the ink tasted so foul it burned, and I played my last card. I spit the entire contents straight into Mother's face. The black ink clung to her pale cheeks and dripped onto her pink gown. Everyone was silent. Aunt Clara covered her mouth, and Dr. Patterson turned to observe. Mother opened and closed her mouth so many times she reminded me of our cow chewing cud.

"Yes, well," Dr. Patterson said, breaking the silence. "I suppose that answers that." He closed the cabinet and returned to his seat.

Aunt Clara fidgeted with her handkerchief and offered it to Mother, who tried in vain to clean herself off. "Doctor, she is ill. Surely you can do something for her."

Dr. Patterson stood up, walked to the front of his desk, and looked down at us. His palms were white as bleached linen and his nails as clean as a baby's. "I believe in a regimen of rest, diet, baths, fresh air, occupation, and as little medicine as possible. We have patients from only the very best of society here. That being said, there are some seriously wounded women in this house, Mrs. Larkin. Women who have addictions, mental illnesses, sexual illnesses, and some who have been unable to overcome some trauma. They aren't the type of people Isabelle would come into contact with in Oak Park. Are you sure you want your daughter exposed to them?"

Mother's voice was muffled by the handkerchief she used to clean her cheeks. "I just want my girl well. If you can heal her, I don't care about the cost." She lowered the handkerchief and looked at me. Mother sounded so effortlessly loving, I wanted to believe her. Yet, if she truly wanted me healed, the power was hers.

"Is there a way you could separate her from the . . . frailer women?" Aunt Clara asked. "I have no doubt she'll recover quickly."

Mother added, "I am willing to pay extra for private accommodations."

Dr. Patterson raised his hand and stopped the conversation. "We have space in our residence wing. As there are no other patients there, she would be confined and safe. However, she will be quite alone, aside from Mrs. Patterson and me."

Mother took advantage of his brief pause. "She is an independent girl. She'll do just fine there, but are you sure you can spare the room? It is your residence after all. What about your own children, Doctor?" Mother's tone gnawed at me. She didn't care about his comfort, only her reputation and whose idle tongue might ruin it.

"We have but one child, who is away at school. I assure you, we have plenty of room. I would not make such an offer if we did not." Dr. Patterson kneeled before me and took my hands in his. "Our residence is on the first floor, and the spare rooms are upstairs. Will you be comfortable living without any neighbors?"

I doubted he knew how much respect he'd earned with that question. It was the type of thing Papa would've asked. I nodded, still keeping my head down. My mouth still burned from the ink, and my head was beginning to ache from the bitter taste.

He cupped my chin in his hand. "This is the question, child—do you want to get well?"

I felt, rather than heard, Mother and Aunt Clara inhale as they also waited for my response. I pondered my answer. How would people who had lost themselves answer this? What answer would guarantee my safety?

Dr. Patterson's eyes bored into mine, and I felt him searching for my answer.

Suddenly, Katerina's screams filled my mind. There was no healing for me. No matter what I did, I couldn't find any way out. Here with Dr. Patterson was my new home—for however long it took.

No, I replied with a shake of my head. I did not wish to be healthy.

While Mother let out a gasp, Dr. Patterson dropped my chin and scribbled something on his papers. "Regardless of this choice, you'll be a good girl and do what you are told?" he asked.

I nodded immediately. That was a small price to pay for protection.

Dr. Patterson moved back to his chair and rang a small bell.

Instantly, a knock sounded from the door, and a moment later a man stepped inside. "Dr. Patterson?" he inquired. "You rang for me?"

"Yes. Please escort this girl to the Rose Room and ask Mrs.

Patterson to come see me." He returned his attention to me. "Samuel is my assistant and will take care of you. Follow what he says like a good girl. Welcome to Bellevue, Isabelle."

Samuel offered me his arm, not seeming to notice Aunt Clara's sadness nor Mother's ink-marked face. I wondered how long it would take to get the ink completely off. I took his proffered arm and left the room. Relief flooded my veins. I had done it. I was safe in Bellevue's walls.

"So, your mother has an interesting way of putting her face on." Samuel glanced at me from the corner of his eye. When I didn't respond, he pulled a handkerchief from his pocket and handed it to me. "Black teeth are not typically attractive, but on you they are. . . . Well, I'm sure you're much prettier without the stains."

Despite every instinct, I smiled at his remark. It might not have been a compliment, but it felt good to smile.

At my reaction, he seemed to relax and insisted, "Dr. Patterson and his wife are good people. If you have problems with those stains, I have a good baking soda mix in my office."

I dabbed at my mouth, ruining his white handkerchief. No matter how young or kind he was, I'd have to remember to keep alert. One wrong move and I'd be discharged and back in Gregory's arms. I shuddered.

"It is a bit drafty, but with summer around the corner you'll be warm soon enough." Samuel gestured up a staircase.

Once on the second story, he led me down a corridor and to a tall oak door.

"This is your room. I'll have your trunks sent up." Samuel flushed as he spoke. "Welcome to Bellevue. I hope it's all you need."

CHAPTER 10

When I awoke everything taunted me. The sun shone from the wrong direction and my bed felt unfamiliar. The white bedspread was simple, but the down filling kept me warm. The wallpaper had a pale flower pattern, something Mother surely wouldn't approve of. Wallpaper was for servants and those who couldn't afford to have such designs painted onto the walls themselves. Yet, as I gazed at the pattern, there was a texture to it that you could never imitate with paint.

I rolled over, trying to push Mother from my mind.

This was ridiculous, I scolded myself. Mother had already proven how little she cared for me when she turned a deaf ear to what had happened. It was time to learn how to manage my life without her guidance.

The wood was cold beneath my feet as I slid to the floor and fished for the chamber pot. Lifting the bed skirt, I found only darkness staring back at me. I threw a blue dressing gown around my shoulders before slipping from my room and running down the stairs to find the outhouse.

Once I reached the first floor, the scent of coffee and cinnamon wafted from the kitchen. My stomach rumbled in hunger. I didn't recall eating dinner. For a moment I was torn between my desire to eat and the need to relieve myself, but in the end I kept to the original course and fled outdoors.

The early glow of sunrise illuminated my path from the porch stairs to the outhouse, but I still felt like a mouse sneaking cheese from the kitchen. As I opened the wooden door of the outhouse, the smell of lemon and lye assailed my senses. At the very least, it was clean. I closed the door and lifted my nightgown.

As I sat a twig snapped just outside the door. My breath froze in trepidation. *Pull yourself together, Isabelle! Mother told everyone we were traveling for the summer. Gregory trusts her. You are safe.*

I quickly finished and pushed the door open. Instead of swinging easily, the door butted against something and closed in my face with a sharp creak and a thud. My heart hammered as I realized I hadn't been imagining it. There was someone out there.

"Oh!" a congested voice exclaimed. I peeked out through the door, revealing a woman in her twenties still in her day gown with puffy eyes and a runny nose sitting on the outhouse stoop. "I didn't realize you were in there."

I shrugged and slipped out onto the stoop. The woman was clearly upset, but it wasn't wise for me to stay. I hadn't yet met any of the patients, nor decided if or how I'd communicate with them. If this woman was a patient, how did she sound so normal? Avoiding eye contact, I took a few steps toward the house, but she sniffed in such a miserable manner that I turned back around.

"Will you just sit with me a moment?" she asked. Her dress hung on her as if it had been made for someone else. Her cheek bones protruded out while her eyes appeared sucken into her face. I wondered if she had been physically ill recently. I couldn't leave her in distress.

"I'm Marilla," she began when she realized I was going to stay. "I don't recognize you. Are you one of the girls who stays in her room all day? Have I heard you shouting at night? Surely you've heard my name mentioned of late. I'm sure they've been looking for me."

Even if they had formed a search party, I'd known nothing of it. I shrugged again and sat on the stoop beside her, feeling her black wool skirt rub against my bare arm.

"They didn't look for me?" Marilla's voice raised an octave. "B-but I ran away. Surely they care a little."

Ran away? Was she an inmate or servant, and what had forced her to leave? Even more puzzling, what had brought her back? I longed to ask these questions, but I couldn't. My ruse would only work if everyone believed it. Silence was part of my ploy. I'd only just obtained safety; I'd not risk it.

I slid closer and patted her shoulder. A sad smile pulled at her lips. Crickets chirped all around us and, after a moment, she shook her head and knocked my hand away.

"Never thought I'd be back here. Joe, that's my husband, should've been overjoyed to have me home. But when I opened the door, there was another woman wearing *my* apron, washing *my* dishes. Joe didn't even apologize—just got mad and insisted I return here till he signs my release papers. Thing is, he never visits . . . never told me why he put me here in the first place. I don't know if he's ever going to come get me."

She fell silent again. I swallowed, hoping to put some moisture back in my throat. Two things battled for my attention: If this woman ran away from here, what was so bad she couldn't stand to stay, and who had to sign papers for me to be released? Who held that power over me?

"Do you think he's replaced me?" Her voice was so soft; I knew this was her true fear. How strange that the first person I met was willing to run away to be with her husband, when I was here avoiding my fiancé.

We sat in silence as the sun continued to crawl up from beneath the horizon. The kitchen door screeched open, breaking the silence.

"I knew I heard you, Mrs. Farthing!" A nurse rushed down the porch steps. Her red hair was still flowing down her back; she must've rushed from her room to collect Marilla.

"Oh, Agatha," Marilla exclaimed and jumped into her arms.

Agatha rubbed Marilla's back for a moment before she noticed me. "And what are you doing out here, Miss Isabelle?"

Surprised by her knowledge of me, I pointed toward the outhouse, but Marilla sniffed loudly and replied, "She was talking with me."

Agatha lifted her eyebrows. "Talking?" She gave me a knowing look. I turned away from her; she knew too much about my "illness" without having met me. In the real world such forwardness would be curtailed, but here such societal rules didn't apply.

Marilla stepped back and looked down at me. "She's a wonderful listener."

"Now *that* I'll believe," Agatha said, laughing. "Time to get you in bed, Mrs. Farthing. Isabelle, your breakfast will be in your room shortly." She put an arm around Marilla's shoulders and led her inside, leaving me on the stoop of the outhouse.

I let them have a sizable lead before dusting off my robe and heading back inside. The smells of breakfast were nearly overpowering, and I couldn't bring myself to move from the kitchen doorway. The kitchen was enormous. Herbs hung alongside pots over a large wooden table in the center of the room, while another table with six stools occupied an entire wall. The metal stove in the corner was an orchestra of boiling water and crackling fire. The shelves and countertops were cluttered with spice jars and dried herbs.

"Well, don't just stand there. Come on in," a woman ordered as she scrubbed a pan in the wide sink. Her back was to me, and I wondered how she knew I was even there. "There's a bowl of porridge on the table. Agatha was supposed to take it up to your room, but she's a bit behind this morning. You're welcome to eat with me."

When I still didn't move, she turned around and put her hands on her hips. "That food isn't going to eat itself. Now get in here and sit."

I didn't want this woman to think I was stupid, so I followed her orders. The porridge was still steaming and had brown sugar sprinkled over the top. Without waiting another moment, I lifted my spoon and dug in.

The cook wiped her hands on a towel and walked over to where I was sitting. She wasn't heavy like our cook back home, but wasn't thin like Mother either. Her figure was like her smile, warm and loved. Her gray hair showed signs of auburn, and her eyes danced with amusement despite the flour and egg on her cheek. I liked her immediately.

"So you're the child who joined us yesterday evening," she said, eyeing me. "I wonder what they will do with you."

My eating slowed. Now that I was living here, perhaps I should wonder what I would fill my days with as well. I'd been so intent on arriving, I'd given no thought beyond that.

"If you ever need someone to pass the time with, you are always welcome here." She dried her hands and moved to work on her rolls just as another woman burst in. I wondered if Cook had known she was coming.

The woman had an air of authority about her, created in part by her tight bun and high cheekbones. Recognizing her from the family portrait on Dr. Patterson's desk, I assumed this was Mrs. Patterson.

Putting a pile of dishes on the table, she turned to me and shook her head. "You certainly leave a unique impression on people. Marilla is up there telling Agatha every detail of why she left, and she's normally quieter than you! It's good you distracted her enough for us to find her, but don't expect me to thank you for that."

I filled my mouth with a spoonful of porridge to avoid answering her. I swallowed under the pressure of Mrs. Patterson's gaze.

"She's just a girl, and a good girl from what you've said," Cook interrupted. "Let her finish her breakfast before badgering her." I paused my chewing to see the slap I was sure Mrs. Patterson was going to give Cook for her impertinence. That was how Mother handled mouthy servants. To my surprise, Mrs. Patterson simply walked over to my side of the table.

Mrs. Patterson tilted her weary head and examined me head to foot. Given the questioning crinkle of her brow, I don't think I gave her much to be impressed with. Perhaps I did look a mess, but she herself was hard to look at. Her gray gown was so starched and straight that it made me wonder if she ever sat or even bent over.

"Agatha is busy so I will dress you this morning. Give Cook your bowl when you are done and return to your room. I'll be there shortly."

I did as she ordered. Once I was out of the room I heard Cook ask her, "What are we going to do with such a young lady?"

I wondered the same thing.

CHAPTER II

My mind swirled with the morning's events, and it wasn't yet eight o'clock. As I returned to my room, hoping the privacy would be calming, I was once again disappointed. Everything was wrong. Things were too clean and too sparse for comfort. I hadn't packed any of Papa's letters or my paintings. The only personal item I'd brought from home was my copy of *Jane Eyre*. Where had my mind been? I was supposed to feel safe here, not lost. Slowly I backed into a corner and covered my face with my hands.

Moments later Mrs. Patterson flung open the door without even announcing herself and stalked over to the wardrobe. Her face was damp with perspiration, and a rogue hair had fallen from her stiff bun. Though thin, she filled my room with an authority that I dared not cross. As she fixed her hair, I allowed myself a good look at her. It was clear that she had once been pretty, but now there were too many lines streaking her face for her to look anything but stern.

"Don't just stand there, girl. Get that nightgown off you!" She opened my wardrobe and pulled out a sage afternoon dress. "What were you doing in the outhouse, child?" she asked.

She knew I didn't speak, so why did she persist in asking me questions? I ignored her and lifted my nightgown over my head. The skin on my arms and thighs prickled in the cool air as I stood in the barest of underclothes.

"Surely you had chamber pots where you lived before?" she asked, grabbing my gown and tossing my clothes in a basket by the door.

I nodded. Mrs. Patterson must have thought me dumb.

She sighed. "Then why didn't you use yours? We keep two in each room for just such . . . emergencies."

I opened my mouth slightly. How could I tell her that there was no pot in my room? Was this the point at which I should behave insane or find a way to answer? I shrugged again and hoped she would simply hand over my dress.

She did not.

Standing to get my dress, I was surprised when she held my clothes out of reach. "Listen," she began. "Now I don't care if you speak to them or not, but I expect answers to my questions."

I crossed my arms over my nearly naked breasts and glared at her. For a moment we stood in my small room, eyes locked. Mrs. Patterson's gray dress blended into the shadows until she was merely a head, floating in the air. She needed to learn that I deserved to be here. I grabbed a strand of my hair and yanked it out and tried not to wince as my scalp pinched. Then I grabbed another and another and another. My scalp screamed for relief, but I couldn't stop until Mrs. Patterson saw that I was a patient, not a girl to boss around.

After a few minutes of watching me, she grabbed my hands, held them together to stop my actions, and said in a soft, clear voice, "Listen, Isabelle. Perhaps you've fooled your mother with this act. Now, I don't care if you go bald, and I don't care if you're vocal, but we *will* find a way to communicate."

Her straightforward nature was oddly reassuring. I suspected that as long as I did what she needed to be done, she'd leave me alone. That was a bargain I was willing to make. I walked over to the bed and lifted the dust ruffle so she could see under it. With one hand, I made a sweeping gesture and then gave her a pointed look. She had to squint to make out the shapes under the bed, but my meaning was clear.

"Well, that explains things," she said. "I will make sure you have two by this evening."

I nodded my thanks. Without another word, she held the gown out in front of her and had me dressed in no time. She pulled my corset laces too tight. I rolled my shoulders until I found a comfortable posture.

When it came to my hair, I had absolutely no say. She yanked my hair back with a brush and began twisting and pulling until it was in a neat bun identical to hers. It was unfortunate, as I'd done my own hair for years now and was much more original than she. "There," she said as she dug the last hair pin into my scalp. "Now you are ready to join the others and start the day."

I didn't move from my stool. "Joining the others" was not something for which I'd prepared. I imagined a dozen giggling women corralling me into a corner and begging me to speak. Or worse, a dozen women chained to their chairs, howling and moaning to be understood in a world that made no sense to them anymore. I turned away from Mrs. Paterson and wondered why I had chosen to be left here, surrounded by women whose husbands didn't want them or who screamed in the night from imaginary pain.

Mrs. Patterson sighed and knelt in front of me. "Isabelle, no one is going to hurt you here. We all have a duty in this world, and yours is to get well. We will give you the tools, but you must do as we say."

I looked into her gray eyes and realized that she felt sorry for me. Heat raged through my chest. The anger was enough to push the fear from my mind and gave me the strength to face my fellow inmates. No one was going to pity me.

Mrs. Patterson grabbed my hands and pulled me to my feet. "Dr. Patterson and Dr. Deston are away on consultation in the city today so therapy is canceled. However, you'll find that today will be like any other day. In the morning we do work for the less fortunate. Today we are mending clothes. You've been taught to sew, haven't you?" Before I could nod she continued, "No matter. One of the ladies can teach you if you cannot. It will do you good to be around people."

I followed her out of the room as I wondered how sewing ever helped anyone feel better.

Mrs. Patterson led me down the staircase and into the main hallway where Marilla stood waiting, shifting a card between her hands. Agatha had braided Marilla's hair down her back and dressed her in a pale pink day gown. The change made her look even younger than before, and I suddenly missed Lucy so much it hurt. I was incarcerated and had no way of knowing what my best friend was enduring. Was she packing for her trip yet or had her mother forgiven her? Was there another suitor on the horizon? So many unknowns with no way to obtain answers.

Marilla interrupted my thoughts and held the card out to Mrs. Patterson. "This arrived for you a moment ago."

Mrs. Patterson pulled the card out of the envelope and clucked her tongue. "I must respond straight away. Isabelle, find a basket and make yourself comfortable. I'll only be a moment."

Marilla grinned. "Don't worry. I can take care of her."

Although Mrs. Patterson's lips pressed tightly together, she agreed before walking away down the hall.

"Agatha told me you can't speak," Marilla said as she grabbed my arm and pulled me toward the front parlor. "I can't imagine that, but I won't bother you about it none." I clenched my jaw.

Behaving like we were bosom buddies only made me feel more alone, but I needed someone to be my guide, and Marilla was willing.

She smiled and walked through a circle of chairs toward a pair of empty ones in the far corner of the room. Cherry bookshelves lined the walls on either side of a fireplace, but were almost completely blocked by the circle of chairs and baskets that dominated the space. If the windows had been opened, it could've been a friendly room, but the lack of outside noise and fresh air prevented any joy.

The few women scattered within the circle didn't look up as we entered, but I could feel their silence press down on me as if they were a pack of hungry wolves. It didn't matter whether I liked Marilla or not; I now clung to her like a life vest. Once I sat down she handed me a sewing basket and pulled out a child's nightgown for me to hem.

"Looks like some women just can't stay away," a blond lady to our right smirked.

Marilla didn't reply, but her fingers shook as she tried to thread the needle. Mrs. Patterson had said she was a quiet woman, but watching her among the other patients, it was obvious that it went deeper than that. Marilla was ashamed.

An elderly woman in a large chair by the fire said, "Seems to me her problem isn't staying away, it's keeping her man happy."

Marilla's cheeks burned red.

"What would you know of that, Mrs. Allan?" the blond woman asked.

"Some of us have intuition. One look at her and I knew she'd be back one way or another."

Mrs. Patterson entered at that moment, her stern presence silencing the conversation. My heart broke for Marilla. They had no need to be cruel. After all, each of them had been brought to Bellevue for a reason. The fact that Mrs. Allan picked on any of us made me instantly wary of her.

"Start your mending, Isabelle. The orphans cannot clothe

themselves," said Mrs. Patterson, sitting across the fireplace from Mrs. Allan in a wooden rocking chair.

I nodded and began a row of stitches. Whoever had started this nightgown had stitched uneven and sometimes crooked lines. I should've pulled them out, but without knowing who had started the work I didn't want to risk insulting someone, especially if that someone was one of the women sitting in this circle. If they were so eager to ridicule Marilla, what might they do to me?

Mrs. Allan whispered something to Mrs. Patterson, who frowned and shook her head. Marilla snorted slightly. Marilla whispered so only I could hear. "Every time the doctor is gone, Mrs. Allan tries to obtain more tonic from Mrs. Patterson. Even though it is her addiction that forced her husband to admit her here, she never feels she's had enough."

My stomach revolted at the thought. Who would want to feel drugged all the time?

"Is the doctor gone to town today?" one of the other women asked before cutting thread with her teeth. Her skin was an unhealthy pink, and her hands shook. She reminded me of Demitri, the local drunk. I'd never met a woman who was afflicted with that condition. I could hardly look her in the eye. Was this a rest home or a house for addicts?

"Of course he is," another spat. "Looking for new patients, no doubt."

"Silence," Mrs. Patterson interrupted. "I won't tolerate any gossip." The women bowed their heads in such a way that I gathered this wasn't their first scolding.

I pulled the thread through the fabric in a smooth motion, then took a moment to look around the room. Through the double doors, a nurse sat at a table in the drawing room, helping another woman with a puzzle. The woman's head jerked to the right over and over in what appeared to be an obsessive twitch. The nurse's eyes caught mine and darted from the patient to me. She flashed an exasperated look my way before standing up and closing the doors.

"You saw her?" Marilla asked, nodding toward the patient in the opposite room.

I shrugged. The nurse's reaction confused me. There was nothing wrong with observing my surroundings.

"That's Jesminda. She has good and bad days, but her constant twitches and stuttering are off-putting. I avoid her whenever I can. There's something not right about her," Marilla said, and the other women nodded their heads in agreement. Even Mrs. Patterson let Marilla's gossip slide.

Mrs. Allan pinched the bridge of her nose. "I can't remember the last time my head hurt this bad."

"It's the heat." Mrs. Patterson continued to sew and rock her chair. "You'll be fine if you keep working. In a little bit, I'll fetch us all some lemonade."

That was not what Mrs. Allan wanted to hear, for she dropped her sewing in the basket and stood up. "No," she demanded, "it is not the heat and having to sew is only making it worse. I need—"

"Hush," Mrs. Patterson interrupted. "You will be fine. Now. Calm. Down."

"I will not *hush*," Mrs. Allan spat. She lunged at Mrs. Patterson and grabbed her wrist. "I know what I need and you know it, too. Now give it to me. Give me th—"

"Isabelle!" Mrs. Patterson cried out. I blinked, startled to be involved in this argument. "Go to the kitchen immediately." When I didn't move, she stamped her foot. "Do as I say, young lady, and leave. Now!"

I didn't wait another moment. I bolted from the room. I doubted Mrs. Patterson was one to raise her voice often, and I dared not disobey her. I didn't want to know how much further Mrs. Allan was willing to go to get what she wanted.

CHAPTER 12

Mrs. Allan's high-pitched hollers propelled me down the hall to the kitchen. Even there, in the back of the house, her voice carried. Before I reached the kitchen door, Cook poked her head out and grinned at me.

"Mrs. Allan's begging for her 'mineral elixir' again, is she? Every time the doctor is away, she tries to guilt Mrs. Patterson into giving it to her." Cook stepped back into her domain. "You'd better get in here before she finds you loitering in the hall. Heaven help who crosses her after this."

Cook stood over the stove stirring a pot. On the table sat a pitcher of lemonade, which made my mouth water.

"Hello again, Isabelle," Agatha said. I'd been so focused on the beverage I hadn't seen her sitting at the table.

"You're having quite the day. First Marilla, now this." Agatha grinned. "It'll calm down. Most days are routine here."

Mrs. Allan's screams finally subsided, but the silence troubled me almost as much as her crying did. I'd read enough novellas to know about sanitarium silencing techniques. Restraints and drugs used to keep control over patients. Yet, the people here had shown me nothing but kindness. Novellas were only fiction.

"Pour yourself some lemonade and have a seat," Agatha said, patting the table in front of her. "Mrs. Patterson will come retrieve you when everything is calm again. You are too young to be a witness to Mrs. Allan's rage."

So, I'd been sent from the room because of my age. Little did they realize all I had seen in my life.

"If you weren't a voluntary mute, you could stand up for yourself and tell Mrs. Patterson you're not a little girl." Cook's voice had an air of amusement to it.

I nearly choked on my lemonade. Voluntary mute! Was that how they labeled me? Such a meager title for all I'd been through. Their assumption meant they didn't believe I had actually lost my mind. Beads of sweat threatened to break out across my forehead. If they discovered my ruse, Mother would have me wed the moment I returned! The back of my throat ached at the thought. I'd have to find a way to avoid that. Clearly, simple silence wasn't enough. I'd have to show everyone more, but when the time was right. A display too soon after these comments would only prove I was calculating.

Agatha must've sensed my distress, for she waved a dismissive hand at Cook. "Don't worry about Cook. She's just nosy. She reads all the files." She paused. "And no one thinks you volunteered to come here. It's just a medical term. None of us want to be here, but a job is a job."

"Speak for yourself," Cook interrupted. "I'm proud to be here. Proud to help these women get back on their feet. It's more than a job to some of us."

Agatha stared down into her lemonade. In the silence Cook returned to stirring whatever was in her pot.

Hoping to appear confused, I kept my expression blank and my gaze out of focus, but inwardly, I thanked Agatha. She didn't have to relieve my worries, but she did. Watching the exchange of glances between the two women, I realized they'd been in disagreement over this issue before. Agatha met Cook's raised eyebrow as if to duel, but Cook returned her attention to the stove.

Looking at Cook's rounded back and the flour handprints that covered her rear end, I couldn't help but smile. She turned around quickly and caught me appraising her.

"Don't you look at me like that, missy. I'm too old and too good a cook for them to ever fire, especially over some silly papers." She dropped her smile. "But, I am sorry for you. What an awful thing to believe of your fiancé!"

For a moment the wind was knocked out of me. Cook didn't question my story, but accepted what I had witnessed. Amazement clouded me. I jumped for the stove where a pot was about to boil over. Using the edge of my gown, I grasped the handle and moved it to the far burner, and with my other hand, I fanned down the heat.

"Well, look at that—this one's useful!" The shock was clear in Agatha's voice. The more she spoke, the more I detected the slightest Irish accent.

With the subject of my past dropped, Cook put an arm around my shoulders and led me back to the table, where she placed a big bowl in the center. In it was a huge pile of green beans waiting to be prepared for dinner, but even though I waited patiently, Cook didn't say exactly what she expected me to do with them. I was beginning to see how hard it was going to be to not be able to speak.

Cook tossed a gingersnap into her mouth before grabbing a bean from the bowl, popping each end off, and putting it on the table.

"You never shucked peas before?" she asked. I couldn't tell if she was upset or amused, so I shrugged and followed her lead.

Agatha frowned at this, her hair catching the sunlight streaming through the window. "Give her a chance! You didn't tell her what you needed done to them."

Cook let out a long sigh. "You're right. I'm sorry, Isabelle."

Agatha reached into the bowl and tossed me a couple green beans. I twisted off each end, adding them to the pile.

We kept working like that when Agatha asked, "*Can* you talk?"

"Agatha, don't be rude. Isabelle, she's sorry. Sometimes Irish folk don't have the best manners."

"Now wait," Agatha interrupted. "I was born here. Don't give the girl a reason to dislike me. I work just as hard as anyone else."

Mrs. Patterson entered the kitchen suddenly, and Agatha squared her shoulders. "Agatha, Mrs. Allan is in room twelve. Please make sure she remains there," Mrs. Patterson ordered.

Agatha pulled her eyes away from Cook. "Yes, Mrs. Patterson." She fixed her skirt. "It was good to see you again, Isabelle," she said before exiting the room.

Cook cleared her throat. "Would you mind if Isabelle stays here with me? She's proving useful."

Mrs. Patterson looked at the bowl of beans. "That would be helpful. Without the doctors, it is hard to keep everyone content."

"Isn't that always the way of it?" Cook asked.

Mrs. Patterson appraised me. "Are you comfortable in the kitchen?"

She acted like I was some kind of silly puppy, but I nodded so she'd go away. As she followed my motions, disappointment read all over her face. She turned to Cook and sighed. "I wish she would speak. I don't know what's blocking her."

Cook kept her eyes on me and smiled sadly. "When she's ready, she'll speak."

Mrs. Patterson glanced once more at me before nodding to Cook and swishing out of the room.

"I'm right, aren't I?" Cook inquired once Mrs. Patterson was gone. "You will talk, when you're ready?"

I thought about it for a moment and then nodded. At some

point Gregory would give me up, my life would return to normal, and I'd be safe, and then I'd be able to speak again.

"Good," Cook said, patting my hand. She poured herself a glass of lemonade and sat down in Agatha's vacated spot. "Do any of your friends know where you are?"

I shook my head. Of course they didn't. Anyone with half a brain knew that for one to make it known they were being committed to a sanitarium was to commit social suicide. I raised an eyebrow and looked at Cook with condemnation.

"Don't you give me a look like that, Miss Isabelle. I'm not so daft that I don't know what people would be saying about you if they knew. But I'm also not so stupid to think that a young lady like you wouldn't still confide in a good friend if she had half a chance."

I thought of Lucy and sighed. She was the only person with whom I could confide such a horror, but there was no way I could do so now. She was probably in New York City by now, and it was all my fault. Despite that, thinking of Lucy brought a small smile to my lips.

"Praise the Lord!" Cook cried out, nearly making me fall off my stool. "She can smile!"

Her exclamation was so overly dramatic that, despite myself, a small caw of laughter escaped my mouth. The sound cut through the air in the kitchen, pausing our conversation.

I waited, still as a tree, for Cook to demand an explanation—or worse, demand that I confess my deception—but she only held my gaze for a moment then drained her glass of lemonade as if nothing had happened.

"Dr. Patterson doesn't understand the healing effect a friend can have. If you want to write to your friends, you just give me the letters. I'll see that they make their way out discreetly."

My hands fumbled with a green bean and fell limply to the table. There was nothing I could trust to paper. If Gregory was visiting Lucy's house at all he could read my letter. Or Mrs.

D'Havland would read them and show them as punishment to me. I couldn't be too careful. My world felt incredibly small.

Cook reached across the table and covered my hands with hers.

"Isabelle, I realize you've had a terrible time of it lately, but remember that a good friend will be there for you no matter what. Don't go through life thinking that everyone is against you."

Her eyes intensified, like clouds in a stormy sky.

"Do you understand me, dear?" Cook asked. I nodded, letting her calmness soothe me.

"All right then. Do you like apricots?" My mouth salivated at the mere mention of my favorite fruit. I nodded. "Then I'll show you how to make my famous apricot cobbler for dessert."

She walked across the room and pulled a basket of apricots from a shady corner. Tossing me one, she began her instructions. Although I listened enough to follow her, I was overcome with my thoughts. Cook was right; a friend could provide healing. I could at least give Lucy my support if not my confession. If I hurried, perhaps she'd get my letter before she was sent away.

CHAPTER 13

The grandfather clock chimed midnight. I'd burned nearly two inches of candle and had only "Dear Lucy" written on the page to show for my efforts. Shoving the paper away, I leaned back in my desk chair and rubbed my temples. The small candle flame forced hypnotizing shadows to dance across the page. To this one friend I'd confided my lifelong dreams, my frustration in Mother's various shenanigans and flirtations, even my own embarrassing inability to keep my female troubles from staining the bedsheets. All that I spoke effortlessly, but I couldn't bring myself to pen this apology, let alone all that had happened to me.

The tree's leaves rustled outside my window. I walked over to open it and let the cool night breeze air out my room. Sitting on my bed, I gazed out at the moon illuminating the path that cut across the lawn. The bright light cast shadows over the property. No one was visible, but anyone could be lurking. I tried to see through the darkness, but I only felt the breeze. I shook the apprehension from my head. It was time to focus and complete my letter.

Yet, no matter what I wrote, my emotions didn't come across. Written words couldn't express my sorrow or fear. I thought again of Marilla and the mockery she faced from the other women. If I told Lucy everything, would she shun me forever? The paper was heavy in my hands as I rested my head back on the window well.

A light bobbed down the street and was accompanied by the rhythmic clip-clops of approaching horses, making my ears twitch and stomach flip. A buggy pulled up to the house and two men in dark jackets emerged. I licked my fingers and pinched out the candle flame. Peering around the edge of the window frame, I glanced into the courtyard below. Immediately, I recognized Dr. Patterson's bald spot glowing in the lamplight, and Samuel's wavy brown hair. I adjusted myself again to be sure they wouldn't see me and strained to hear their conversation.

"And I'm saying that she is ill." Dr. Patterson spoke with authority as he stepped out of the buggy. "You heard the behavior the witnesses described. Spending money without thought, hallucinations that her son is on his deathbed, and then insisting that there is a plot to murder her. She needs our help."

"Needing help is one thing, sir, but taking your mother to trial to have her committed is quite another. What is Robert after by making such a spectacle? This is going to be in the papers!" Samuel's voice was crisp with passion. "This could ruin her." Shadows darkened his face as he stood and waited to climb out of the carriage.

Who were they speaking of? I had no idea. None of the women I had met matched their description.

"That isn't for us to say. Our job is to take care of her and assist in what ails her."

"She's had a sad life." Samuel's hair shone in the moonlight.

"Grief is an odd thing, but I don't believe that is all this is. The woman is seeing things that aren't there and is squandering her money to speak to the dead." Dr. Patterson rubbed a hand over the horse's mane. "If nothing else, she needs a period of rest and reflection. We can give her that."

I held back the curtain and continued to peer out from the corner of the window.

Samuel waved his hand. "You're playing with fire, sir. She was our president's wife and worked hard to save many during the war. If we aren't able to cure her or at least help her, our reputations will be at stake. Are you willing to put that on the line?"

The president's wife was coming to Bellevue? What ailed Mrs. Grant? Dr. Patterson's laugh made me twitch. "My dear boy, when you get to be my age, you'll learn how little others care about reputations, especially if you just do your job. Mrs. Lincoln will be well taken care of here. Now please, Samuel, put the horses away. I need to see my wife."

I slid down so my head rested on my pillow. Mary Lincoln was coming to Bellevue! Not our current president, but Abraham Lincoln's widow. Since the war there had been numerous reports of her odd behavior, but Papa forbade me from reading gossip. He'd known her during the war and regarded her of the highest caliber. Lucy saved the articles for me and we read them together in her room. Such silliness. Reports of frivolous spending, convulsive shopping, and a scandalous auction of her belongings a few years back. I hadn't read much of her since the great fire in Chicago four years ago. Given her odd behavior since the war, it wasn't all that shocking that she needed rest. Yet, that anyone could be sent here for something as common as grief surprised me. Perhaps being locked up here wasn't as terrible as Marilla had made it out to be. If someone of that caliber was coming, it couldn't be.

Wasting no time, I grabbed the pen and wrote in the moonlight:

Dear Lucy—

Words cannot express my sorrow for what you must be enduring. I don't know which would be worse, marrying that boring man or being forced to move and start over in New York.

It's my fault. If you hadn't followed my advice, you'd not be in such trouble now.

If it's any consolation, I've ruined my life as well. If you write back, I'll make you privy to the details.

I miss you, my friend,
Izzy

My fingers itched to write more, but I couldn't confide in her, not yet. Mine was too big a story to not know who was reading it. I folded the letter and sealed the envelope.

Tuesdays were for gardening and before I could tie my dress laces, there was already a line of women coming out of the building and taking tools off the gardening cart. My eyes skimmed over the handful of women, looking for someone I'd not yet seen, but there were no new faces. Mrs. Lincoln must not have arrived yet. Marilla glanced up at my window and waved to me. I forced myself to smile before backing out of view.

Tucking Lucy's letter deep in my pocket, I ran down the stairs and into the kitchen. Cook was on her hands and knees scrubbing the floor.

I glanced out the window into the garden. Seeing how close Mrs. Patterson was, I promptly shut my mouth and instead stamped my foot to get Cook's attention.

Cook looked up immediately. Her smile for me was genuine. "Isabelle, what a surprise. You should be outside, dear."

I pulled out my letter and pressed it into her hand. She

glanced down and quickly shoved the envelope in her pocket. Her callused hand squeezed mine.

"I'll put it in the mail today," she promised. "Better get outside before Mrs. Patterson comes looking for you."

Once outside I quickly blended myself into the group of women standing before Mrs. Patterson. Despite the fact that patients tended to them, the gardens of Bellevue were just as beautiful as ours were at home. Roses climbed up the trellis and bloomed in bright colors. Other flowers had sprouted as well and looked as if they might open any day. Clearly, Mrs. Patterson knew how to lay out her plots. Mother refused to let me associate with our male servants, which meant I had never learned about gardens or horses.

The other ladies immediately walked to their plots and knelt on pillows next to the narrow brick walk that outlined the curving flowerbeds alongside the building. I observed how they moved with purpose. Bringing things to life was a therapy I understood.

Mrs. Patterson said nothing to me, but put a trowel in one hand and a sack in the other. Then she glared at me for a moment before saying, "Weed that bed beside Marilla."

She pushed me toward the front of the house where there were only a few women working. I was close enough to overhear Marilla and Mrs. Allan's conversation, which was quickly becoming animated. Pulling my gloves on, I dug into the earth and listened as they discussed the latest trends in ladies' gloves.

As I eavesdropped, dirt snuck its way through my gloves and into my nail beds, while the dampness of the ground seeped through my skirt and petticoat. My dress, petticoat, and apron were soon wet and clung to my knees. Standing, I grabbed the fabric and shook it out. As I did so, I turned to look back toward the front of the house.

Standing on my tiptoes, I could see down the two blocks that led to the main road. Squinting slightly, I made out a buggy piled high with trunks and boxes making its way toward us.

Of course it was nothing fancy enough for a lady to ride in, but I was sure it meant Mrs. Lincoln was on her way. She was legendary for living in excess. No one else would pack so much for a stay here.

Remembering the day's task and not wanting to attract Mrs. Patterson's attention, I turned to finish my plot, but instead found myself face to face with that odd girl, Jesminda. Her lips moved in short, staccato motions, but I heard nothing. Her eyes met mine as she approached me. Judging by the way Dr. Patterson secluded Jesminda on her bad days, he considered her more disturbed than many of us. I wondered if she was someone to emulate. Our eyes met, and I sensed she wanted to say something, but her lips quivered too much.

A few feet away, I saw Mrs. Allan touch Marilla's arm and point to us. I turned back to Jesminda, nearly jumping at how close she stood. Reaching out, she grabbed my wrist and refused to let me go. I pulled back, but she held tighter and grunted.

All thoughts of my prepared act vanished as my heart raced in fear. This girl was odd, perhaps truly insane, and she was after me. Her lips moved, but no sound came out. With her free hand she hit the side of her head until it continued to jerk side to side and her muttering became audible.

"Dirt, dirty girl. Dirt."

Her nails dug into my arm until blood was visible, yet she retained her grip on me. I tried to gesture at Marilla for help, but she jumped to her feet and ran toward the other side of the building. I prayed she sought Mrs. Patterson and not avoidance of me.

"Dirty dirt, dirty dirt, dirty dirt, dirty dirt," Jesminda said over and over.

My legs tightened as if to flee, but my eyes were on Jesminda. Her gaze bore into me as if I were her anchor to reality.

"Dirty dirt, dirty dirt," she continued in a louder voice. She couldn't stop repeating the words.

I could feel everyone in the garden staring at us. Not just

the women, but the flowers, mosquitoes, and grass blades all seemed to turn their attention to me: the dirty girl.

This was my life now, waiting for new patients and being frightened by the others. My breath became staccato, and my ears rang.

Jesminda's repetition elevated. It was too much. There was silence for a moment, and then I let myself go limp and fall to the ground as a scuttle of activity filled my ears.

"Poor child," Mrs. Allan cooed from one side as Marilla said from the other, "What's the matter with you, Jesminda!"

There was a large thud as someone dropped beside me and their strong, cold hands took hold of my face.

"Isabelle," Dr. Patterson shouted. I did not respond. "Isabelle!"

Still I did nothing.

"Shall I fetch the smelling salts?" Marilla asked.

I twitched my head slightly. Smelling salts were disgusting!

"No, she's coming to," Dr. Patterson said. I fluttered my eyes open ever so slightly.

"Is she all right?" Marilla asked.

"She'll be fine after a good rest. You girls continue to work. Mrs. Patterson will put Isabelle to bed."

It took all my self-restraint not to sigh in relief at those words.

Mrs. Patterson held an arm tight around my waist as she led me through the halls to my room. I accepted her support and hoped she'd allow me to stay inside for the remainder of the day. I longed to ask what affliction Jesminda suffered from, but could do nothing to refute Mrs. Patterson's opinion of my condition. Let her think me frail and weak. As we started up the great staircase, she supported me even more.

"You should regain your strength quickly," Mrs. Patterson said, holding my bedroom door open. "Spend the rest of the morning here resting."

I nodded and immediately sat on the bed. Leaning over, I worked on unlacing my boots.

Mrs. Patterson paced in front of me. Then her face softened, and she started to rub her hands together. "Listen, Isabelle. Many of our patients are here for a rest, a separation from society, but others need more. No one will harm you here. You will become accustomed to life here in time. You will find its rhythm." She cleared her throat. "We'll see you at dinner."

My boots slipped off with a thud and I lay down. My actions cued Mrs. Patterson to return to the garden. Her words, however, lingered in my room like spirits. She spoke as if I'd be here forever. I wondered if that was what it would take.

Once I knew she was gone, I got up and opened my door so the room didn't feel like it was swallowing me. Then I returned to my bed.

Sometime later, the sound of something being dragged woke me. I wondered what the Pattersons were having moved into their residence. Then it dawned on me. I was in their residence. Was it possible Mrs. Lincoln would be housed here as well? Staying here did offer solitude from other patients. I forced myself to stay abed and hoped that stillness would conceal my spying. After a moment, I could see the backside of a man slide in and out of my sight as he pushed and pulled something down the hallway.

"No one needs this much baggage. I don't care who you are or used to be." The man pulled his end of the trunk toward the room across the hall. His graying hair explained the small groans he made as he moved the trunk. His companion appeared in my view. A few tendrils of brown hair were barely visible beneath his cap. His shirtsleeves were rolled up to his elbows, and red suspenders pressed against his shoulders as he pushed the wooden trunk. His tall frame appeared in my doorway as he backed into my room.

The two men worked hard to get the trunk to move; with

each tug they forced it and the younger man deeper into my bedroom. I tried not to react, but there was a *man* in my room. Mother would've been scandalized, but my skin prickled with excitement. *Silly girl*, I thought. *There's nothing improper happening. He probably doesn't even know you're here.*

As he pulled the trunk, I watched his legs flex, examined the neat crease in his blue trousers, and wondered if his face was as attractive as the rest of him. He was tall and slender, the very opposite of Gregory's muscular frame. I doubted he was much older than me.

Finally the trunk was straight enough to be pushed into the opposite room, and the men stood up to take a break before they finished. The older man glanced into my room for the first time and jumped back in surprise.

"There's a girl in there, Samuel," he said.

I slid back against the wall, wishing to make myself invisible. I had spent the last few minutes listing the attractive qualities of Dr. Patterson's assistant doctor. That same man was now in my room, and despite my humiliation, I couldn't help but admire his thighs. I shook the attraction from my mind.

Samuel turned around and pulled the hat off his head. His manners were that of a gentleman. I couldn't keep the smile from my face.

"Miss Isabelle, I didn't see you," Samuel stuttered. "I would never dare disturb your privacy intentionally."

Not wanting him to leave, I held my hand up and shook my head to show him I wasn't angry.

"Our secret then?" Samuel asked. I lifted a finger to my lips and nodded. He grinned.

"Sam, give 'er a push, will you?" the older man grunted.

"'Course," Samuel replied, tipping his hat to me and resuming his stance against the trunk. "What do you suppose is making it so heavy? You've never needed help before."

"Well, who knows what she's decided to bring. You know what they say about her."

I sat up on the edge of my bed as Samuel replied, "What do they say?"

"She brings the house wherever she goes. She's spent President Lincoln's savings on silly gowns and stupid curtains. Someone even said they saw her buy ten of the same tablecloth. Trunk is probably full of coal in case we run out. If her husband only knew, he'd roll over in his grave."

President Lincoln's savings. I'd heard of her eccentricities, but hadn't known it had gone that far. It made Mother feel better to scoff at the one woman whom Father had held in high esteem. Again, I wondered what had put her here. She'd endured his death for years, why now?

"Don't be too hard on her, Ewan," Samuel said, stretching his back now that the trunk was in place. "She's lost all her sons except the eldest, and was sitting right beside our president when that tyrant shot him. I'd say she's allowed to be a little eccentric."

"Well, she's plum crazy now," Ewan replied. "I'll get the last trunk myself."

There was *another* trunk! I leaned toward the door for a better look into the hallway.

Once Ewan left to go retrieve the trunk, Samuel turned and rested against my doorframe, blocking my view. "Don't pay attention to anything Ewan says. He puts too much stock in his wife's gossip. Mrs. Lincoln is no crazier than any of us. She's just bereaved and lonely."

I nodded at his words, but inwardly shuddered. If people spoke of Mary Lincoln with such disdain, how would they treat me when I got out? If I got out. Again, I reminded myself that this was my life now. Yet, instead of feeling relief, tears of frustration threatened to overwhelm me. What had I done?

Heat rose to my face, and I slipped off the bed and onto the floor. I'd ripped all prospects from my life without a true thought to the consequences. Gregory's hands on Katerina's throat sped through my mind and I knew I'd make the same choice again, but the tears refused to abate.

I'd nearly forgotten Samuel was there until he offered me his handkerchief. He lunged so his other foot remained in the hallway. If anyone saw, my reputation would be intact. He believed I still had a reputation to salvage. Optimistic fool.

"Things may seem desperate now, but they will get better." He shook the handkerchief. "Take it. Please."

My face felt sticky with tears. I took it from him. "Thank you," I said.

My ears thudded with the silence. Why? How could I have let myself speak to him of all people? He was Dr. Patterson's assistant, a doctor himself. Surely he was obligated to tattle on me. I swallowed the lump in my throat and waited for the questions to start.

Samuel hadn't moved either, but he watched me with an intensity I'd never experienced. Without warning, he rocked back on his heels and stood up. "Keep the handkerchief as long as you need. I'll have Agatha send up some water for you."

I looked up at him and nodded.

Stretching his arms, he gazed toward the main stairway. "Sometimes what Dr. Patterson doesn't know is for the best. We all have our reasons for being here. I'll not press you for yours." He tipped his hat and left down the servants' staircase.

Had Samuel just assured me that he'd tell no one of my slip? If so, did that mean he saw through my act or not? I wiped my face with his handkerchief and returned to my bed. I wasn't sitting long before the swishes of satin and clomping of shoes echoed into the hallway. Mrs. Lincoln had arrived.

CHAPTER 14

"I am too old for such traveling," an elderly woman moaned. "My bones ache."

"Mother, I used only the very best to bring you here," a man replied. Their footsteps echoed from the stairway. It was clear from his tone that this was not her first complaint of the day.

"Oh, yes, only the best for your insane mother. Even the best sanitarium, just as long as it is far away from the city where you live and do business." From my bed, I could watch the black hoop skirt sway back and forth as the couple moved slowly down the hallway. The style of her gown gave her away. Mary Lincoln hadn't been seen out of mourning since President Lincoln died. I'd thought it was desperately romantic of her, but now that I'd seen it, it just felt sad. A decade had gone by and still she mourned. It broke my heart.

Her wailing startled me. "How could you do this to me? What would your father think of this embarrassment?"

I slid from my bed and moved toward the doorway, my curiosity giving me the strength I needed. So this was the woman Father spoke of so often, the one who nursed him to health. I had to see what she was like for myself. Being careful to stay hidden in the safety of my room, I peered around the corner. She came slowly down the hall, favoring her left side. Her movements were so careful and measured, I could almost feel her pain.

She was now standing in the hallway, her hoop skirt taking up nearly half the space. Given all I'd read of her clothing obsession, I was surprised to see she wore an old-fashioned hoop. Father had described her as the epitome of high fashion, that even as she tended to his bullet wound, she managed to stay soil free and nearly floated from bedside to bedside. Her skin, he said, was soft like porcelain and her touch healing in its gentle nature.

The woman in front of me was not someone of whom Mother should be jealous. Her cheeks were puffy and pressed oddly together by her bonnet's ribbon. Her hair was dark gray, but lined in white. I looked closer at her gown and noticed sections in front were wrinkled, like she had been clutching them in her fists.

"You have not been well, Mother. You speak of spirits pulling out your eyes and write frequently as if I am on my deathbed. This is not normal. I cannot stand aside and allow for this to continue. Father would not want you to remain ill." Robert Lincoln glanced about the hallway, as if looking for someone to confirm his words.

I suddenly saw my mistake. This wasn't some play I was watching. The real Mary Lincoln was mere feet from me and shuffling closer every moment. I was sure to be found eavesdropping. I slid to the floor, let my head roll to one side, and closed my eyes. Hopefully she'd think me a patient who slept in odd places. Stranger things had happened here.

"What's this?" she demanded. I gave up and opened my eyes. "A young spy come to laugh at poor Mary Lincoln? How dare you follow me here! I'll have none of that. Turn your pad in. I want no reports of me here! Give me your notes!" She lunged into my room with the agility of a tiger.

I clamored to my feet and scuttled away from her arms. Her hoop knocked over my side table, and she paused a moment to watch its contents fall. A glass broke when it hit the floor, but no other harm was done. She must not have found whatever she thought I had, for she hobbled around the table still searching. My legs pressed against the bed as she advanced toward me.

"Mother," Robert Lincoln shouted from my doorway. Mrs. Lincoln paused, but her eyes did not leave mine. In two strides Robert had his arms around Mrs. Lincoln's shoulders. "She is to be your neighbor, Mother. Can't you see that? She is only a curious patient."

Her eyes didn't leave mine as she said, "I want no more spies, Robert. I've suffered more than my share in this life."

The intensity of her gaze made my eyes water, but I dared not look away.

Thank heavens, Dr. Patterson arrived. He sighed and glanced from Mrs. Lincoln to me. To my surprise, he turned his back on President Lincoln's widow and came to pull me away from the bed. Even more shocking, I trusted him enough to follow.

"This is Mrs. Lincoln," he told me. "She is here to rest, same as you. It'll be good to have a neighbor, will it not?"

He paused for a response so I nodded.

"Mrs. Lincoln, this is Isabelle. We've given her these special accommodations because her mother didn't want to expose a woman so young to the other women's conditions. Will you force me to protect her from you as well?"

I scarcely breathed as I waited for the response. Mrs. Lincoln's face turned red, and she brushed Robert away from her. "I am no animal, Dr. Patterson. I will help you protect this girl's young mind."

Part of me wished she saw my strength, but mostly I felt relieved. This was the woman Papa had spoken of—one who had control of herself and cared for others.

"Good," Dr. Patterson said. Then to me he said, "Go ahead and lie down, Isabelle. I'll send Agatha up to attend to you soon."

I obeyed, but not before I saw the curious look Mrs. Lincoln gave me. The moment my door closed I heard her say, "She's a quiet child. That is a rare quality indeed. Your wife could learn a thing or two from her, Robert."

It was Dr. Patterson who replied. "We do not comment on the other patients, Mrs. Lincoln, but she'll be little bother, I'm sure."

"My head," Mrs. Lincoln moaned again. Even though both of our doors were closed, her voice was clear. "It feels as if Indians are hacking it apart with hatchets." She was so bereaved that my own scalp throbbed in sympathy.

I pulled a pillow over my ears to stifle the cries that came from across the hall. At first I felt bad for Mrs. Lincoln but hours later I was at my wit's end. I'd not had a wink of sleep. Dr. Patterson may have assured her that I'd be silent, but I wish he'd given me that same promise.

Finally, one of the nurses went to her. They were too quiet for me to hear, but as the sound of her weeping slowed, I knew Mrs. Lincoln had calmed down. I could feel my shoulders relax and waited for sleep to drag me in as well.

I longed for soothing dreams, but instead, I was bombarded with images of Katerina's dead eyes staring at me. In the dream, I moved closer to her. With horrifyingly rigid movements, she gripped my hands and let out a shrill scream. Her blue eyes pierced my mind like beestings.

"Beware," she exclaimed. "You failed to aid me. Now Gregory roams free. Do not be fooled. This could be you."

I tried to free myself from her arms and apologize, but her

limbs became tree branches and their leaves covered my mouth. I strained against the tree's grip, but it refused to let me go. Desperate, I looked for Katerina, but she had gone.

The sun was barely up, but there was no more sleep for me. I pulled *Jane Eyre* from the nightstand and lost myself in her troubles until breakfast.

When I walked into the dining room that morning, Jesminda, Mrs. Allan, Marilla, and a handful of other patients were already seated and passing a jar of jam among themselves. The table was laid out with orange juice, milk, breads, and assorted jams. I took a seat at the closest end of the table and reached for a slice of bread from the basket in front of me.

Jesminda pushed the basket toward me and gave me a small smile. Her head twitch was hardly noticeable. I put two slices on my plate and smiled my thanks in return.

After a moment of silence, Jesminda scooted close to me and said, "I'm so sorry I scared you. Sometimes I have episodes of . . . illness. I hope we can start fresh."

She spoke so articulately I could hardly believe it was the same person who had been so out of sorts the day before. I nodded to indicate I'd heard her and was rewarded with the same soft smile.

"We should ask her," Marilla said, gesturing to me. I paused in the middle of reaching for the butter. "She lives in the residence, after all."

Mrs. Allan smirked as she turned her gaze to me. "We could ask her many things, but she'd not reply to one of them. Isn't that so?"

My tongue followed the line of my teeth as I did my best not to reply to her comment. Mrs. Allan had a way of heightening my frustration. She was right, of course, but that didn't make it any less annoying. I sliced off a slab of butter with my knife and busied myself with spreading it across my bread.

"Don't discount her so quickly," Marilla said. Then to me, "You'll answer our questions, won't you, Isabelle?" A piece of her brown hair fell from her braid. She tucked it behind her ear. She hadn't eaten a bite off her plate, just moved the food around so it looked eaten.

For a moment I was tempted to ignore Marilla as well, but I remembered her grief at her husband's cruelty and didn't have the heart to disappoint her. I nodded.

"See, she isn't stupid, just quiet." Marilla pinched Jesminda's hand playfully. Mrs. Allan must have said similar things about Jesminda.

My silence never seemed more to me than a symptom of my supposed insanity, a reminder to all that I wasn't well. I never imagined that it would make me seem unintelligent. Father had worked so hard to educate me, and now I'd gone and made people believe I was daft. Pulling myself up straighter, I stared down the table at them and awaited their questions with what I hoped was a look of startling intelligence.

Mrs. Allan took a long sip from her juice glass before fixing me with her eyes. "There is really only one question to ask. Did someone move into your hallway yesterday?"

A smile pulled at my lips.

"And who was it?" Mrs. Allan asked, leaning forward on the table.

Before I could do anything, Jesminda blurted, "Is it true? Is Mary Lincoln herself living here now?"

"Don't you answer that, Isabelle," Mrs. Patterson demanded from the doorway. She took two loud steps into the room and placed a hand on my shoulder. "These ladies know how to mind their business, don't you, ladies?"

They all nodded their heads, but I caught Mrs. Allan rolling her eyes.

Mrs. Patterson sighed. "But to answer your question, yes, Mrs. Lincoln is spending some time here. I hope I can trust you all to make her feel at home and to give her the privacy she requires."

"Of course," Mrs. Allan said. "We all need our privacy. It is all some of us have left."

"Yes, thank you," Mrs. Patterson agreed curtly. I wondered if she was trying to avoid another confrontation.

There was a long silence in the room, only interrupted by Jesminda's noisy smacking as she chewed her breakfast. I took a few bites of my bread. Marilla continuously wiped her mouth with her napkin. The more I thought about it, I didn't think I'd ever seen her eat a meal. I wondered if the doctors noticed her lack of appetite.

A knock came from the front door that caused every head to snap in its direction. There were muffled voices, and then Agatha appeared with an envelope in her hands.

"Mrs. Larkin and Mrs. Haskins will be visiting within the hour," she said, handing the envelope to Mrs. Patterson.

Despite Mrs. Patterson standing behind me, I jumped to my feet and dropped what was left of my bread to the plate. Mother and Aunt Clara were coming to visit? A stillness crept over me as I considered the only reason imaginable for so soon a visit: Mother had decided to release me from both Gregory and Bellevue. It had been a week, enough time for her to see what life might be like with an inmate for a daughter. I clung to that idea and dashed to my room to dress.

CHAPTER 15

With my best dress laced around my tightest corset and the bustle Aunt Clara gave me, I was the vision of propriety. The rose fabric lay straight down my front and pulled back into layers of ruffles down the rear and smooth lines across my sides. The sleeves puffed over my shoulders and buttoned gracefully up my arms. Although I could not breathe freely, it was worth it when Aunt Clara and Mother entered the parlor and tears came to Mother's eyes as she took me in.

I stood in front of the fireplace, my hands held in front of me. The pink shine to my dress stood out against the dark brick behind me. The scene was set for her to apologize and beg me to return home with her.

"I'm pleased you've remained a lady here," Mother began, glancing around her. "It is too bad they don't have a proper chair for you, but we can't have everything, can we?"

I hadn't a clue as to what she meant, so I just smiled. Aunt Clara's starched skirt shuffled loudly as she came to my side. Taking my face in her hands, she kissed each cheek, stepped back, and smiled at me.

"Dear me, you look well. Look at her cheeks—do you see

how they've gained more color? I told you this place would be good to her." Aunt Clara settled into an oversized rocking chair.

Mother perched on one of the settees and sighed. "Yes, rosy cheeks will bring many suitors for my insane daughter."

Why was she still insulting me? She should be asking me to forgive her by now.

Aunt Clara winced at Mother's rebuke, but quickly regained her charm. "There is someone for everyone, even if it mightn't be who we originally intended." She winked at me, and I allowed her a small smile in return.

"Don't put such thoughts into her mind. Her future is decided. All she needs is to focus on finding the truth through the thick fog of lies she's allowed to fill her head. Then she and I can return home."

These words put a nail in the coffin of my hope.

I ignored Mother and returned to my seat. The other ladies were outside working in the gardens, but every once in a while I caught one of them blatantly staring into the window, looking at me. For some reason, their spying comforted me. Mother waited patiently for me to turn around. For all I cared, she could wait forever. Luckily for her, Mrs. Patterson appeared.

"Mrs. Larkin. Mrs. Haskins. We've been expecting you. I do apologize for not receiving you properly, but I've been tending to another patient."

I glanced toward them and saw Mother's face light up. "I read about the Widow Lincoln's trial. Is she about today?"

Only I could be so stupid not to see the truth. Of course, Mother had come to gawk at Mrs. Lincoln. After all of Papa's stories, how could I imagine she'd stay away? I counted my blessings that my own admittance wasn't based on the result of a trial. Any annoyance with my neighbor's nightly outbursts flitted away. She had reason to suffer nightmares.

Mrs. Patterson patted my shoulder, forcing my concentration

back to the parlor. "Your daughter has made excellent progress in the past few days. Perhaps your time would be better spent attending her, or would you like me to get Dr. Patterson so that the two of you may discuss her case?"

Mother's face turned red. In a small, controlled voice she asked, "She's making progress?" When Mrs. Patterson smiled, Mother jumped from her seat and demanded, "Then why is she not speaking yet? That is what we are paying you for, after all."

"These things take time, Mrs. Larkin. Isabelle will come around when she is ready and not a moment before." Mrs. Patterson looked at me. "Perhaps a stroll about the grounds will entertain you both."

"Is Mrs. Lincoln walking the grounds this morning?" Mother asked, returning to her true agenda.

I turned to the window so she wouldn't see the hurt pinching my expression.

"Don't be rude, sister," Aunt Clara insisted. "We are here for Isabelle." My heart went out to my aunt for pulling Mother back.

Mother glared at Mrs. Patterson. Then to Aunt Clara she insisted, "I would like to meet the woman my husband spoke of so often. I would like to meet Mrs. Lincoln."

Aunt Clara fidgeted with the strings of her handbag. "Now, now. If they say she's indisposed we ought to believe them."

Mother practically snarled at Aunt Clara. To Mrs. Patterson, she demanded, "Is it true what the papers say? Is she so insane that her own son had to send her here? Was there really a trial? It seems too dramatic to be true."

"Sister, stop this." Aunt Clara grasped Mother's arm and pulled her back. "This is wrong."

Before Mother could ask more questions, Mrs. Patterson said, "Mrs. Larkin, this is not a zoo. We do not gawk at the patients here. If you do not wish to visit with your daughter, you should go about your day's business."

"Well, actually, that reminds me, I ought to be going." Mother tipped her hat to Mrs. Patterson. "Just stopping in to see that Isabelle was being looked after. Wouldn't want her to be overlooked because of the Widow Lincoln."

"Isabelle, I am glad you appear to be doing so much better," Aunt Clara said, pulling me toward her in a hug. "We will be back to visit soon."

Mother embraced me as well, though her arms were stiff. "I hope you are working hard. We both know that where there's a will, there's a way."

Aunt Clara linked her arm through mine as we walked out to the carriage. She held me back as Mother climbed up the steps and took her seat.

"You do what you need to do and come home to us." She kissed my cheek and then climbed up next to Mother. Aunt Clara motioned to the driver and the horses clopped down the road away from me.

"Let's get you out of that ridiculous outfit, Isabelle," Mrs. Patterson said. I nodded and started up the stairs to my room.

Once there, Mrs. Patterson stripped me of my corset and gown, placing me back in my gray afternoon dress. Without another word, she simply left me alone to my thoughts.

There were things to do in my room, cleaning and straightening, which would be productive for my mind, but I couldn't bring myself to do anything. Instead I lay on my bed and succumbed to my disappointment. Sobs shook me and made the room spin.

After a few moments, I heard shoes on the floor of my room.

"Are you all right, child?" Mrs. Lincoln asked.

I shook my head, though the answer should have been obvious.

"Would you like to talk about it?" she asked.

I shook my head again, allowing my sobs to rattle my chest.

I expected her to leave me to my misery, but instead my bed

creaked and sank beside me as she sat down. Strong fingers grabbed me around my rib cage and pulled me up toward her chest, and she rocked me back and forth.

"There, there, child. Let the tears out and restore yourself."

"Thank you," I sighed out loud as I closed my eyes and allowed Mrs. Lincoln to rock me.

Dr. Patterson tapped his fingers against the desktop, waiting for me to start speaking. It was our little game. Every other day we met and he treated me like I was normal and I tried to show him he was wrong. In previous sessions, I had pulled on my hair, rocked back and forth, and made assorted clicking sounds, but I was tired of making such a fuss. Instead, I sat, dragging my fingernail across my shirt cuff. Having worked on it for thirty minutes, I had achieved the beginnings of a tear, which was a shame since it was my favorite blouse. A small strand of string appeared in the fray, which I grabbed and pulled. No one cared what I looked like in here anyway, so why preserve a silly shirt? As I pulled, the hole grew until I could put my pinkie finger through it.

"Well," Dr. Patterson started. "Perhaps we should talk about the servant girl."

Despite myself, I froze. Never before had he tried to discuss anything so personal. Only Cook had referenced that incident, and with her it seemed different somehow.

"Catherine or Carmina? Her name must be here in my notes somewhere." He flipped through some papers. "Cassidy? Cassandra?"

"Katerina," I whispered. For an instant, I could smell the wet, musty smell of her small home. Her eyes still cast their blame on me. I shivered.

It was Dr. Patterson's turn to freeze. His fingers were halfway through my file and his brown eyes on me. His lips twitched as if trying to conceal a smile.

"Yes," he soothed. "Tell me more about her."

As he waited for my response he pressed his fingertips together, making a pyramid with his hands. I knew that look—it was the same one Father had given me when he thought he'd caught me in a lie. Dr. Patterson thought he had me, thought he was about to break me.

There was no way I'd let that happen.

Thinking of Jesminda's fits, I repeated Katerina's name over and over in a muttering, frantic way. Then, just to prove my point, I tore a chunk of fabric from my sleeve and calmly folded it into halves over and over again. When it was small enough, I shoved it into my mouth, chewed, and swallowed.

Dr. Patterson reached forward to stop me, but he was too late. His hand dropped onto the desk and his eyes widened. When he didn't move I grabbed my broken sleeve again and tugged hard on the tear. A second piece quickly came free. The first was still sitting precariously in my throat, but I kept the discomfort from my face. Instead, as I prepared to swallow another piece, I twisted my foot beneath Dr. Patterson's desk, trying to release some of the pain.

Lifting the fabric to my mouth, I met Dr. Patterson's questioning gaze. His skin had turned a bit green and his lip curled in distaste. He finally declared, "Oh, stop. I'll not make you speak."

Still, I shoved the piece of fabric into my mouth, though this time I only pretended to swallow.

Twirling his pen around his finger, Dr. Patterson pursed his lips. "If you ever wish to return home, you'll have to speak."

Good reason not to, I snarled inwardly.

"And, clearly you can speak, if you've a mind to."

I'd have to fix his impression of that.

"Mrs. Lincoln says you spoke to her." His declaration nearly choked me, and I couldn't stop coughing. "Can you tell me about that?"

Leaning back in his chair, Dr. Patterson waited for me to reply. Slowly, I obtained control of myself. The damage was done, however. He knew Mrs. Lincoln's story was plausible, if not true. I returned his gaze, hoping to regain some footing, but it was no use. Mrs. Lincoln had given the doctor the winning card.

"All right, that is all for today, then." Dr. Patterson turned his back to me. "I'll have Agatha give you a bath to help calm your soul this afternoon."

Before he could change his mind, I bolted from the room.

CHAPTER 16

Back in my room, I slammed the door behind me. Everyone was at dinner so there was no one to hear my rage.

How had I become so lazy? Barely here for three weeks and I'd slipped by speaking to no less than three different people, one of whom had betrayed me to Dr. Patterson. I threw myself on my bed and hugged a pillow to my chest.

To have someone hold and rock me was soothing, but it wasn't trust and now never would be. I couldn't afford to trust in the wrong person.

Rolling to my side, I hugged the pillow tighter and stared at the tree branches moving in the wind. They reminded me too much of the oaks outside my window at home.

A pair of voices outside brought me back to myself. They were low and raspy.

"I'm tellin' you, mate, she's here," one said.

The bushes rustled before another man replied. "You must be mistaken, man. No respectable woman stays here."

I rolled my eyes. Apparently it didn't take much time for the press to start stalking Mrs. Lincoln. No wonder she was so paranoid.

Perhaps if they were reported to Dr. Patterson he could kick them off the property. I leaned out my window and marked their images in my mind. Barely had I noted their brown suits when the shorter one nudged the plump one and pointed up to my window.

"Gallagher insisted she was with that aunt of hers, but I knew better! There she is! See her?"

I dropped from view and tried to catch my breath. Gregory hired men to find me? The thought sent shivers over me. He must have suspected something was amiss and that meant one of two things—either he missed me or he suspected I knew something. Either way, it wasn't good for me.

Well, I'd not lie like easy prey for him to surprise unawares. No, I'd sacrificed too much to let Gregory beat me now.

With as little sound as possible, I slid from my bed and grabbed my hand mirror.

Keeping a lookout behind me and checking every corner made for a slow descent to the first floor. After only a few minutes, I was exhausted. What were Gregory's spies after? I slid the mirror around the final corner and descended the staircase. Once I was sure no one was there, I pocketed my mirror and ran down the stairs. Surely, they'd not look long; it'd be dark soon.

My foot hit the smooth wooden floor and, despite my grip on the banister, my foot slipped and landed me on the ground. Hard. As I rubbed my buttocks, a familiar swishing sound came down the hall, announcing Mrs. Lincoln and Mrs. Patterson. For a moment they stared at me, taking in my disheveled skirt and awkwardly sprawled legs.

"Didn't think you were a clumsy one." Mrs. Patterson frowned. When I didn't respond, she grabbed my elbows. "Let's get you up, then."

She had me on my feet in one pull and promptly moved around me, spanking the dirt and wrinkles out of my skirt. As she hit the left side of my skirt the mirror slid out of my pocket and shattered on the floor.

"Heavens above," Mrs. Lincoln exclaimed, backing away from me. "That's seven years' bad luck!" She crossed herself and continued retreating until her back was against the wall.

I patted my hair, which was out of place from my fall, pretending I hadn't noticed Mrs. Lincoln's outburst, but deep inside I was relieved. Her mood swings were too extreme for me. I didn't want to remind her of my foolishly spoken words. Perhaps her superstitions would keep her far away from me. Yet, without the mirror, I had no way of seeing who was around the bend—no way of protecting myself from the unseen.

Mrs. Patterson had a harder time hiding her annoyance. "Isabelle, you're late for dinner. Be off with you."

I nodded and scooted out of the hallway and around the corner, and waited for them to pass.

"Someone needs to protect that child," Mrs. Lincoln said.

Mrs. Patterson sighed as she responded. "Yes, yes. We watch all our patients. Now, you're due with the good doctor."

My breath was thick in my throat as their footsteps grew softer and softer. Mrs. Lincoln had defended me to Mrs. Patterson. No one but Papa had ever protected me like that before. Was it possible I'd misunderstood what had transpired between her and Dr. Patterson? Perhaps she had more integrity than I thought.

Instead of making a right to the dining room, I took a left. The sun was setting fast so I darted out the front door. There were no buggies parked from Bellevue all the way down the street. Of course, those men would be pretty poor spies to leave such obvious clues behind them. I leaped from the porch onto the gravel path and darted to the side of the building.

My heart drummed through my ears, but I ignored my fear. The tall oak on the south lawn loomed over me, its shadow making it seem darker outside than it actually was. I spun around a few times, but saw no one. The yard was freshly cut and no footsteps betrayed its lines. Disappointment fought with relief as I realized they were gone. Surely their task wasn't so dire if they'd already left. Regardless of anything, Gregory would soon know where I was staying. Just the idea of him trying to locate me sent heaves of disgust through me. What was he after? My only hope was that he'd find the sanitarium too far beneath him and disassociate from my family. I hoped that, but I knew I'd not get off so easily.

I trudged into the bushes below my window, hoping they left behind some token that would identify them. I had some jewelry that might convince them to forget they saw me. Gregory couldn't harm what he couldn't find. The bushes weren't fully grown in yet, but the soil was freshly turned. Despite some footprints, I found nothing.

What did I expect to do if I came upon them, anyway?

Shaking my head at myself, I stepped out of the bushes.

"What are you looking for?"

I jumped and spun toward the sound of the voice. There was no one to be seen. Twice, I turned in a circle trying to locate the man whose voice had called out to me, but it seemed I was alone.

"Over here, in the window." Samuel's hands rested on a window ledge to my left and he grinned down at me. "No woman I know would ruin their dress unless it was for something special. Can I help you?"

I held up my hand to tell him no. My skirt was torn, but as it matched my blouse, it mattered little.

Samuel's face clouded at my disapproval. "Oh, well then. If you'd like to go bush hunting again, please invite someone along. It looks charming, but you shouldn't be alone at dusk. You never know what danger lurks about." He winked at me. If anyone else had scolded me, I would have felt irritation, but Samuel's tone made it clear that his concern was genuine. He cocked his head to one side. "Cook made fried chicken. It's a specialty of hers. I'd hate for you to miss it. Come inside."

As soon as he mentioned her dish, I thought I could smell the chicken and my stomach growled. I nodded.

"Good. Let me know how you like it." Then he ducked his head back inside, closed the window, and disappeared from sight.

The following week, my work time was spent in the kitchen. I couldn't decide if it was punishment for not speaking further to Dr. Patterson or a privilege from Mrs. Patterson for being so helpful with Cook. Either way, I was just grateful for Cook's cheer and that I didn't have to do any of the other chores. As I entered the kitchen the oven's heat slapped my face.

"Isabelle," Cook exclaimed. "Thank goodness you are here. I'm all a mess this morning. Could you run and get me four eggs from the henhouse?" She didn't stop chopping as she talked. "I dropped the ones I got this morning."

I swallowed, my heart jumping to a canter. I'd heard nothing more of Gregory's spies, but I doubted they were done. If there was one thing I knew about Gregory, it was that he only hired the best, so the fact that there might be men out there who were watching me, but whom I could not readily detect, left me unsettled. The hens' roost was directly behind the house, where it was shady most of the day, and was invisible from the street. I was halfway there when someone called out my name.

"Isabelle, wait a moment."

I looked over my shoulder and found Samuel following me. I hesitated before stopping altogether. "Good morning," he said, running up to me until we were side by side. "Where are you off to?"

I pointed to the wooden chicken coop a dozen yards away. He nodded. "Dr. Patterson said he'd given you time to work with Cook." Ah, so it was a punishment.

His tone led me to wonder if there was more he wanted to say. I let my stride match his. He rested his hands on his suspenders.

"How is Mrs. Lincoln as a neighbor?" he asked.

I shrugged. There was something in the way he asked the question that told me it wasn't what he really wanted to ask. As we approached the coop, he pulled a handful of breadcrumbs from his pocket and threw it on the ground. Immediately, the hens congregated at our feet, pecking at the crumbs.

"Listen, Isabelle," he began.

Samuel drew a line in the dirt with the tip of his boot. "I just wanted to tell you that I won't tell anyone about your speaking. Whatever the reason for your silence, it's your business, and I won't intrude. I don't know what it is, but I trust there is a strong reason. Hopefully one day you'll trust me with your secret." Even the hens stopped clucking as he spoke. A breeze whipped across my face, forcing my eyes to water at its strength. "You remind me of my sister. She'd go quiet whenever she had a problem she couldn't solve. She'd get the same expression you get when people expect a reply. She died from a fever years ago. I think it was she who inspired me to pursue medical school."

He stepped forward and took the basket from me, his fingers brushing mine. Though I could barely breathe, he didn't seem to notice. His words meant more than I expected. He saw *me*— not just an insane girl.

"I'd like to be your friend, Isabelle, if you let me." He opened the gate of the chicken coop for me.

I entered the yard, feeling the chickens' feathers against my ankles. Samuel darted back and forth, startling the chicks outside. Grinning, I walked toward the henhouse and quickly took four eggs. Placing them in the pocket of my apron, I returned outside to put them in the basket Samuel was holding for me. But, as I stepped back out into the sun, Samuel was nowhere to be found.

He reappeared from the side of the shed a moment later, a smile brightening his face. "Your bouquet, my lady," he said, bowing heroically. In his hands was the basket, now filled with baby chicks, all fuzzy and new.

My stomach fluttered, and I inhaled in surprise. Taking the basket, I held the chicks close to me, feeling them tumble over one another. Samuel grinned as he watched me. Despite his genuine nature, a small voice warned me that this was wrong. The last thing I needed was a romantic entanglement. I couldn't let my emotions distract me from the reason I was at Bellevue. Namely, my own survival.

Gently, I pushed the basket back into Samuel's hands. I nodded slightly to Samuel and turned to leave. From the corner of my eye I saw him slip back into the henhouse and return without the basket.

"Isabelle?" He was serious again when he caught up with me. "Have I offended you?"

I shook my head. He kept pace beside me as I walked back to the kitchen.

When we reached the kitchen door, he placed his hand on it and gestured for me to stop. "I'm sorry to have overstepped my bounds. It won't happen again. But I really would like to help you." He opened the door for me. "And not just because I'm a doctor."

As I entered the kitchen, I nearly walked into Dr. Patterson. Samuel bumped into me when I froze in place. To be sure I didn't break the eggs, I scooted past the doctor and placed them in a bowl on the table.

"There you are, Samuel," Dr. Patterson said, relief spreading over his face. "I need you to administer the medications this afternoon."

Samuel nodded and unrolled his sleeves, buttoning them at the wrists. "Of course. Anything else I can do?" he asked.

Dr. Patterson waved his hand in the air as if dismissing the question. "Attend to the patients as needed. I must tend to business with Mrs. Lincoln this morning. She is—" He looked at me. "Unwell."

Samuel nodded. Then, to Cook, he said, "You will look after Isabelle?"

I turned to glare at him. I neither needed nor wanted someone to "look after me." Cook, who had been fussing at the sink this whole time, came to my side.

She patted my back, saying, "Isabelle is a solid girl. But, yes, we'll be fine together."

Samuel nodded, ignoring the odd look Dr. Patterson gave him. "Then I shall be on my way," he said.

The men left, but as they turned down the hallway, I heard Dr. Patterson ask, "What was that regarding?" But I didn't catch Samuel's reply, as Cook chose that moment to begin jabbering.

"Those two, always so busy with something. Never mind their comings and goings, dear, we will keep to our tasks." She handed me a pile of onions and instructed, "Mince these."

I nodded and got to work, careful to keep my head as far from the fumes as possible, for I hated onion tears more than anything.

As I chopped, I heard the bushes outside the kitchen rustle. I froze. Straining my ears, I listened for Gregory's men. Two squirrels leaped from the bushes and chased each other across the lawn. Loosening my shoulders, I tried to calm down, despite the anger that seethed inside me. Gregory had managed to ruin my solace at Bellevue and I had no idea how to get it back.

CHAPTER 17

It had been nearly three weeks since I had discovered Gregory's spies, though I hadn't found one piece of evidence that they had actually existed. Perhaps he had only charged them with uncovering where I had disappeared to and wasn't actually worried about any knowledge I might have of Katerina's death. Regardless, I refused to give up my search and subjected myself to a game of croquet with the other women in the hope of finding footprints or something else amiss.

As we took a break on the side porch, Agatha brought a tray of lemonade for us. Mrs. Allan, Marilla, and I settled into chairs and sipped the cool liquid. At the back of the property, Samuel was walking with Jesminda, who was twitching and jerking. His eyes met mine, and he grinned as he waved. I returned the gesture. Marilla was pointing out shapes she saw in the clouds when the porch door opened and revealed Mrs. Lincoln herself. Her short frame lumbered down the porch steps and toward our small party. Mrs. Allan's face reddened and Marilla's mouth dropped open in surprise. If Mrs. Lincoln saw their responses, she didn't acknowledge them. Instead she came to my oversized chair and demanded, "Move over, girl." She insisted on settling herself in a chair beside me.

Marilla and Mrs. Allan stared wide-eyed at the former first lady. She didn't often spend time with the other patients, and I wasn't sure what to make of her interest. When we were alone she pretended to be kind, but she tattled on me to the doctor. Was she here to extend an olive branch—or something else?

"I hear your daughter will soon be married," Mrs. Lincoln said to Mrs. Allan, whose face quickly fell.

"Yes." Her voice wavered. "She is to be wed next week."

"How joyous for you," Mrs. Lincoln exclaimed. "Weddings are such happy occasions. Where did your daughter purchase her wedding trousseau?"

Although Mrs. Lincoln's words seemed genuine, Mrs. Allan's chin quivered nonetheless. The silence felt so long that I was tempted to speak just to rescue Mrs. Allan, but just as my heart began to race at the prospect, she finally spoke.

"My daughter has told me little of the details. The truth is . . ." Mrs. Allan inhaled sharply. "The truth is I shall not be in attendance at the wedding."

"What? Don't you want to go?" Mrs. Lincoln's eyes widened. "But, she's your daughter."

Mrs. Allan shook her head. "Of course I want to, but . . . she's decided not to invite me. I'm too much of an embarrassment." She raised a handkerchief to her mouth.

This was a side of Mrs. Allan I'd never seen before; I didn't even think it existed. Despite all her hurtful comments, no one deserved to be shunned from their own family. I moved to the seat next to hers and put my arm around her shoulders.

Mrs. Lincoln's cheeks flushed in obvious frustration. "You are not an embarrassment. You are her mother." She lurched to her feet. "I shall take care of this myself."

"No, ma'am, no." Mrs. Allan pulled on her hand to make her retain her seat. "Please, do nothing."

Mrs. Lincoln paused, looking uncertain. "Very well, but you only need to ask."

Just then, Agatha came running to the back porch.

"Isabelle," she called out. "You're needed in the parlor straightaway."

This could mean only one thing: Mother and Aunt Clara had come for a visit.

Mrs. Lincoln turned her hard gaze to Agatha. "Whatever or whomever needs her shall have to wait. Isabelle just started her lemonade. She'll join you when she's finished."

Agatha's face fell. "But I'm to bring her. She has visitors."

Mrs. Lincoln snorted. "Anyone who doesn't give proper notice of their visit deserves to wait. If Mrs. Patterson disagrees, she can talk to me about it."

The lemonade sloshed in my shaking hand, but I stayed firmly in my seat. Mrs. Lincoln was right. If Mother didn't think enough of me to give me time to prepare, then she could wait until I finished my drink.

Before I entered the room, I smoothed my skirt and adjusted my blouse, hoping I was presentable.

Mother and Aunt Clara were sitting side by side on the chaise longue with backs so straight they looked like statues. Mother wore a gray gown trimmed in lace. Her primness meant only one thing: They had come with news.

Agatha shut the door behind me for privacy. Everyone knew a person could hear each and every word through the doors, so I don't know why she bothered.

"Isabelle." Aunt Clara stood and walked toward me. I tilted my cheek toward her, and she kissed me. "How are you feeling, my dear?"

I didn't respond.

"See how her cheeks are pink and healthy instead of horribly pale?" Aunt Clara returned to her seat. "That is surely a good sign."

I glanced in the mirror above the fireplace and touched my cheek. Did I actually look healthier?

Aunt Clara twisted the handle of her handbag around her finger. She was getting agitated. They had something to tell me. Had something happened to Lucy? I sat on the chair opposite them and waited.

Mother cleared her throat. "We have news, Isabelle. Gregory has written to ask permission to call upon you. He is to visit a colleague in St. Charles next month, and he misses you terribly. He'd like to accompany us to church. He must have spared little expense to uncover our trip to visit Aunt Clara. It's horribly romantic. I couldn't refuse." She avoided eye contact and stared at the floor. "Dr. Patterson says you've improved. I am sure you will enjoy this visit with Gregory. It may clear whatever is blocking you. He didn't mention your ill health in his letter, so our rouse for your whereabouts is secure." Mother's chest swelled with pride, or relief.

My ears buzzed like a hornet. Gregory was coming here with Mother's blessing? It was not to be endured! My hands grasped my skirt, and I stood up. I paced back and forth in front of Mother and Aunt Clara. My skin heated with unspoken frustration. I'd been fooling myself this entire time. As long as Gregory was free, I'd never be safe.

Mother cleared her throat. "Gregory wished for me to tell you that he's missed you. He wanted to visit sooner, but it was impossible for him to get away from his business obligations. You know how dependable Gregory is. Once he's committed to something, there is little anyone could do to change his mind."

Aunt Clara smiled. "A fine quality in a man."

My mouth went dry. They were right. Gregory had already killed once. What would stop him from coming after me? He'd kill me as soon as he realized what I knew, and I couldn't find any way to stop him. My legs gave out and I collapsed to the

floor. I'd been fooling myself this entire time. I wasn't safe anywhere so long as no one believed me.

"What's wrong with her?" Aunt Clara cried as she looked
around for someone to assist her.

"Stop it, Isabelle," Mother said. "Be still, please." She dropped
to the floor next to me and tried to wrap her arms around me,
but I shoved her off.

The memory of Gregory's face loomed in front of me. His
brown eyes were cold, despite the smile on his face and the
wind in his hair. Gregory was a killer.

Heavy footsteps sounded as Samuel came into the room.
"What's going on in here? What has Isabelle so upset?" He knelt
beside me. After a moment, he grasped my wrist and paused,
and then started to count out loud. "What on earth happened?
Her heart's racing."

Mother flashed me a pained expression, but quickly found
her defense. "She was supposed to be getting better, but I give
her what should be happy news and look at her. What else am
I paying you for but to heal her?" Samuel stood and glared at
Mother. He never got to speak, for Mother had given me an
idea.

From my spot on the floor, I cried out and pulled at my hair
until all the pins fell to the floor, causing my hair to fly loose all
around me. I rocked back and forth, keeping my face covered
by my arms.

Aunt Clara twittered about the room. "Perhaps this is too
soon. We should tell Gregory to delay a week or even perhaps
a month."

Samuel knelt back by my side. To my mother he said, "You
invited him here?"

Mother flicked her fan open. "Of course not *here*. No one
knows she's here, let alone her fiancé. I'm not stupid, Dr.
Deston."

Samuel's strong voice filled the room. "You mistake my

meaning, ma'am. Regardless, she is not ready to see him. She's clearly distraught because of the invitation. Who knows how she'll be when presented with the man. Don't put her through this."

"No, I think this is the exact enticement she needs," Mother persisted. "If she doesn't work hard to improve, she will then have to show her condition to the man she is to marry. It is up to her to avoid her own embarrassment, and I know how much she wants to keep her stay here out of the town gossip. So . . ."

My rocking ceased as I listened. I wondered if Mother's opinion would change if she realized that she had just opened the door to a murderer.

I played the only card I had left: I pretended to faint.

Dr. Patterson chose that moment to come in. Since my eyes were closed, I could see nothing, but the long silence was telling. I'd worried them, or at the least confused them.

"Samuel, take Isabelle to her room. Have Agatha stay with her the rest of the afternoon."

Strong arms wrapped around me and pulled me from the ground to carry me up to my room. As we left, I heard Mother say, "Perhaps she will feel better in the morning." There were no good-byes.

CHAPTER 18

The following day brought little change to my mood. I couldn't bring myself to do anything. If my sanctuary was no longer safe, why even try to pretend? I'd done all I could to keep Gregory away and yet he found a way to harm me even at Bellevue.

For lunch Agatha insisted I eat outside. "Fresh air will do you good," she promised.

She brought a tray of lemonade and sandwiches with us and sat beside me in the patio chairs under the large oak tree.

Despite the tree's cover, the sun shined warmly upon our part of the yard. It felt good not to be layered with flimsy shawls or handling a dainty umbrella, but rather to let the sun shine upon me without restriction.

Agatha took a bite of her sandwich and leaned her head back into the sun. "I love these days. The warm sun and cool breeze . . . It's perfect."

I hadn't thought that way since before Bellevue. Looking up at the clear blue sky, I tried to release the tension from my shoulders. Just as I was ready to fully relax, a twig snapped by the neighbors' lawn. I jumped and was immediately ready to run.

"There she is!" a man gasped, his voice muffled by the tall, thick bushes. "Isn't she the loveliest thing you've ever seen?"

"She is pretty," another voice agreed.

Neither man sounded like the spies I'd heard outside my window. I glanced at Agatha, but her eyes were still closed; apparently she hadn't heard them. Unable to warn her with my words, I instead lurched to my feet and grabbed a fork off the tray. I jabbed Agatha hard in the arm. She squealed.

"Isabelle!" she exclaimed. "What the devil got into you?" She rubbed her arm where I had jabbed the fork.

The fork fell from my hand. Agatha glanced from the fork to me. She clasped my hand in hers and pulled me back into the chair besides her. "Everything is fine. Take a deep breath and calm down."

Before I could respond, the bushes rustled again and two men stepped through. The shorter of the two raised his hand and called out, "Agatha!"

Her head spun so quickly I thought she was upset, but her face exploded in a smile.

"Elbert," she exclaimed. "I didn't expect to see you until next Friday."

Elbert ran the last few steps and kissed her cheek. "I couldn't wait. Besides, Colin here leaves town tomorrow and I wanted him to meet you before the wedding."

"Shhhhh!" Agatha released my hand and pressed a finger to her lips. "I haven't told Dr. Patterson yet."

"You will tell him before the wedding, won't you?" Elbert shifted from side to side. "I know you love it here, but—"

Agatha pressed her hands to his lips. "I will tell him just as soon as we have a date set."

Silly girl, I scolded myself. *Agatha is engaged to this man. She is the woman they were talking about, not you.* I shook my head at my foolishness and stood up.

Agatha grabbed my hand and drew me to her side. "This is Isabelle, Elbert." Then to me she said, "This is my fiancé, Isabelle. I trust you won't give us away and tell Dr. Patterson until we are ready?"

She looked at me and grinned. I nodded. She knew I wasn't going to tell anyone anything.

Glancing back at the door, she explained, "Dr. Patterson said that you are to rest for the remainder of the day. Can I trust you will go to your room?"

I put my hands together and then pressed them to my cheek, indicating I wished to sleep, and left her with her betrothed. In truth, I was suddenly tired. Tired of watching over my shoulder and tired of being silent.

When I returned to my room there was a letter waiting on my pillow.

My eyes glistened with joy as I tore open the letter. Lucy's messy scrawl filled the pages. Before I'd even read a word, I felt a weight lift from me. Lucy mustn't hate me if she'd taken the trouble to send me such a letter.

I read:

> *Dearest Izzy,*
>
> *Where are you? One day you were here, the next Abigail said you'd left town—without leaving word for me! Is something wrong?*
>
> *Oh, Izzy, my life is falling apart. I followed your advice, yet Mother is still marrying me off to some New York City gentleman. Mother tells everyone she can that she snagged a millionaire for me, but all I can wonder is why my reputation means so little to him. What kind of man marries a woman who says she's lost her virtue?*
>
> *If I could, I'd tell you face to face, but for now, this letter must suffice. I need Patrick. He is the man I will spend my forever with . . . him and no one else!*
>
> *So, I bought a ticket and am leaving tomorrow. I know*

*this means I may never see you or my family ever again,
but I have to go. I don't know how long it will take, but I
will have the life I want. Please forgive me.*

*Below, I've included the address of the hotel I'll stay in
while waiting to marry Patrick. Please write, even if it's
to chastise me.*

I miss you, my dear friend.
Lucy

I crumpled the letter in my hands.

"Good for you, Lucy," I said aloud, despite the uneasy feeling in my stomach. She was giving up her whole world for Patrick. In my entire life there wasn't anyone I'd make so great a
sacrifice for—except perhaps Lucy.

Grabbing a pen and paper, I wrote out every detail of my
ordeal for Lucy: how I had seen Gregory kill Katerina, how
I suspected that he knew I had witnessed it, how I came to
be at Bellevue, how Mother refused to see things my way, and
finally how I feared for my life. Even though, way out West,
Lucy would be so far away from anyone we knew, my heart
still skipped a beat as I folded the cream-colored pages and
considered the prospect of gossipy eyes finding my letter. But
Lucy deserved to know every detail, and I felt a great weight
had been lifted in confessing everything I knew to my beloved
and most trusting friend. I blotted the ink of the address she'd
given me on the front.

Once I'd laid my life so completely out on paper, I couldn't
think clearly. Taunting me, the trees outside my window blew
back and forth. They knew my secret. They reminded me that
they were holding my soul in their branches. If I laid one step
beyond them, Gregory would have me. This building was both
my salvation and my prison. I opened my mouth to cry, but
there was nothing left.

The next thing I knew, I was being rocked. For a moment, I

assumed it was Agatha, but as the woman holding me hummed, I recognized Mrs. Lincoln's soft tunes. Her cheek lay against my forehead.

"There you are, child. You seem yourself again." She pulled away and looked down at me. "Why, whatever frightened you?"

My face was wet, my hair matted against my cheeks. I tried to make a sound in response, but nothing came out. Instead I sighed and rested against her warm shoulder. Was I truly going mad? What had happened that I should need to be rocked like a child?

Her normally stern face relaxed in sympathy. "Is there a reason for it, dear?"

I could not lie to her. I nodded.

"Will you tell me?" She pulled away from me and lifted my chin. "I know there is a reason you don't speak, but nothing is gained from suffering fear alone."

I paused. At some point I'd have to trust someone, or at least try. Even though I had written everything out to Lucy, she could not help me from where she was. I needed someone here to be on my side. Before I knew it, the words came pouring out. I explained how Mother was forcing me to visit with Gregory, despite my being unhappy with him. I stopped short of sharing the whole story, however. I wasn't ready to trust her that much.

"Mother will not understand anything. All she cares about is her reputation and the silly ladies she calls on. I am second to everyone and everything. Now . . . Now . . ." I couldn't bring myself to speak the truth of Gregory. "Now she is doing the worst possible thing for my health."

Mrs. Lincoln shushed me. "You poor child. Is there anything I can do?"

I shook my head. Agatha grunted in the hallway, and something clinked on a tray.

"You need a break from this place," Mrs. Lincoln declared

hurriedly. A fervor overcame her, and she patted my knee excitedly. "Tomorrow. Tomorrow I shall take you for a carriage ride, and you'll feel better. The fresh air will do us both good."

Time away from Bellevue, alone with Mrs. Lincoln. The idea both relieved and terrified me.

CHAPTER 19

The carriage jostled to and fro, forcing me to concentrate on how I sat in order to avoid knocking against the sides. We rode down the river walk alongside dozens of carriages, ladies and men on horses and casual couples walking with their heads tilted in private conversations. Here, among Batavia society, Mrs. Lincoln and I looked the very essence of propriety. The smell of summer was in the air as were the river bugs, which crawled over my sweaty skin. Across from me, Mrs. Lincoln's eyes had glazed over. Despite the bouncing of the carriage, I leaned forward and placed my hands on her knees. Immediately, she blinked and turned her attention toward me.

"I'm glad you've come with me today, Isabelle. I've gone for rides nearly every day and felt so isolated from the beauty around me. All these people are having normal fun. They don't see how close they might be to illness. But with you here, I feel a part of their gaiety. Like I've a friend to spend time with as well. I no longer feel alone." Mrs. Lincoln looked around us at the others who rode along the lane.

Two girls sat on the grass, their heads together and their

braids dangling as they giggled. I'd have given anything to be that carefree again. If only I could have gone back and done it all again, surely I'd have done better.

Mrs. Lincoln focused on me. "Now, tell me of your mother. Why is she forcing this man upon you?"

Behind her, the driver's shoulders twitched. My stomach flipped uncomfortably. Disappointment filled my chest. I wouldn't be speaking to Mrs. Lincoln today. I couldn't risk giving Gregory more information.

"Isabelle, we are far from Bellevue's prying eyes. You can speak freely."

I can't, I thought and turned my face away from her pleading eyes.

"God gave you a voice, child," she urged. "Use it."

It was as though she had slapped me. Her mood swings forced me to admit that her son may have had reason to seek help for her. Perhaps it wasn't all about the money after all. Our eyes met, and the world faded away. For a moment it was only the two of us. The challenge she presented to me hung in the air between us, like a threatening storm. I glanced around, hoping for some excuse to avoid giving in to her.

"There is no one here of importance. Talk to me," she urged.

Trees blurred as we passed them by, the branches brushing against the top of our driver's head. I gestured toward the driver and shook my head. I wouldn't allow anyone to undermine me so easily. I'd worked too hard to have my safety snatched away from me in a careless moment. Mrs. Lincoln sighed.

"Isabelle, that man doesn't care if you speak or not. He doesn't even know who you are." She didn't understand what danger I faced, I reminded myself. However, I couldn't explain it to her without risking exposure.

Men with bowler hats and pronounced mustaches walked beside us in the shade of the morning. Ladies with bustles and parasols glided past, unencumbered by heavy thoughts. I longed for my life back, for the time when I could walk through the day without fear or regrets. One of the men caught my eye and tipped his hat at me. For a moment, my breath caught in my throat, but then he turned to another woman and gestured similarly. I turned my attention away from him, hoping to blend in with the other afternoon riders.

Mrs. Lincoln adjusted her gloves and smoothed her skirt as she watched me. I knew she was waiting for me to speak, but I'd been too weak already. And here we were in public; I couldn't let go where anyone might hear. My silence was the only weapon I had. My beating heart reminded me of what would happen if I gave in to her request. Gregory was out there waiting for me.

I looked into Mrs. Lincoln's eyes and shook my head. Then I covered my mouth with my hand, making sure she understood my meaning. Instantly, her face tightened, and what little smile she had for me disappeared.

"Isabelle, I brought you with me for a nice ride. We are away from the doctors and all the staff. Talk to me. I want to be your friend."

Her eyes were earnest as she took my hand. But there was nothing she could've done to make me speak. The previous night was a fluke, one I'd do my best to avoid in the future, especially now that Gregory had plans to try to see me. I had to be vigilant. The way she pushed me to talk made it all too clear how little she actually understood.

Again, I shook my head and covered my mouth.

"I see," she said. "You only wish to speak when it pleases you. No matter what strings I had to pull for our little adventure. Well, just see if I try to soothe your nightmares again."

I opened my mouth in surprise. I never would've expected the nastiness that seethed from her. Her friendship was indeed a precious gift, but I had to protect myself. She snapped her fingers and directed the driver to return home.

We rode back to Bellevue in chilling silence.

Upon our return, I ignored every bit of propriety I'd ever been taught and jumped out of the carriage, leaving the woman to gawk behind me. I held my skirt high as I ran to the back of the house and burst into the kitchen, my mind whirring. No matter how I longed for her friendship, the price was just too great.

Agatha, Cook, and Samuel were all sitting on stools around the wooden table. I walked over and sat down.

"What are you doing back so soon?" Cook asked.

Agatha looked around us. "I thought you went for a ride with Mrs. Lincoln today?"

I ignored both of them and sighed. Samuel shifted his stool so there was room for me to sit comfortably. I pulled an orange toward me and began peeling it. They continued their conversation, but my ears were buzzing so loudly I couldn't hear a thing. Mrs. Lincoln's pain reverberated through me. She was lonely too and I'd hurt her.

Perhaps if she had insisted earlier that I speak I would've complied, but I couldn't be caught speaking now. Not only would Dr. Patterson release me, but if the spies knew I was only pretending to be insane they would report it back to Gregory. I had to be sure no one questioned my stability.

"You've gone pale, Isabelle," Samuel said, putting his hands in his lap. "Is everything all right?"

No, I wanted to say. *I'm so tired. It feels as if Gregory's eyes have followed my every step, and Mrs. Lincoln is angry with me. And Lucy . . . everything is ruined.* But I said nothing. Instead, I clasped my hands in my lap and squeezed. Long ago I'd hurt my hand and if I pressed the right spot, incredible pain erupted up my arm. I needed the pain to help me.

"Marilla's feverish today. Isabelle appears flushed. Perhaps an illness is spreading through the patients." Agatha looked slightly alarmed. "I'll give her some tonic."

Samuel nodded, but didn't take his eyes off me. They all cared for me. Realizing that made the deception harder, but it had to be done. They could not view me as a friend. I was a patient. I jammed my thumb against my knuckle and gasped. A wet, warm streak ran down my cheek. I inhaled sharply. "You all right, child?" Cook asked.

Gregory's visit pressed against me, and I could feel the threat as if it were a being all its own. It would crush me if I was not careful. Crying wasn't enough. They had to see me as more than weak.

Cook and Samuel spoke in hushed tones to one another while Agatha rifled through the small medicine cabinet in the kitchen for the tonic.

Without warning I clenched my hands into fists and pressed them against my temples. Cook's whispers stopped and I felt the attention turn to me. While they watched, I beat my fists upon my head. The pain in my one arm still reverberated.

"Stop her!" Agatha shouted as she slammed the cabinet closed.

Samuel lunged toward me. His strong grip stopped my self-abuse and he wrapped his body around me so I couldn't move at all. I'd seen him hold other patients like this after an attack, but it was different experiencing it. Had Katerina felt so helpless with Gregory? The very thought made me squirm to get away, but Samuel's grip didn't loosen. My ears buzzed and my throat itched. I shouldn't have tried to deceive these people. I needed to get away.

"Isabelle, relax," Samuel whispered.

"You're safe, dear," Cook agreed.

From the corner of my eye, I saw Agatha pouring a spoonful of tonic. She came toward me, a look of determination on her face. I'd had enough of tonics. Dr. Carson's always seemed to knock me out and I'd have none of that now.

I tried again to get free, but Samuel was just too strong.

"Hold her still," Agatha demanded.

"I'm trying," Samuel replied. "I won't hurt her."

Agatha tried to take my chin in her hand, but I bucked away.

"STOP!" I screamed at the top of my lungs, expelling all the air inside of me until Samuel released his grip.

Cook and Agatha stepped backward.

"Apparently she *can* speak," Agatha whispered.

Cook nodded, her eyes never leaving my face.

Samuel didn't respond to them. His eyes were focused completely on me, his hands supporting my back, easing my shuddering.

A moment later, Dr. Patterson burst into the room. He looked from Samuel to me. I was still leaning back on Samuel, and my breath was ragged.

"What is going on in here?" Dr. Patterson demanded.

Cook raised an eyebrow at me as if asking permission to tell him. I shook my head so slightly I wasn't sure she would see it.

"It was I, Dr. Patterson," Cook said. Samuel paused momentarily, but then agreed.

"It's my fault, doctor," Agatha added. "I bet Cook she was too weak to yell with a patient's force."

Dr. Patterson smirked. "Well, next time you choose to play your little games, please make sure the kitchen is clear of patients."

Samuel nodded. "Very sorry, sir. That was bad judgment on my part."

"See that it doesn't happen again." Dr. Patterson swooped out of the room.

Cook was still watching me when Samuel said, "You lied to him."

"Sometimes that is the way things happen." She took the two steps toward me and lifted my head so that I met her eyes. "There is a reason this girl doesn't speak."

She searched my face, but I gave away nothing.

"What could've happened to make someone mute?" Agatha was again speaking as if I were not in the room.

"Isabelle will tell us when she is ready," Cook promised. "Won't you, my girl?"

Seeing no other option, I nodded.

CHAPTER 20

If Mrs. Lincoln meant to keep away from me, she did a rather poor job of it. Instead of pretending I didn't exist, she had Dr. Patterson order me to accompany her on another outing the very next day. I knew she would ask me to speak once more and that I would let her down again. Yet, Dr. Patterson told me he believed it would be good for me, and I needed to keep his good opinion. There was no way out without damaging my safety. It seemed a pointless task to join her, but I couldn't find a way out of it.

"Mrs. Lincoln has surely taken a shining to you," Agatha said as she watched me eat breakfast.

I shrugged.

"Well, be glad for it. It's a change of pace. That's got to be nice."

Again I merely shrugged.

"Well, the other patients are jealous. They spoke of little else while you were gone yesterday." Agatha collected my dishes onto her tray and looked me over. I patted my mouth with a napkin and placed it on top of the dirty pile.

With a wink, she lifted my tray and disappeared out the door. I took my hat and pinned it to my head, taking care that the ribbons fell down my back properly. At the least, Mrs. Lincoln would have no complaints about my appearance.

Our ride into town was silent. Mrs. Lincoln waved to certain couples as the horses clopped along the river walk. The ride seemed easy until the driver veered off the river walk and onto the main road away from town. Despite myself, I jolted at the sudden change.

I patted Mrs. Lincoln's knee and gestured around us, hoping she'd explain herself. Instead, she met my eyes and shrugged with the same hard expression I'd given her so many times. I held her gaze for a moment and hoped she'd take pity and say something, but she did nothing. I turned away and crossed my arms. If her only reason for having me join her was to force me into speaking, I'd have none of it.

After a time, Mrs. Lincoln's face relaxed and she sighed. She reclined on the carriage bench and pretended to ignore me, but I could tell she was listening for the slightest noise from me. I also settled back into the carriage and forced a serene expression onto my face. Two could play her game.

The Fox River rippled to my right, full of mother ducks and their ducklings. Many of the babies were growing up, tufts of feathers erupting atop their heads. Despite Mrs. Lincoln's anger, these adolescent ducks made me smile inwardly.

It was nearly an hour later when the driver pulled the horses to a halt. We stopped in front of a dark brick building with a second-story wraparound porch. Bright flowers dotted the entry stoop while vines hung from the railing above. It was garish. It brought to mind the time Father took me to New Orleans with him. I wondered whom we were calling upon.

Mrs. Lincoln was helped out of the carriage first, and then the driver assisted me. I stayed close to Mrs. Lincoln, hoping she'd explain why we were here. The bustle of her skirt was larger than normal, in the European style. This was no ordinary visit.

"Shall I return for you, Mrs. Lincoln?" our driver inquired.

She turned around with one hand raised. "No, please wait for us, Joseph."

He nodded and turned his attention to tending the horses.

Mrs. Lincoln said nothing to me, but glanced over her shoulder every few steps to make sure I was still with her. Before we even reached the front door, it sprung open as if they'd been waiting for us. In the doorframe was a woman of Mother's age in a dark purple gown. Her hair was pulled back, but messy, as if she had slept recently and had forgotten to check the mirror. Her face showed a dreamy expression, as if she were one half in the till. "I have been expecting you, Mrs. Lincoln," the woman declared in a breathy voice.

Mrs. Lincoln let out a long sigh. "I've heard much of your talents, Madam Rosetta. Is the spirit with you today?"

"Oh, yes." Madam Rosetta's voice rose in pitch. She placed a hand to her forehead and declared, "The spirit feels very strong today." She rested her eyes upon me, and I saw a glimpse of tension cross her face. "The girl . . ."

"Is mute," Mrs. Lincoln said, touching her lips with a finger.

A short pause passed between us as if they expected me to open my mouth and refute Mrs. Lincoln. Naturally, I disappointed them.

"We do not bring strangers into the circle. It disrupts the communication," Madam Rosetta said.

"This is not negotiable." Mrs. Lincoln placed a hand on my back. "I shall not sit without her."

For a moment, Madam Rosetta gave me a sour grimace, but quickly changed her countenance to a soft smile. "Of course. I can make an exception for one so strong in the power." She took my hand and gasped. "Someone has done you a grave ill, my dear."

"How do you know that?" Mrs. Lincoln took my other hand and mimicked Madam Rosetta's hold, trying to learn the same things she had. I pulled both hands away and shook the uneasiness from my shoulders. Papa always said mediums were phonies, but the idea of someone seeing into my soul made my skin crawl.

Madam Rosetta glanced to the sky. "Ah, the sun is well placed. Shall we go inside and begin?"

Mrs. Lincoln and I followed her into a dark hallway and then an even darker parlor. All the curtains were closed, and the only light came from a candelabra on a side table. The walls and furniture were various textures of maroon, giving a unique aura to the room. The only other thing with any color was the dark gray fireplace, which stood open and empty. There wasn't even a pile of wood in it.

We sat at the five-sided table, and Madam Rosetta held out her hands for us to grasp. Once we sat, the door shut, bathing us in deep darkness. Mrs. Lincoln's hand was wet beneath mine, but Madam Rosetta's was as light as a feather, as if she expected to float away.

"Dear spirits," Madam Rosetta began. "Speak to us and fill the room with your greatness."

The room was so still I doubted we were even breathing. Mrs. Lincoln's hand shook. I tried to hold her tighter to give her strength.

"We need a sign," Madam Rosetta continued, her voice low and strong. "Show us you are with us."

We waited a moment. I glanced from Madam Rosetta to Mrs. Lincoln in the flickering light. Both of them had closed their eyes, and Mrs. Lincoln was muttering something to herself. I stared behind her at the candelabra, which cast shadows about the room. The flames momentarily doubled in size before they went out, and we were left in near darkness.

"Oh dear," Mrs. Lincoln exclaimed. Her excitement was palpable, though she stayed seated.

152 / *Sarah Barthel*

"Yes," Madam Rosetta sighed. "They are here." Her voice remained as even as before. It was eerie how little emotion she showed.

"Who?" Mrs. Lincoln's voice shook with longing. "Who is here?"

"Show yourself, spirit," Madam Rosetta demanded.

There was a soft chill against my back as if someone had opened a door. Then I saw it. A tall figure in a top hat was circling the table.

"Abraham!" Mrs. Lincoln exclaimed and began to rise.

"No!" Madam Rosetta insisted. "Do not make any sudden movements or break the circle, for the spirit may leave."

In the darkness, I saw Mrs. Lincoln nod as she grasped my hand even firmer than before. "Just . . ." she began. "Just tell me if it's my Abraham."

"Spirit, are you he?" Madam Rosetta requested. "Tap once for yes, twice for no."

Almost immediately a single knock vibrated in my ears. Impossibly, President Lincoln's spirit was there—in the room with us. He continued his restless walk around our circle. Mrs. Lincoln hunched forward, nearly overcome with emotion. "I've waited so long to contact my beloved. So long," she whispered.

I kept my grip firm on her hand so the spirit wouldn't leave.

Mrs. Lincoln tried to take the spirit's hand, but he moved before she could touch him.

As I studied Mr. Lincoln's figure, there was something off-putting about how he stood. He swayed as if off balance and hiccupped every few moments. I watched his hands and twisted around to see more clearly in the darkness. The figure stepped away from the table and into the darkness of the large room. Mrs. Lincoln was still leaning down, presumably praying or crying, and Madam Rosetta was staring into the ceiling. A faint *shush* sound came and again I felt cold air on my back. Squinting in the dimly lit circle, I spied a dark figure behind me.

"Stop!" I exclaimed. Before the "spirit" could vanish, I jumped to my feet and grabbed the tall man. Once I had him, I could just make out the outline of the fireplace.

"What's this?" Mrs. Lincoln's tone was flat.

"Pass the light," I demanded as Madam Rosetta exclaimed, "Sit! The spirits will shun such energy."

As Mrs. Lincoln passed a candelabra to me, I dug my nails into the man's skin. "Don't think about running," I threatened. He turned to the wall.

The firelight flickered against the fireplace. On first glance, I thought I'd made a fool of myself, but then I saw a slight crack in the corner. I let go of my prisoner, crouched down and pushed against the back of the fireplace. It opened in an almost silent *whoosh*, revealing a small room of costumes.

"Explain this!" Mrs. Lincoln demanded.

"I . . . uh . . ." Madam Rosetta stuttered. "Maria!"

The man turned from the wall to face us and then slowly pulled the top hat and beard from his face, revealing himself as a woman. She hiccupped once again before belching loudly. Mrs. Lincoln took a step back and shook her head.

"I believe I've seen enough," she said, taking my hand and pulling me from the room.

Madam Rosetta was on our heels. "My dear Mrs. Lincoln. That was an unfortunate trick my sister played on us, and I will make sure she is punished. Perhaps next time we will have real luck and—"

"There will be no next time," Mrs. Lincoln interrupted. "I will not be back here again."

Madam Rosetta's eyes turned to slits. "I am not the only fool here. You said that girl was mute. Perhaps you are not as honest as you seem, either."

Mrs. Lincoln turned from the door and weighed Madam Rosetta's words. She sighed. "Perhaps a spirit guided her tongue. If anyone asks, I shall tell them of the healing powers of your room, but nothing of your sister."

My mouth dropped open. Mrs. Lincoln was bribing this fraud just to keep my secret.

"Yes," Madam Rosetta agreed. "The spirit clearly moved the girl." Her posture relaxed, and I knew my secret was safe.

Mrs. Lincoln nodded and opened the door. Sunlight flooded on us. Then she pulled me toward Joseph and the carriage.

I hadn't dreamt; in fact I had barely slept. Lying in bed later that night, watching the trees move back and forth across the moon was all I could manage. Helping Mrs. Lincoln during the séance had awakened something within me, and it was banging against my chest.

I had no idea how long I'd been lying down when my door creaked open and the familiar smell of coconut and lavender filled the room. Mrs. Lincoln didn't pause at the door, but walked straight to my bedside. I sat up against my pillows and made room for her to sit beside me.

The moonlight danced off her face, and the darkness concealed her wrinkles so that she looked like a young woman. This was the woman Father described and, I was sure, whom President Lincoln fell in love with.

"My friend," she said, taking my hand in hers. "My nurse is sleeping so we have a little private time."

She paused and stared down at our interlocked fingers. Her thumb moved back and forth thoughtfully. I was about to ask why she had come when she spoke once more.

"I should've liked a daughter," she whispered. After a pause she asked, "I know what speaking today could cost you. Why did you do it?"

Why indeed? "I don't really know." My voice was raspy from lack of use. "Papa always said he owed his life to you. Thaddeus Larkin, perhaps you remember him? You nursed him during the war. He spoke often of your intelligence and your kindness. I couldn't let you be taken in by those pranksters."

"I nursed your father?" Mrs. Lincoln sat back and sighed. "That was a long time ago. Before . . . well, I was a different person then." Her eyes shifted.

Leaning forward, I laid my hand on her knee. "Not so different. The woman Papa described was kind, caring, and full of life. You are still that person. Living here—it brings out the best and worst in us. You are still the woman Papa admired. I think he'd be proud that we've become friends."

"I worked with many men during the war. I'm sorry, but I don't think I remember your father."

I held up my hand to silence her. "I remember Mother reading the lists of injured and dead men. I didn't think that you'd remember him."

"All those men." Her eyes clouded over. "Can we speak of something else? I don't want to invite nightmares."

"Of course," I replied instantly. I'd listen to stories of the war all night if she'd share them, but I knew better than to press.

Mrs. Lincoln turned something over in her hand and said, "It's taken the better part of the day to decide how best to repay you for helping me expose those charlatans today."

As she closed her mouth, her hand opened. I looked down and gasped. Lying against her white skin and swollen knuckles was a pair of drop pearl earrings. The top pearl was round and small, but the bottom one was nearly as big as my thumb. Not even the jewelry Mother was saving for my wedding was as rich as these.

I moved my hand out to touch them, but paused, feeling suddenly presumptuous.

"F-for me?" I asked.

Her eyes were moist. She nodded.

"Why?" I asked. The earrings were in my hands now and

their smoothness was like heaven to my fingertips. I longed to rush to the mirror, hold them to my ears, and watch them dangle.

"I know your suitor is coming to call. Perhaps if you wear these, he will see you've not lost your value."

It was as if she'd thrown a bucket of water over my head or singed my hand with an iron. The earrings fell from my hand before I could find the sense to simply give them back. Luckily they landed on my dressing table.

Mrs. Lincoln's face tightened. "Do you not like them, Isabelle?"

I picked the earrings up and returned to the bed. The woman beside me looked suddenly self-conscious. I knew I needed to answer quickly, but her mentioning Gregory's visit froze my mind.

"They are everything I could wish for," I said, finally.

Mrs. Lincoln brushed a lock of hair from my face. "You are too pretty to fear anything. He'd be a fool not to love you."

"I do not wish him to love me." My voice was crisp in the darkness. A breeze came in through the window.

"But he is coming to see you—surely that means something."

Yes, it could mean any assortment of things, but I doubted the primary reason for Gregory's visit was mere affection. Mrs. Lincoln would only understand that if I entrusted her with the truth of what happened. Closing my eyes so I wouldn't see the skepticism on her face, I began to tell her my story. I left nothing out, from the stone that had led me to the scene to hiding under the bed to seeing Gregory and Lucy the following day.

"You see why I can't tell anyone else," I said when I was done. "No one is going to take my word when my own mother and Dr. Carson think I'm a liar." I clenched my hands into fists, waiting for her to poke holes in my story.

The silence that filled the room was thick. The moonlight had gone from dark blue to highlighted pink. Morning was near.

Finally, Mrs. Lincoln spoke. "You are sure of what you saw?"
I nodded.

"Oh my dear child," she exhaled. With those words she enveloped me in a hug and lifted the stone wall that had weighed my spirit these past months.

"And he's arriving next Sunday?"

"Apparently we are to attend church with Mother and Aunt Clara."

"So we have a bit of time. I shall do what I can." She clenched her hand into a fist and pounded my mattress as if it were Gregory's dark heart.

Suddenly, I was overcome with fatigue. Mrs. Lincoln, however, was as alive as I'd ever seen her. She spoke to herself as she rose from the bed and walked away. If there was one thing I knew, it was that Mary Lincoln could save people. She had nursed Papa back to health and now she would save me as well.

CHAPTER 21

Marilla passed me a pair of scissors and the cream thread. My white stitches were gleaming against the cream fabric, and not in a good way. I accepted her suggestion and pulled my work out to start over. It was Saturday, but we were to stay active every day. Dr. and Mrs. Patterson thought it was the best way to keep us sane, but it was becoming repetitive. Mending, weeding, croquet games, cooking, and long, soothing baths . . . there was more to life. My mind wandered to Gregory's impending visit the following day, but I pushed it away. Mrs. Lincoln would have a plan. An early heat wave had kept some, including Mrs. Lincoln, to their beds. A few other patients chose to tend to the weeding despite the heat. Our divided forces left just Marilla and me in the parlor, although she barely let a moment go by without filling it with her observations.

"You are so still, Isabelle," Marilla said. "I couldn't sit as you do for hours at a time." She smiled to herself. Just as I pulled my last stitch out, she slid closer and put her hand on my knee. Looking at her, I stopped rocking and tilted my head inquisitively.

Marilla looked to each of the doorways and swallowed as she returned her gaze to me.

"Can I tell you something?"

I put my work down, giving her my full attention, and nodded.

"You won't tell anyone?" she asked.

I shook my head.

"My sister sent this to me." Marilla fished in her apron a moment before retrieving a newspaper clipping and placing it in my lap. "She won't visit me as she's still young and doesn't want the taint on her, but she cared enough to warn me."

The ladies in the garden were giggling so loudly we could hear them inside. I pushed their amusement away as I picked up the palm-sized clipping:

> *Thomas Shelton is to marry Vanessa Naringo in two months' time. The bride's trousseau is being sent from Paris. His first wife abandoned him and was admitted to the Bellevue Sanitarium. Shelton's family and friends wish him better luck with Miss Naringo.*

Marilla fixated on my face as I read the notice. Never had I read such a poorly worded and spiteful announcement. Truthfully, I felt bad for Miss Naringo for choosing him. I didn't doubt he worded the announcement himself to make sure Marilla was further hurt by the news. I dropped the clipping into her basket and wrapped my arms around her. The moment I did this, she let out a small whimper.

She pushed me back, her eyes wide and desperate. "Then you think it's true? You believe he's . . . divorcing me?"

My grip on my mending slackened. That he was divorcing Marilla was a given the moment she returned to Bellevue. Had she been so naïve not to realize that? My expression must've said it all for she took a steadying breath and pulled herself as tall as possible.

"Well . . . good riddance." Her voice was shaky. Gesturing

around the room, she said, "I live better here than I ever did with him."

I nodded. However she could justify getting over him was better than grief.

Samuel cleared his throat as he entered the room. Instead of his usual work clothes, he wore a three-piece tweed suit, and his hair was combed like a proper gentleman. The cut of the suit highlighted his broad shoulders and tall physique.

"Marilla," he said. "Dr. Patterson told me of your news. Would you like to talk?"

She glanced at me and then back to the work in my lap. "Actually, I think I'll be all right. Isabelle is a good listener."

Samuel smiled at me. I looked up and felt my face flush from his gaze. "Yes, I hear that often. Still, I'd like to talk. It is a shocking way to hear such news."

Marilla stood, but didn't move. "I can't leave Isabelle alone."

"Isabelle would be fine alone," Samuel said. "But she's needed in the kitchen. I hear she has mail to read." He winked.

My stomach flipped. That message could only mean one thing: Lucy had replied. I gestured my departure to Marilla and tried to thank Samuel with a look, but as it made me feel moony, I gave up and left the room.

Once I had gotten the letter from Cook I secreted myself away to my room. The shadows from the tree created patterns on Lucy's letter. I lay on my bed and reread her words, my heart beating a little slower.

> *Dearest Izzy,*
>
> *Your letter was incredibly shocking! Yet, I dare not doubt you. Gregory murdered Katerina. The very thought sends chills over my very being!*
>
> *And you, my dearest friend, are locked up in an asylum. What are we to do? I don't know how quickly I can get to*

you, or if I even can. The pastor will be in town this Sunday,
and Patrick and I shall finally become man and wife. If I
leave now, it will be months before he will be back, and I
can't return unmarried. You and I both know that.

Please know I am with you in spirit. My support and
my love are always with you. This shall pass. I don't know
how or when, but it will.

I'll write more soon,
Lucy

At least one of our lives was progressing. It was time to protect mine. I walked across the hall to Mrs. Lincoln's room. Left
alone all day to think, she must have found a way to help me.
Before morning I needed to know the plan. Her oak door was
shut, and the knob wouldn't budge. I knocked hard. After a
moment, I heard the swishing sounds of a skirt rustling.

"Yes?" Nurse Penny asked as she opened the door a few
inches.

I opened my mouth and froze. This was Nurse Penny's typi-
cal time off. She wasn't supposed to be there. I knew Mrs. Lincoln would find a way to dispose of her once she saw me.

Nurse Penny shook her head. "I'm sorry, but Mrs. Lincoln
cannot be disturbed."

I stood on my tiptoes, trying to get a look at my friend, but
Nurse Penny placed a hand on my arm and said, "She is resting.
Don't make me send for Dr. Patterson to restrain you as well."

Her words did their duty, and I stepped back from the door,
which was promptly shut.

For an instant I was defeated, but then I pulled myself together and reminded myself that this was Mary Lincoln. She
had promised to protect me, and I knew she wouldn't disappoint. Even her fiercest critics admitted she was a woman of her
word. She wouldn't abandon me in my hour of need. All I had
to do was trust her.

CHAPTER 22

The dreaded day finally arrived.

Agatha pinned my hair and dressed me in my finest church dress before excusing herself to aid the other patients. With Mother arriving any moment, I slipped across the hall and knocked on Mrs. Lincoln's door. When no one answered, I tried the knob. This time it gave easily, and I opened it.

Slipping inside, I was surprised to see that the room was empty. I had no time to search for her; Aunt Clara and Mother were surely waiting for me downstairs by now. I ran back to my room and wrote Mrs. Lincoln a hurried note saying I'd gone to church and was thankful for her aid. When I read it over again, it didn't convey the depth of my gratitude, but it would have to do.

When I returned to her room, I realized I had never seen it so neat. All of her trinkets were packed away, her bed was made without so much as a wrinkle, and her perfume bottles stood in a straight line. The only mess in the room was her desk. Papers lay haphazardly upon the surface. I walked over to the table and picked one up. In a messy scrawl she demanded aid for a friend who had details about a murder. Many lines were crossed out or written over. There were almost half a dozen different drafts of the letter. Clearly she'd put thought into how she phrased my dilemma. I'd put my trust in the right person. Perhaps she and one of her friends were apprehending Gregory right now.

I tucked my note into her stationery box so she'd be sure to find it and rushed out to meet Aunt Clara and my mother. I didn't know how Mrs. Lincoln planned to help, but I knew she would come through.

As Aunt Clara's carriage made its way down Wilson Avenue, I twisted my handkerchief between my fingers, my pulse beating in my ears. If I didn't watch out, I'd vomit, but even that wouldn't stop Mother. Neither Mother nor Aunt Clara had spoken a word to me. There was nothing they could say that would make me forgive them for putting me through this. What was worse was that it seemed Aunt Clara knew they were doing wrong, for she was continuously biting her lip and glancing at Mother. Between the two of them, I couldn't decide which woman was more unforgivable.

We turned a corner, and the church was before us. I searched the grounds of the tall white building for Mrs. Lincoln or anyone she might have sent to protect me, but there was no one. People stood in small groups of three or four, laughing as if today didn't spell disaster. Without Mrs. Lincoln, it slowly occurred to me that I was actually going to have to see Gregory. My skin prickled at the thought.

My heart beat so loudly I could hardly hear the horses clomping or the trees swaying in the wind. However, I was not blind to Aunt Clara giving Mother an obvious poke to the ribs.

Mother adjusted her gloves and cleared her throat. "Isabelle, do not embarrass me," she began. "Gregory traveled a long distance to see you, and you should be grateful. More than just your childish fantasies ride on this match continuing. You were very fond of him once. Perhaps he can win you over again."

I glanced at Aunt Clara and hoped for her to rescue me from Mother's lecture. Surely she knew something was amiss in this courtship, but she was too busy scanning the crowd in front of the church to pay me any mind.

I was dreading seeing Gregory's tall frame standing above the crowds, but I was relieved that so far I didn't see anyone even slightly resembling him. I shifted my attention to the other carriages and looked for Mrs. Lincoln or some sign of the help she promised. She had connections. Perhaps she'd gotten the sheriff to intervene. But no one familiar or abnormal stood out. Our carriage pulled to a stop, and the dread I'd suppressed crept over my heart.

"Do you understand, Isabelle?" Mother's quavering voice communicated her nerves.

I nodded simply to stop her from saying more. I was rewarded with a curt smile before she rose and got out of the carriage. How had I been so foolish to not have a plan in case Mrs. Lincoln couldn't help? I'd been so focused on trusting her and her connections that it never dawned on me she could fail.

I prayed for God to protect me. If He truly knew all, then He would not allow Gregory to reenter my life. He would turn Aunt Clara's and Mother's eyes to see the devil in Gregory. I wouldn't have to endure this meeting and would be free to return home. My true home, not the sanitarium.

As Mother stepped from the carriage, Aunt Clara tilted her head and gave me a kind look. "Your mother wrote him that you have been battling laryngitis and may not speak. Even so, will you at least try for me?"

Her voice was loving and soft, but I turned away from her, searching the street for my savior. Any savior. Then, as Aunt Clara climbed out of the carriage, every hair on my arms stood on end.

Gregory had arrived.

He stepped out of the square white church and made his way toward us. The wide brimmed hat, bushy mustache and perfectly fitting suit all looked the same, but I was finally able to see past the good looks and charm. His every move was choreographed to make people admire him. He fiddled with a pocket watch as if nervous, but was all smiles as he took Aunt Clara's hand and kissed it.

The muscles in my arms twitched as I watched him. He had destroyed my life, as surely as if it had been my neck he had strangled, and yet he behaved as if he had no blame upon him. A woman walked past our carriage and nodded to me. I repeated the gesture before realizing that I'd seen her before, while out riding with Mrs. Lincoln. Looking over the crowd, I noticed a few other familiar faces and I smiled. These families had influence and would remember me as Mrs. Lincoln's companion. If things became too unbearable, all I had to do was loudly betray where I'd been living and Gregory would be sure to give me up. I'd have little value if my ruinous circumstances were exposed before such influential people. I smiled. If nothing else, I had this plan of action.

"Why, Mrs. Haskins," Gregory preened to Aunt Clara. "You haven't aged a day since I saw you last." His baritone voice was as smooth as ever. "I hope you've been enjoying Isabelle's visit. Hopefully you haven't gotten her into too much mischief." He winked at Mother.

"You do like to flatter old women." Aunt Clara giggled like a schoolgirl and covered her mouth with her perfectly gloved hand. I wanted to retch.

"Is your husband about?" Gregory asked.

Aunt Clara shook her head. "He had an important meeting in the city, but he will be back this evening."

She guided his attention to Mother, who was standing nearby on the wooden sidewalk in front of the church. He took her hand as well, and I noticed how her cheeks flushed at his touch. How did she not see through his act?

Mother and Aunt Clara stepped aside and watched as Gregory approached the carriage and offered me his hand. I smiled politely at him, but didn't accept it. For all I knew, that was the hand that covered Katerina's mouth and suffocated her. Where was Mrs. Lincoln's promised aid?

It was time to accept that it wasn't coming. She'd been too sick or sedated to fulfill her promise. I was alone.

"Do let me help you, Isabelle." He offered me his arm again. "The service is starting soon."

His hand was nearly at my eye level and he clearly wasn't going to move so I could get down without him. Mother's eyes darted around us, but Aunt Clara watched me, waiting to see what I'd do. I refused to take his hand. Instead, I placed my hand on his shoulder, so I could launch myself out of the carriage. I didn't even wobble as I landed. Mother rewarded me with a glare. She grasped Gregory's arm and led him toward the church entrance.

"Clara and Walter have attended here since they were married," she explained. "The building dates back to the turn of the century." Mother gestured to the tall windows.

"It is beautiful," Gregory agreed.

The church bells sounded from the tall spire, and we fell in line to enter the building.

"Batavia is unique," Aunt Clara replied, taking Gregory's other arm. "Mr. Haskins spent his youth here and always said it was where he wanted to spend the end of his days." They walked arm in arm.

"He was lucky to have a wife who was so accommodating," Gregory said.

"Wives are best when helping to fulfill their husband's dreams," Mother said. I nearly rolled my eyes at how they were both hanging onto him, as if otherwise he'd run away.

Gregory laughed. "Surely we men aren't so bad."

Aunt Clara smiled. "You will find there is much to love and hate in government, Mr. Gallagher." Then she lifted her hand to her face again and sighed. "I nearly forgot. Mr. Haskins is having some men over for dinner this evening. They are very interested in meeting with you."

He held the door open so we could enter the church. Most of the congregation was already seated in the pews. The morning sun streamed through the large stained glass window behind the pulpit, casting warmth throughout the supposed sanctuary. But even here, in a house of worship, I felt unsafe and exposed, unable to ask for help from anyone around me.

Gregory followed us down the aisle. "I would be more than happy to join you for dinner," he gushed to Aunt Clara. Then, as an afterthought, he added, "So long as Miss Isabelle will join us."

Mother grabbed my elbow and drew me close. "Speak," she whispered in my ear. I allowed myself a small smile and shook my head. Despite her words, Mother would quickly regret it if I spoke. I'd make a scene so grand they'd tell the story for months. *If* I spoke, that is. To accomplish what I needed would ruin any chance I had at a real life, and I wasn't quite ready to give up my hope. Not yet.

"I'm so sorry, but Mr. Haskins specifically said it was to be a gentlemen's dinner," Aunt Clara said quickly.

We stopped and slid one by one into the family pew. Despite all attempts otherwise, I found myself seated beside Gregory. He took my hand in his, and I could feel the strength in his grip.

"Perhaps a stroll would brighten your day, Isabelle," Mother offered when I said nothing. "I'm sure Gregory would oblige."

"Actually, I was hoping to accompany her on a carriage ride." He turned to Mother. "You see, after I heard she'd been ill, I thought a carriage ride along the river might be more to her liking than a walk, so I hired one this morning. Does that sound nice, Isabelle?"

All I wanted to do was scream, "NO," at the top of my lungs. Instead I put an indifferent expression on my face.

"Always the demure one," he said, clearly taking my indifference as modesty.

Aunt Clara and Mother exchanged a look before Mother said, "Despite her illness, I think a carriage ride is just what Isabelle needs. It would be unfair for us to take up all your time this afternoon."

My stomach flipped. Alone with Gregory.

The pastor stepped before the congregation in his white robes and began the service.

"Let us pray," he said somberly.

And I did.

CHAPTER 23

As the congregation followed the minister out of the church I refused to leave. I hadn't thought of an acceptable way to get rid of Gregory and couldn't move until I had. In front of me, Gregory offered Aunt Clara his arm. Since he had discovered that Uncle Walter was in town, his attention had rarely been diverted from her. I was embarrassed to admit how it chafed me that Gregory would get to see my dear uncle and I would not. Mother grabbed my arm, pulled me from the pew, and directed me outside and into the morning sunlight.

As we passed him, the minister took my hand in turn and said, "Peace be with you, child."

I stared into his brown eyes, silently pleading that he'd realize the danger I was in. He didn't hear my prayer. Instead he grasped Mother's hand and repeated his blessing as he did for everyone around us.

Gregory and Aunt Clara waited beside a white, open-top carriage with a red stripe around the side. The inside was covered in velvet, which, if you had asked me, was absurd for a summer afternoon. Despite my fear, the horse's proud stature made me want to give him a carrot like I did with my own horse as a child. That thought was short lived, however, as the Negro coachman stepped down and opened the door.

"Your young man awaits you, Isabelle." Aunt Clara seemed nervous. She glanced at Mother, but didn't say more.

I cursed myself for trusting my fate to another. It was foolish of me not to plan my own escape, but I couldn't change the past. My options were limited: cause a scene so hysterical that Mother would be forced to restrain me and return me to Bellevue, or confront Gregory.

Looking back and forth between Mother and Aunt Clara, I decided to make one last plea.

I pulled on Mother's arm and led her away from the carriage, gesturing to Aunt Clara and Gregory that we'd return. She followed me, but I was sure it was only to keep me from making a scene.

"What is it, Isabelle?" Mother asked once we were at the other side of the church and clearly out of view.

I wanted to tell her. My mouth opened and I waited for the words to pour out, but they didn't come. Instead my throat tightened, blocking any sound from escaping. Perhaps I had been playing mute too long, and now my voice was truly gone.

"You have to speak, child," she said. "I cannot understand breathing."

Tears welled in my eyes, and I could not prevent them from spilling over. I punched my chest once to unblock my voice, but nothing happened. It was a cruel fate that once I needed to speak I could not.

Mother looked horrified. "Isabelle, pull yourself together. We cannot let him see you so distressed!" She glanced around and put a hand on my back. "Please, child. Calm yourself."

I glanced toward Gregory's carriage and shook my head back and forth repetitively. Just once I wished Mother would think of me first.

She gripped my chin and forced our eyes to meet. "This is too important for your flights of fancy. Now. Calm. Down."

I tried to swallow the lump in my throat, but it only expanded.

"Isabelle," she whispered. "This is enough. No one is going to help you. You have to control yourself. Now, you are going for a ride, and you will be normal and that's final. Understand me?"

She was right; no one was coming to help me. I had no other option but to take matters into my own hands, for there was no one left to trust. A chilling calm filled my body and pushed all panic aside. Indicating I understood, I nodded my head to Mother.

"That's better. Gregory is waiting." She turned to go, but then looked over her shoulder at me. "Don't forget. None of this foolishness today."

I nodded again. Today was time for action. I would finally reclaim my life.

I did not linger for her, but returned to the carriage myself.

"Thank you for waiting. Isabelle and I were saying a prayer." Mother's face was serene as the lie passed easily through her lips.

Gregory nodded and twirled his hat in his hands. "I've always admired your close relationship."

I turned away from the look that passed between them. The lump returned to my throat, but I swallowed it away. This was not a time for tears. I must be brave.

To assure Mother stayed behind, I said, "Yes, mothers and daughters ought to be close."

Aunt Clara gasped and covered her mouth with her handkerchief, but Mother merely nodded. I believed she'd pat her back if she could and congratulate herself on a job well done. She had broken me.

"I told you she was better," Aunt Clara whispered. "I knew the laryngitis was gone."

Gregory, clearly not understanding what was transpiring, looked from them to me, his brow crossed. I wondered if he thought it was an act, or if he thought something was amiss beyond my stay at Bellevue. Surely he'd read the report from his spies. Mother's and Aunt Clara's eyes were fixed on me so tightly they didn't see his confusion.

I sighed and explained, "Excuse them. I've been ill for a while, and they weren't sure if my voice would ever come back. They can be so dramatic."

Gregory laughed and stepped closer to my side.

My resolve wavered, but I forced myself to stand my ground. Never again would I back down from this man. "You mentioned a ride by the river." I gestured toward his carriage.

To prove my decision, I strode past everyone, lifted my skirt high enough to annoy both Mother and Aunt Clara, and stepped into Gregory's carriage. Mother was wide-eyed, but did her best to ignore my behavior. Despite myself, I smirked.

"I think someone wants to depart!" Gregory was cheery as he kissed both Mother's and Aunt Clara's hands. Then he leaped into the carriage and settled next to me. I could feel the warmth of his body, but it chilled me. The devil was beside me.

"I'll have her back for lunch." With one motion, he ordered the driver to move forward, and we lurched away from the church.

"We'll wait for you at the house," Aunt Clara called out as she waved after us.

The bouncing of the carriage forced both of us to wobble on the bench. As we swayed down the street, Gregory leaned back and put an arm around my shoulders. Twisting away, I pulled my shawl around me tightly.

"I know your mother felt you needed a break from all the wedding planning, but it's lonely without you at home." His smile was full of perfect, straight teeth, complete with dimples.

I raised an eyebrow at his words. More like he had no one to accompany him to his dinner engagements. A large bump in the road made my teeth bang together.

"I miss you, Isabelle. This long absence has made me realize how much I care for you." I looked at him, finally. Given all he'd done, I could not believe he was saying all this. He continued. "I've discovered that . . . well . . . I love you, Isabelle, more than I thought possible."

It was the first time such a declaration had been made during our courtship. It was not how I imagined it. I searched his face for some sign of rehearsed actions or vengeful lying, but all I saw were his brown eyes staring at me. He reached out and took my hand, his large fingers cupping my palm. Suddenly, it was hard to breathe.

If he had said this months ago, it would've made me happy and warm inside. But he chose today to declare his love, and all I felt was empty.

Our carriage turned, and we moved along the riverbank among other couples in their Sunday best. I occupied myself with our surroundings as I tried to decide how to confront him. It wasn't something I could simply blurt out. Luckily, Gregory continued to chatter about folks at home. Above us the foliage was lush and green. The river glistened in the morning sun, the gurgling easy to hear. Its coolness brushed against me.

Couples of all ages dotted the lane, some strolling, others in carriages, and even a few on bicycles. The bicycles entranced me for a moment, for they were a rare sight. Then, looking around, I realized what fortune had dropped in my lap. Surrounded by people, out in broad daylight, Gregory would be stupid to make a scene. And Gregory was not stupid.

He took my hands once more.

"Have you not missed me at all?" His voice was soft, barely above a whisper.

Clearly he expected me to declare my affection for him in return, but I was not some foolish woman to be swayed by a few kind words. Nor was I desperate to hold onto him, not anymore. I, more than anyone, knew what kind of man he was. "I know what you did."

His eyebrow twitched. "What do you mean?"

I pulled my hands out of his grasp. "I know what you did."

"Isabelle." He reached out to touch my cheek, but I tilted away from him. "Whatever you've heard, you are mistaken."

"Whatever I've heard?" I stopped a moment, refusing to be baited with his lesser crimes. I needed him to admit it. I needed him to look at me and tell me that he killed Katerina.

I sat up straight. "I was there," I said. "I was outside her house. I know what you did." The carriage jerked suddenly. Let the driver hear, the more the better.

For a brief moment Gregory's smile faltered, and he blinked. Then he pulled himself back to normal and folded his hands in his lap. His fingers were locked together so tightly, his knuckles whitened.

"I've no idea what you are referring to. Perhaps I have indulged in one indiscretion, but you'd be hard pressed to find a man who hadn't. She is the past, you are my future." As he spoke, he also glanced toward the driver, and I knew he was worried about being overheard.

"I know what you did." My voice quivered as I repeated myself.

Gregory's eyes narrowed. "What is it you think I did?" He placed his hand on mine and squeezed in such a way that I couldn't move a finger. "I'd be careful of what you *think* and pay attention to what you know."

"I-I-" My mouth went dry and my lips froze. Was this how it started with Katerina? My chest rose and fell as I tried to find a way out of the situation. I should've known better than to confront him so directly. "I know you hired spies to find me."

Gregory smirked and chuckled. It wasn't what I wanted to say, but it was the only thing I could force out. I prayed he'd give me the proof I needed to accuse him.

"Isabelle, is that what's causing your sullen mood?" he asked. "You and your mother left so quickly. I was worried. You were ill and so many terrible things had happened already. I had to know you were all right. I hired *investigators* to make sure you were not in danger. I hired them to protect you."

"What did your investigators discover?" I asked in my prettiest voice. Two could play the betrothed game.

Gregory grunted and adjusted his legs. If I wasn't mistaken, he hadn't anticipated my question. No proper girl would want to admit she was in a sanitarium, let alone discuss it. I tucked back a strand of hair and waited for his response.

"Well, they . . . um . . ." He cleared his throat.

"They what?" I pushed in my most innocent voice.

"What they claim is impossible." Gregory adjusted his collar. "It was a breach of your trust and a total waste of money."

I wanted him to admit what he must suspect on some level—that I was a patient at Bellevue. If I wanted him to try to get out of our engagement, I had to show him how my prospects had changed.

I lowered my lashes in mock shame and said, "I suspect I know what they uncovered."

Gregory gulped. "Oh?"

"They told you I was in a sanitarium, didn't they?" I folded my hands in my lap and tried to behave like a demure and devoted lady. I wasn't yet ready to show him my insanity act.

"They *said* you were in Bellevue Place." He avoided my eyes. "But I, of course, thought they'd found the wrong girl. You're not insane."

"Did they explain why I was at Bellevue?" I asked, ignoring his dismissal.

Gregory's eyes narrowed again. "No. I fired them for incompetence. You are not insane. Look at you . . . you are healthy." Surprised, he loosened his hand, and I was able to free myself from his hold.

"Yes, I've been living there these last few weeks." I took a breath and forced my eyes to him. "No one knows, but I fear gossip will soon spread. I thought it only right that you hear it from me."

Gregory was still for a long moment. "I'm so sorry, Isabelle," he began.

Knowing our breakup was coming, I tried to control my face. He couldn't see my relief when he gave me the terrible news. He continued. "I had no idea that attack affected you so deeply. I've been insensitive and negligent in my attention to you."

"What?! No!" I moved as far from him as possible in the carriage. "Don't you see what folks will think when this is found out? People will shun me. The life you want will be impossible. I—"

"We can overcome that," Gregory interrupted me. "You shouldn't give up your life because of one incident. Those that love you will stand by you and the rest will quickly forget. We will be fine. I love you."

His arm slithered around me, but there was no place for me to retreat. My last card had been played and it was worthless. Gregory was willing to risk his career for me. The strangeness of that confused me. Even so, our engagement had to end. Before the carriage ride was over, I'd be free of him.

"You are not the man you say you are," I said softly. "I know what you are capable of."

Gregory pulled away from me. "What do you mean?" he asked.

"I witnessed Katerina's murder."

The color slowly drained from Gregory's face. "Y-you witnessed her death?" His voice broke.

"Her murder," I corrected him. My heart pounded so hard I could feel it against my blouse. "I told you I was there."

"And what did you see?" Gregory whispered.

I paused. Then, not able to turn back, I replied, "You know what I saw."

Gregory swallowed and glanced at the driver before stammering, "H-how would I know?"

Our eyes locked for a moment. "You strangled her."

Gregory coughed. "I see now why they locked you in that asylum. Why on earth would I do such a thing?" His voice was loud enough to carry in the open air. More than one person turned to look at us, then returned to their own amusements.

His easy dismissal was fuel for my anger, which overpowered my fear. I grabbed his knee so he'd pay attention. "I saw you, Gregory. Don't deny me the truth."

The driver's head twitched as I spoke.

"I had no relationship with that servant." Gregory's voice was crisp. He grabbed my wrist before continuing. "Why would I kill a girl I don't know?"

His eyes bored into mine as he pulled me close to him. His breath was wet on my cheek and smelled of old coffee. I turned my face away, and he made his grip firmer.

"I know where you are living. Don't think I won't use that information," he whispered.

"So long as I never see you again, it matters little to me," I replied quietly.

I didn't expect the hurt that shadowed Gregory's face. As if he hadn't realized that I could ever choose anything other than him. After a moment, the hurt melted from his face, replaced with anger. He grabbed my other wrist and pulled me to his chest.

"And you believe me capable of such acts?" His grip burned as I tried to get free, but he had me under his control. I couldn't even struggle unless I wanted to break my arm. Words were my only weapon; perhaps they always had been.

"I know what I saw. I'll never forget it either."

"So that's it, then. It's over." His grip slackened slightly.

"Over?" I repeated. "You killed someone. Don't you have anything to say about that?"

Gregory glanced around us. "Keep your voice down."

A maroon carriage passed us. The two women kept an eye on us as they whispered to each other.

"Is that it?" I spat. "Can't have the neighbors talking. That is your only concern to my words? I've agonized over this moment and the Gregory in my mind is *always* more interesting than this."

"Isabelle, please." Gregory pulled on my hands, trying to get me closer to him. "Please, calm down so we can discuss things."

"Let go of me," I shouted. His grip was too strong. I stood, still tugging on his grasp.

"Darling," Gregory's voice elevated.

"I am not your darling." The heel of my boot bore down on his foot. As he gasped and shook, his grip lessened so I regained my freedom.

The moment I was free, Gregory looked up at me. "Sit down!"

His eye twitched and his ankle shook. Gregory was not as in control as I thought. I glanced ahead of us quickly. The river walk was coming to an end. If the driver took us to a less populated part of town, there would be no stopping him.

In as strong a voice as I could muster, I whispered, "Follow me and I'll scream every detail. I don't care if they believe me or not." As I spoke, I located the door handle, jostled the door open, and then, once Gregory looked properly frightened, I jumped out.

CHAPTER 24

A few screams and shouts came from nearby riders, but nothing I could comprehend. My ears buzzed with the exhilaration of flight. My feet hit the ground with more force than I expected and I twisted to one side in surprise. My ankle collapsed beneath me and I landed on my right hip, with my arm breaking my fall. For what felt like ages, I tried to find my breath and move.

For a moment I wondered if Gregory would still try to come back and help me, but he didn't. As I scrambled to my feet the driver of his carriage yelled, "Yah!" and the horses broke into a gallop so quickly that Gregory toppled back in surprise. Had I frightened him so much that he had decided to simply abscond?

I walked to the dirt path on the side of the road, ignoring the obvious comments from passersby and waving off offers of help. The carriages moved on quickly, and soon I blended into the crowd beside the river, my dramatic scene quickly forgotten.

Now free from Gregory's control, at least for the moment, I didn't know where to go. Mother and Aunt Clara were preparing lunch at Aunt Clara's house, but the very idea of returning there was nauseating. I couldn't go backward like that.

A pair of horses came clopping up too close beside me and I darted off the road, landing in a bush, my heart racing. I looked up. The coach was filled with elderly ladies with poised hats and gay laughter. One pointed at me with concern, but I waved for her to keep going. Inwardly, I scolded myself. Foolish to think with one confrontation, I'd forfeit my fear of Gregory. There was no guarantee he was done with me. Just because he'd fled didn't mean he wouldn't return. Gregory was a determined man and now he knew everything. The only thing that possibly held him back was my situation at Bellevue. I turned south. If I walked carefully, I could make it back in good time.

Carriages continued up and down the road beside me. It took all my concentration to keep my head forward and move onward. Gregory had driven north and my instincts said he wouldn't return here to make a scene.

I walked through the crowd trying to figure out what his next move might be. Gregory must have a plan. He was too smart to just return to Oak Park and move on. There were too many variables. The only thing I was fairly sure of was that he wouldn't come after me in public again. Then, as I passed by the General Store, someone grabbed my arm.

"Let me go!" I exclaimed. I would not be taken by him again!

"Isabelle, it's all right." The grip slackened, yet my eyes remained closed. I could not bring myself to turn and confront him.

People commented all around us as I struggled to pull my arm away.

"Isabelle, it's me. It's Samuel." He released me, and I opened my eyes. My heart still pounded in my ears, and my skin throbbed where he had held me, but I was safe. It wasn't Gregory. I took a deep sigh and tried to make myself stop shaking.

"What's scared you so?" Samuel's face tightened.

"I . . . He . . ." I couldn't make any explanation make sense.

The crowd around us grew until it blocked the entrance. I was forced to step away from Samuel when some people nudged their way through the crowd and into the store.

A clerk came outside. "Are you all right, miss?"

I nodded. "Of course." Standing next to Samuel, I felt silly for making such a spectacle.

"Very well. Then, please clear the entryway." He walked back to his duties, and the crowd went back to their business as well, leaving Samuel and me alone.

A few of the women clucked as they passed by, and my cheeks flushed at how disheveled I appeared. My sleeves were wrinkled, and there were a few rips in the bottom of my skirt. A large section of my hair had fallen to my shoulders. I twisted it around my finger to put it back in place when a bolt of pain radiated down my arm. I dropped my hair and winced as pain jolted through my elbow and up to my shoulder.

Samuel noticed the motion, and his eyes clouded over with worry. "Isabelle, you are in pain! I didn't mean to grab you so hard. I—"

I rubbed my arm. "It wasn't you."

Samuel looked around as if my attacker was waiting a few steps away. "What happened?" he whispered.

I stammered, "I . . . I told him I knew, and he grabbed me. I fell. Nothing went right today."

If Samuel thought anything strange about my comments he didn't show it. Instead he waved the remaining onlookers away, offered me his arm, and led me down the street. His bag swung freely from his free hand. I wondered if we looked odd together, me limping in my church dress and him in his rolled-up sleeves and suspenders.

"Who hurt you?" he asked quietly.

I expected him to placate me or argue about the truth in

my words or at the very least question my loose tongue, but his tone and manner evoked sympathy. We reached the end of the block, and he led me to the left. I recognized the large oak tree on the corner. We were walking back to Bellevue, back to safety.

I exhaled and said, "Gregory Gallagher."

My eyes stayed fixed on him and waited for any signs of disbelief, but instead shock and pity covered his face.

"Your fiancé?" he asked.

"Not anymore."

Samuel strode in silence before saying dryly, "That's probably for the best."

Bellevue was now directly in front of us, a short, two-block walk. I stopped walking before we could be overheard by anyone working outside.

"Are you badly hurt?" He took my hand in his. For an instant, despite everything, I felt my skin tingle at his touch. Samuel was all business, however, as he lifted my injured arm out to the side and up and down. "I think you'll be fine. If it still hurts this evening, come see me and I'll wrap it for you."

I nodded.

"And your ankle?" His voice trailed off.

"I fell on it when I jumped out of his carriage. I'll find you if the pain persists."

Samuel looked like he wanted to ask dozens of questions, but he couldn't find the words.

"Isabelle!" The call of an all too familiar voice shot down the lane to us.

"Mother?" She shouldn't be here. She was waiting for me at Aunt Clara's.

She stepped out of her carriage, which was parked in front of Bellevue, and stalked down the sidewalk toward us. She was merely a block away, but I could feel the anger seething from her.

She ignored Samuel and grabbed my injured arm so that I was nearly face to face with her. I cried out from pain. Her fingers had found the exact place Gregory had clutched me not an hour before.

"She is injured, ma'am." Samuel tried to separate us, but Mother positioned herself so as to exclude him from our conversation.

Instead of letting go of me, she gripped tighter, and her nails embedded themselves in my bruises. "When I want your opinion, Dr. Deston, I'll ask it." Returning her attention to me, she demanded, "What did you say to Gregory?"

We both knew what she was referring to. I twisted my arm to get out of her grasp, but she only held tighter. At least I knew where he'd gone so quickly.

Lifting my chin, I replied, "I told him I knew the truth."

Her grip became so tight that her nails punctured my skin, and blood appeared through my thin white sleeve. Samuel's eyes were fixated on her hand, and his eyes squinted as if he once had felt similar pain.

"The truth? You mean your lie!" Mother's voice was so loud I wondered if she had forgotten we were in public. Her grip tightened as her voice softened. "What have you done, Isabelle? How could you do this to me?"

"To you?" I exclaimed.

"As if you don't know how your actions could ruin me as well." Mother gave a disgusted snort. I bit my lip to avoid reacting.

"You are hurting her," Samuel interjected, his eyes still on my stained sleeve. "*He* hurt her."

Mother turned and looked him square in the eye. "She is none of your affair."

Samuel glanced at me as if seeking guidance and I motioned for him to leave. This was between Mother and me. He opened his mouth as if to argue, but retreated to the garden shed, a

184 / Sarah Barthel

place he could surely overhear every word. His slight defiance against Mother gave me strength.

Once he was out of sight, she continued. "Mr. Gallagher wants nothing to do with us now and will surely spread ill will when he returns to Oak Park. He uncovered where you've been staying, and he intends to make sure everyone knows in order to protect himself from your slander. No man will have you now! I don't know what to do with you, Isabelle. This isn't you. You don't lie, and yet here we are. You've ruined yourself, and I don't understand why."

Even with Mother's frantic fears and the trickle of blood down my arm, all I felt was relief. Gregory was no longer interested in my life; I was free. Perhaps he truly thought all he had to do was discredit me in order to keep me silent. If that was true, I could go home.

"But I am well now. I can speak again, and Gregory is out of my life. Let's go home," I said.

Mother's face froze, and she turned a cold eye to me. "*We* are going to do nothing. *I* am going to return home. You shall remain here."

"What?" My head shook in confusion. "Am I to stay here with Aunt Clara?" It wasn't the worst idea. No one knew me in Batavia. I could start over.

"No. I am not releasing you from Bellevue. I told Dr. Patterson I didn't believe it was safe for you to leave until this foolishness had left your mind."

It took a moment for her words to seep in. If she didn't arrange my release, I wouldn't be allowed to leave—ever. Marilla's panic made more sense now.

"But . . ." I began.

Mother released my arm and gave me a satisfied smirk. "Everyone will soon know where you are. You cannot return home after a month or two and expect your life to be waiting for you. It doesn't work like that. However, I will write you. If I play my cards right, our friends will, no doubt, pity the mother of such a damaged daughter. If I act quickly, I shall not lose status." She patted my cheek.

"You cannot leave me here," I said. "There is nothing ill in me. I am your daughter, your flesh and blood."

Mother crossed her arms. "A daughter? Daughters are obedient, loving, and subservient. But you have none of those qualities. Every single thing I've done has been to aid you, and yet you still tried to confront Gregory with your wild accusations. He is a good man, Isabelle. Until you remember that, I have no daughter."

I reeled at her words. "But Mother, he is the reason Katerina is dead."

"Despite all I have done, that is what you still believe? There is nothing to be done, Isabelle. Even if you were to confess your lie now, you'd have to stay here. People must believe you are healed before I can let you come home. I'll not be mocked for harboring a lunatic or worse, a spiteful liar."

She dragged me up the porch steps and through the front door of Bellevue. Mrs. Patterson rose from the sewing circle and greeted us in the hallway. The tall grandfather clock boomed its quarterly chime.

Mother shoved my arm out toward Mrs. Patterson. "I've come to return my daughter to you. She is beyond help. Thus I am returning home for the remainder of her care."

Mrs. Patterson put an arm around me as Mother dropped my arm and stalked out of the house. There was no good-bye, no remorseful glance over her shoulder, no kindness at all.

That was how she left me: shocked beyond tears in the front room of Bellevue, which was now my home. Forever.

CHAPTER 25

Back in the hallway, fatigue overcame me. My arm throbbed and my legs were sore from my fall from the carriage. Despite all that, when I saw Mrs. Lincoln's door open I was overcome with an angry curiosity. She had broken her promise, but there must have been a reason. She wouldn't have abandoned me without cause. Before I succumbed to anger, I wanted to know the reason. More than one figure made shadows over the floor. Mrs. Lincoln's pacing was audible even in the hallway. She only paced when angry, and I wondered who was with her. That she was well enough for visitors ate at my heart. Why hadn't she sent her promised help?

As I approached it was impossible to ignore the raised voices coming from Mrs. Lincoln's room.

"Mother, you are not well. This is where you must live for the time being," a man's voice declared.

"I *am* well, Robert," Mrs. Lincoln cried out. "It is you who are keeping me in here. Why? Do you wish to have all my money? Take it—just give me my freedom."

I was close enough to see into the room as Robert took a step backward at his mother's outburst.

"Your money is far from my mind, Mother," he insisted. "I am worried about your health."

Hand on my doorknob, I peered over my shoulder in order to gain a better view. Mrs. Lincoln twirled a piece of ribbon around her fingers. She threw it onto the table as she demanded, "Speak to Dr. Patterson when he gets back." Mrs. Lincoln stood, walked toward Robert, and placed a hand on his cheek. "Please, aid me. Surely as my son you owe me some allegiance."

Robert stared at his mother and slowly nodded his head. "Very well, Mother. I will inquire after you, but if you are refuted, you must stay here willingly. I want no more of this foolishness."

"They will affirm my well-being." Mrs. Lincoln stood straighter. "I have been the perfect patient."

I decided that I had heard enough and opened the door to my room. I'd gain no answers from eavesdropping. The slight *click* of the doorknob must have alerted them to my return, for immediately they both were in the doorway staring at me.

"Isabelle, a moment, please," Mrs. Lincoln requested. Her face was flushed and her eyes pinched.

Robert stepped back to give me room to enter. Even if I wanted to speak with her at that moment, I couldn't. Just looking at her caused my throat to clog with emotions, but I didn't know how to refuse without damaging my relationship with Mrs. Lincoln further. As always, the blush pink quilt on her bed looked odd in the bleached starkness that was Bellevue, but it looked childish today, not sweet.

"My mother says she's developed quite a relationship with you," Robert began, offering me a seat at the table.

"We have become close," Mrs. Lincoln explained. "Haven't we, Isabelle?"

Mrs. Lincoln sat across from me and folded her hands on the table. "Isabelle, you have nothing to fear in this room; you know that. Robert will not repeat anything that is said here."

To that Robert raked his fingers through his hair. "Mother,

188 / *Sarah Barthel*

you know I cannot keep such a promise." His honesty impressed me.

As Robert paced the room, I avoided both of them by staring at the floor. *Please,* I prayed. *Give me a way out of this confrontation.*

He turned to Mrs. Lincoln. "Mother, this is a waste of time. Even were she to talk, it would matter little."

"Robert, is there a problem here?" Dr. Patterson stood in the doorway and looked in at us. "Isabelle, I did not know you had returned."

I swallowed and turned my gaze to the doctor. His face was expressionless, and that made me feel less safe than ever.

Robert walked over to Dr. Patterson and crossed his arms over his chest. "The girl refuses to speak."

Dr. Patterson shook his head sadly. "That is because Isabelle does not speak. She's mute, Robert." Samuel had not betrayed our confidence. Then in a softer voice, "Your mother believes they have a relationship?"

Robert nodded. "She claims they spend the evenings conversing."

"She had once mentioned something along those lines. Interesting." Dr. Patterson tilted his head in thought.

Mrs. Lincoln was staring at me as the men spoke in hushed tones, as if we were not in the same room. Our eyes met and guilt nudged me.

"Isabelle," she begged softly. "Isabelle, tell them. Tell them how we talk late at night. Tell them of your nightmares and how you saved me from being a fool at Madam Rosetta's. Do not let them think less of me."

Dr. Patterson's head snapped at Mrs. Lincoln's words. "Late night talks? But what about your nurse? Does she not lock you in?"

Mrs. Lincoln didn't hear him; she was focused only on me. "Tell them!" Her voice rose in pitch to the point that she'd sound insane even if she read the Constitution. "Tell them of our talks so I can leave. You are the only one who can. Tell them!"

Dr. Patterson strode to Mrs. Lincoln's side and took her wrist, counting her pulse. "She's overly excited. What on earth put you in such an argument?" He shot Robert a questioning gaze as he soothed Mrs. Lincoln's brow. Her breath was ragged and I wondered if she was in physical pain as well. Everyone knew how quickly her headaches came upon her. "Stay with her while I get a tonic. She'll settle for us."

Not able to take the guilt another moment, I looked from Dr. Patterson to Robert and back to my former friend. Then, as if I were truly insane and hadn't heard the desperation in her voice, I stood up and walked out of the room. Dr. Patterson followed me out the door. Mrs. Lincoln spoke not another word.

As Mrs. Lincoln slept, I curled up on my bed and gazed out the window. There was a breeze that afternoon, forcing the tree branches to blow from side to side. They had not the strength to oppose the wind's will. After the breeze released its grip, a single green leaf broke away and floated to the ground. Why shouldn't I break away as well? Mother had left me; I owed her nothing. I'd have control over my life.

I jumped to my feet and rummaged in my wardrobe for the carpet bag I had brought with me. Yanking it out from the far corner, I began pulling my gowns off the hangers and shoving them into the bag. For a second I wondered if I should fold them properly, but dismissed it as Mother's advice and continued packing. I moved to the vanity table and began doing the same with the powders and brushes. The door creaked open behind me.

"What are you doing?" Agatha shut the door behind her.

"Leaving," I replied, not even glancing at her.

Agatha walked through the room and placed a hand on my shoulder. "Samuel told me what happened and that you were finally speaking freely."

I didn't stop to look at her. If I paused, I'd lose my nerve.

"I wish you had told me what was keeping you silent. Perhaps we could have helped you."

I snorted. "What do you think you could have done?"

Agatha placed her hand over mine and stopped me stuffing a blouse into the bag. "No one should have to go through what you've gone through—but you can't leave." Her young eyes pleaded for something I didn't understand.

I shrugged her off me. "Mother's left me here to rot. Why shouldn't I leave?"

"The Pattersons will come after you." She spoke so simply, I knew it wasn't a lie, but I could not accept her words.

"No, they won't. If they were so concerned about keeping us here, why did they let me ride out with Mrs. Lincoln? Why did they let me out with Mother today? They had no way of knowing I'd come back. No one locks the front door. I could walk out any time." Just to prove it, I rammed my last comb into the bag and snapped it closed.

Agatha sighed. "They let you leave with a chaperone to bring you back. If you leave now, if you flee, they will find you. No one wants an insane woman roaming the—"

"I am not insane!"

Agatha slid a few inches away from me. "Do you think that really matters? Listen, I always knew you could speak. We all did. I knew you weren't deranged, not permanently anyway, but now you're going to have to prove your sanity."

What a flip my life had taken. Twenty-four hours before, I was working to maintain the appearance of insanity, and now I'd have to undo all that and demonstrate that the quality of my mind was good.

"So, I am a prisoner here." I sat on the bed beside Agatha. "What am I to do?"

Patting my knee, she sighed. "I don't know. Ask me how to help Mrs. Allan avoid laudanum or keep Marilla from starving herself. But you don't have those kinds of problems. Perhaps yours is a problem for which there is no assistance. Perhaps you have to find a way out of this yourself."

"Perhaps." I folded my hands in my lap.

Agatha rose and handed the carpet bag to me. "If you unpack now, no one will know."

"I don't care who knows," I muttered.

Agatha reached out and grabbed my chin. "Don't you give them any reason to punish you. Keep your head down. Somehow it'll all work out." She dropped her hand.

"No one will believe me."

"I don't know the whole story. Samuel wouldn't give me the details, but I do know that he believes you. And Samuel doesn't trust many people." Agatha smiled.

"But Samuel doesn't know the whole story either."

"That doesn't matter," Agatha interrupted. "He believes you. No matter what."

"No matter what," I repeated to myself. Perhaps if I told Samuel the whole story, he'd actually believe me. At this point, I had nothing to lose.

I rolled my shoulder and winced. "I think I need my arm bandaged," I said.

"Lord, is it as bad as all that?" Agatha fussed, getting to her feet. "Dr. Patterson is meeting with Mr. Lincoln. Go on to Samuel's office, then. I'll unpack all this for you."

"Thank you," I replied.

Though I knew where Samuel's office was, I had never been there. The further I walked down the hallway, the darker it became. Finally, I reached the last door and knocked. Samuel opened it immediately.

"Isabelle," he said, a smile brightening his face. "How can I help you?"

"My arm isn't improving."

"Ah, of course. Come inside." He stepped back so I could enter.

The office was smaller than Dr. Patterson's and lacked the tall bookshelves, but felt more comfortable. There were plants on nearly every shelf and a landscape oil painting on the wall. On the desk an opened box of colored pencils and a drawing lay in the sunlight. I stepped to his side of the desk and traced the outlines of a tall blue house. The blue pencil was tucked behind Samuel's ear.

"Did you draw this?"

"Yes, it's a small hobby."

"It's lovely." I looked closer. He had drawn small flowers, a willow tree in the distance, and stained glass windows above the front door. "Where is this? Is it here in Batavia?"

Samuel shuffled his feet and diverted his gaze. "Um, no . . . i-it's a home I mean to build one day. It's of my own creation."

It was my turn to be embarrassed. Inadvertently, I'd pried into his personal life. And, despite myself, I wanted to stay. How many men could draw their futures so beautifully?

"I paint as well," I said instead.

"Really? Oil or watercolors?"

"I prefer oil on canvas. I like the smell and texture." I examined his painting. "What is this?" I asked, pointing to a small blob of color in a window.

Samuel ran his fingers through his hair. "A mistake. I left it out a while back and a patient added that detail."

"How horrible!"

Samuel shrugged. "Art is nothing if not fluid."

I traced the lines of his house with my fingernail, then stopped myself. "You are an interesting man, Dr. Deston."

"Not nearly as interesting as you, Miss Larkin."

I blinked and turned to look at him. Had he really said that? He didn't meet my gaze. Instead, he collected his pencils and put them in their case.

Clearing his voice, Samuel gestured to a pair of chairs across the room.

"May I?" Samuel asked, kneeling in front of me. I nodded, and he placed my hand on his knee.

With the most gentle of touches, he turned my hand over and unbuttoned my shirt sleeve. His fingers were cool against my wrist. He didn't say anything, but I heard his breath quicken as he rolled up my sleeve and continued to examine my arm. His fingers moved over the curve of the elbow, and in the silence, his touch was as gentle as a kiss. His blue eyes rose to meet mine, and his breath became uneven as he pushed my sleeve even higher. No other man had touched me like this, skin to skin. After a moment Samuel broke our gaze to look at my arm and gasped. What he saw destroyed the mood.

"He did this?" The anger in his voice was palpable.

My upper arm was polka-dotted in bruises and blood-stained marks from my mother's nails digging into me. "Mother broke the skin, but yes, I believe the bruises are from him."

Samuel shook his head and put his hand over my bruises. "No man should ever harm a lady like this. Why did you ever accept his proposal?" He reached for a washcloth and began wiping away the blood and was careful not to let the water stain my skirt.

"I didn't know he was capable of this. He had a good reputation and political ambitions, which was the kind of man I thought I wanted. Then I witnessed him murder Katerina. That's why I'm here, and why he did this today. I told him what I knew, and he grabbed me. I knew he'd hurt me, so I jumped from the carriage." I held my breath and waited. I'd told him everything. If he was the man Agatha claimed, he'd believe me. If not, well, he and Mother could bond over that disbelief and work together to keep me here. I counted the seconds as he stared at me.

Samuel stopped nursing my arm and considered me. "That was brave."

I waited for him to say something—anything—else. I

counted to thirty in my head. Was he going to deny the truth like everyone else? I don't know why, because when it came down to it I hardly knew Samuel at all, but that was something I could not bear. I jumped to my feet and tried to push past him. "I'm sorry I said anything. Please, I'll just go now."

He caught me by the waist and held me firmly yet gently in place. "I believe you, Isabelle," he said in my ear. "I believe you and will do all I can to help you."

His arms were so strong around me and his body was so near, but while my pulse was racing, all I felt was relief. He believed me. *He believed me.* I fell against his shoulder.

"Thank you," I whispered.

"No," Samuel replied while he smoothed my hair. "Thank you for trusting me." We stood for a moment before he pulled away and said, "Now let me bandage that arm."

CHAPTER 26

Hoping to avoid another confrontation with Mrs. Lincoln, I spent the following day helping Cook cut apples for that evening's pie. The scents of cinnamon and roasting chicken filled the air as I peeled the apples. We sat at the center table as Cook pounded and rolled the dough, while I twirled an apple core between my fingers. The bandage made it so I couldn't cut for long periods, but Cook's good humor was the medicine I truly craved.

"I told that clerk he had to get up pretty early to fool me!" she chuckled to herself. I smiled at her story, but my mind lingered elsewhere.

Agatha was correct. I'd have to prove my sanity in order to obtain my freedom. And speech alone wouldn't do it.

Cook turned her attention to the pile of apples and chopped them all into perfectly formed crescents. She tossed a slice into the air and caught it in her mouth.

"Bet you can't do that!" she exclaimed, apple juice spurting from her mouth.

"I probably can't," I replied as I rested my chin on my hands.

Cook opened her mouth as if to say something and then shook her head. Instead she continued to pound the dough and sing "Greensleeves." The tune soothed my spirits, and soon I was tossing apples in the air as well.

The door slammed shut so loudly that we both jumped. The apple I'd just caught threatened to choke me. Samuel walked in with dirt covering his pants and an awful animal stench radiating off of him.

"No one should have to harness the carriage *and* unharness it in the span of an hour," he grumbled.

"What on earth did you do that for?" I asked as Cook tossed him an apple slice.

"Mrs. Lincoln told Mrs. Patterson that she wanted to go riding and then when everything was ready and waiting for her, she sent word down that she couldn't be bothered." Samuel took a bite and wiped his mouth on his sleeve.

"She's having a hard time, poor dear," Cook pouted.

I bit my lip and glanced out the window. Dr. Patterson had sedated her yesterday afternoon. I had no idea how she was feeling today. I felt my face burn. If I had confirmed Mrs. Lincoln's claims of friendship, would she still feel so destitute?

Cook tossed Samuel another apple slice and grinned when he missed.

"Is Mrs. Lincoln ill?" I asked. Perhaps she had come down with a cold, which would explain her absence.

Samuel shook his head. "Heartbroken. Her son refused her pleas to go home. I believe she is exhausted and unsure of herself."

I could fix this if I put my mind to it. "I believe I am partly to blame for her poor mood."

Samuel blinked in surprise. I had no doubt Dr. Patterson had told him of my involvement.

"Excuse me, but I should have a word with Dr. Patterson." I stood up and wiped the apple juice on my apron.

Samuel nodded. "Before you do that, I think you should know that Mrs. Lincoln had the carriage harnessed yesterday morning as well, but was confined to her room after a fainting spell. I understand she was to attend church." He gazed at me meaningfully.

"Oh," I whispered as the events finally made sense to me. She had planned on coming to my aid herself. She hadn't intentionally abandoned me after all. "Thank you for telling me."

Cook watched us as she pounded the dough harder. "If you'd told us your problems, Isabelle, we'd have done something for you or at least tried."

I looked at my feet and shrugged. "I didn't think anyone would believe me. If my own mother didn't, why would you?"

Cook shook her head as I mentioned Mother. "Sometimes what you believe to be true in your heart is more important than anything else. Regardless of anything else, you were in pain. She should see that."

I glanced at Samuel and nodded. "I know that now."

Samuel squeezed my hand and smiled. He took a great risk in being so open with a patient. Yet, I couldn't convince myself to let go. His warmth radiated in our grasp and gave me strength.

He placed his other hand on mine so he was cupping my hand and said, "From now on you tell us what you need. Gregory Gallagher will not harm you again. I promise."

I truly believed his words, yet it wasn't Gregory who scared me anymore. He could have kept me in that carriage, but I got away. Gregory wasn't stupid enough to get blood on his hands twice; he would hire people to do that for him. My mouth felt dry as I thought of the men Gregory had sent to spy on me. Gregory would move on with his life, find another woman with the proper connections, and move up the social ladder. Then I realized what that meant. Another family exposed to Gregory. Another woman taken in by his false charms.

"I cannot bear to see another life ruined by him."

Cook left her thumping and came to my side. "We will find a way to prevent that fate. Couldn't Lucy tell everyone of Mr. Gallagher's actions?"

I shook my head. "Who would believe it? They think him a hero. Besides, she isn't in town anymore. No, I must expose him another way."

Just then, the front door opened, and Dr. Patterson's booming voice echoed down the hall toward us. Samuel and I rushed to the kitchen entrance in time to see Dr. Patterson escorting a man in a brown suit out the front door.

"How dare you bother our patients with your questions? Don't you understand they need a reprieve from people like you in order to get well?" He gestured toward the open door. "I believe you were leaving."

The visitor bowed curtly before saying, "It's been an honor, sir. I will be staying in town overnight if you change your mind and allow me to visit with Mrs. Lincoln." He then went down the front steps, got on his horse, and rode away.

"The nerve of some people," Dr. Patterson thundered. "Demanding interviews without appointments."

I strode into the hallway determined not to let this opportunity pass me by.

"May I have a word with you, Dr. Patterson?"

If I surprised him, he did not show it, but locked the front door and said, "But of course, Miss Larkin."

"Privately?"

Dr. Patterson led me to his office, which was brightened by the afternoon sunlight. "I'm pleased to hear you speak, Isabelle. The silence was becoming . . . pronounced." He sat behind his desk, folded his hands together, and then looked up at me expectantly. "Now, why did you need to speak with me?" he asked.

"You should know that Mrs. Lincoln and I have shared a friendship. Since she arrived, I've spoken with her many times.

It was dishonest of me to let her son think otherwise. I'd like to remedy that, if I may." I rested my hands on the back of a chair.

Dr. Patterson rubbed his chin. "Am I correct in inferring that you lied to me as well?"

I had forgotten about that. Explaining would make little difference, so I said, "You are correct."

"Well, I'm glad that's cleared up." He pushed a folder away from him. "However, it would've made little difference. Mrs. Lincoln is not yet well enough to leave."

"But her son thinks less of her because of me."

"Perhaps, but I will clear that matter up when I next meet with Robert." He paused. "Is there anything else?"

I glanced at the chair I sat in during our therapy sessions and nodded. "I assume Mother has spoken to you?" I began.

Dr. Patterson pressed his hands together. "She and I spoke before she returned to Oak Park."

I nodded. "Then she, no doubt, told you what happened between me and Gregory Gallagher." I paused. This was the moment. Mother could have made up any sort of story to keep me here, and I needed to know what I had to work with.

"She merely said your engagement dissolved due to your hallucinations. She seemed greatly disturbed by it." He pressed his fingertips together.

"She believes the truth to be a hallucination, but she was not the one who found Katerina. I know the truth about the death and will not be swayed otherwise. Gregory now knows all and has promised to slander my name."

"You have a fierce will, Isabelle," Dr. Patterson said.

I nodded. "Is it true she's abandoned me here?"

"So it seems." Dr. Patterson was completely still, like a cat before it pounces.

"Well, the question then becomes, how do I obtain my release papers?" I prayed I'd gauged the doctor well and did not anger him with my question.

"Release from here?" he repeated. "To go where? Will your mother take you in? Will anyone in this town? You'd be eaten alive by the city." He paused and then added, "Even if you could prove the honesty of your tale, I couldn't in good faith release you knowing you'd have nowhere to go. Best for you to remain here, be a good daughter, and make peace with your mother."

Whether he meant to or not, Dr. Patterson had just given me what I needed to get out of Bellevue. Prove my story was true and have a place to go when I was released. Such tasks did not sound so impossible when knowing the reward.

Reconciling with Mother was a matter for another day.

CHAPTER 27

Moonlight cascaded through my window, leaving random shadows across my bed. I sat in the corner, leaning my head against the windowpane and listening to the wind, my copy of *Jane Eyre* dangling in my hand. Sleep eluded me. Every snapped twig or rustling bush made me jump and search for Gregory's men. It was impossible to believe he was done with me.

I glanced toward my door and saw the soft flames of candle-light whisper from across the hall. I crawled off my bed and tiptoed to my old friend's room.

Mary Lincoln was sitting on the floor in the center of the room, a tall candle next to her. Her long gray hair was not pulled back in a braid, but flowed freely. I still stiffened at the sight of her, but Samuel's words came over me like a balm. At least, she had planned on helping me.

I slipped across the threshold and into her sadness. "Mrs. Lincoln, it is time to sleep now."

Her head twitched, and she looked at me. Those dark, cold eyes bore into me, and for an instant, I was frozen. There were tears upon her cheeks, and her hair was wet as if she were sweating.

"What is the matter?" I knelt to the floor beside her and clasped her hands in mine.

Her eyes were wide. "He said you would come back to me. He promised that you had not forgotten your dear friend."

Her words made no sense. Who was she referring to?

"I beg your pardon?" I tried to get her to stand by pulling on her arm, but the old woman would not budge.

"Abraham. He told me you would not abandon me so cruelly." Her eyes shone in the soft light.

"Your husband? But he is dead." She winced as if I'd slapped her.

I feared she was going to resume crying, but when she turned to me once more, there was a smile upon her face and not a frown. "Some love transcends death, my dear. Such it is for Abraham and me."

We sat on the floor as the candle's flames danced about, turning coat racks and vases into mythical beasts from lands beyond our own.

When her breath had been normal for some time, I pulled away from her and said, "I came to put you back to bed, Mrs. Lincoln."

"Please call me Mary."

"It is time to get into bed, Mary," I repeated.

"Very well," she sighed.

With my assistance, she rose from the floor and shuffled to her bed. Watching her move made me see the ache in her bones.

I expected her to climb into bed, but instead she turned, gripped my hands, and demanded, "Why did you do it, Isabelle? You made me seem far crazier than I am."

The desperation in her voice rekindled my disappointment. Did she actually not know what her inaction had cost me? Perhaps she had intended on coming to my rescue, but she didn't even send someone in her place!

"I couldn't let Robert have that kind of knowledge of me.

No man will ever have the ability to threaten me again. And, I was so hurt that you didn't help me, I didn't know who to trust. You left me alone with Mr. Gallagher. *You* promised to protect *me* and let me down. I didn't know if I could trust your son."

Standing was too much for her, and she sat upon the edge of her bed. "Growing old is a cruel fate. No one had returned my requests so I had planned to come to town and collect you myself, but such a pain came over me, I could scarcely breathe."

"Samuel told me." I sighed. "I guess I should simply be grateful you intended to come, but that afternoon all I could see was the freedom I'd lost and I refused to give anyone more power over me."

Her eyes, which had been black with tears moments before, lightened with sympathy. "You saw him, then? I assumed when you came back from your trip early you were safe. That was our goal. This Mr. Gallagher did not harm you, did he?"

Did Gregory hurt me? That wasn't exactly accurate. I rubbed my bandaged arm. I was not permanently damaged, but my previous life was gone. As I rose to leave, she grasped my hands and refused to let go.

"What happened, Isabelle? What did I fail to prevent?" The clarity in her voice made me smile.

Tears were now upon my cheeks and I paced the room. "He knows that I know about Katerina. I got away, and now he swears to Mother he wants nothing to do with our family."

"She still fails to believe you?"

"Yes and refuses to allow me to leave here."

Mrs. Lincoln's face looked as if she'd found the body of her dead son all over again. "Oh my dear girl, I had no idea." With strength I did not expect from her, she pulled me back to her side and wrapped her arms around me.

My mind screamed with warnings of how she was not to be trusted. But, sitting beside her, allowing her to soothe me, love

204 / Sarah Barthel

was all I felt and all I wanted to know. I forced my anger to disappear and wrapped my arms around her in return.

"I am sorry I betrayed you," I whispered. "I will make this right."

"It is forgotten. We will find another way out of here, you and I," she said. "Abraham will show us the way."

I hoped she was right. Mrs. Lincoln placed a brush in my hand. "Would you mind?"

As I moved the brush rhythmically through her hair, we enjoyed the peace. My mind raced to find another road to safety, but there was no one to corroborate my story. Or was there? Gregory hadn't exactly confessed in the carriage, but had definitely sounded guilty.

"I must go into town," I said.

"To town? What for?"

Pulling her long gray hair back, I divided it into sections and braided it. "I must find the carriage driver who drove Gregory and me. He is the only one who can verify my story."

Mrs. Lincoln turned to face me.

"I can secure the carriage tomorrow, but I've little idea of how to find the man you are after. Do you know the driver's name?" I knew she was trying to help me, but her question pointed to the very thing I didn't know.

"I'll do my best to find out," I said, wishing I were as confident as I sounded.

Knowing how anxious Lucy was about me, I quickly penned a response explaining what had happened and not to worry, that she should enjoy her honeymoon and give Patrick my best. I blotted the ink and put the letter in my pocket. Since I'd be going to town today, I decided to mail it myself. This small bit of independence empowered me.

I'd just finished pinning up my hair when someone pounded upon my door. I searched for my robe to cover my nightdress, but they didn't wait for me to answer.

"Nurse Penny!" I exclaimed, jumping in surprise. She was still in her long white nightgown, and her hair had yet to be combed, for it frizzed around her face like a crown of hornets.

"Thank goodness you're up. Sit with Mrs. Lincoln for me. I must find one of the doctors to get medications for her but if I leave I fear she may harm herself."

I jumped to my feet. "I'll stay with her," I promised. She was running down the hall before I could say anything else.

The hallway was dark as I crossed it into Mrs. Lincoln's room. Her curtains were drawn closed, and she was still abed.

"Mrs. Lincoln?" I said, walking across the room and resting on the edge of her bed. "Mary, my friend, what is the matter?"

At my words, she turned from the wall and met my eyes. "Oh, Isabelle. It is like a tomahawk is beating upon my head. The spirit is inside my head again, ripping off my scalp and sticking pins into my eyes. Can you stop it?" Her voice was weak, and I could see how each word pained her.

I glanced around the room until I located her washbasin. I walked over to it and dipped a cloth in the cool water. Then I came back to her side and laid it upon her forehead.

"With such pain, it is best to lie still and rest. It will go away," I promised, hoping I didn't lie.

Mrs. Lincoln's chin quivered. "I fear the pain shall never go away."

I stroked her bare arm and hummed a waltz. The compress stayed put over her eyes and, after a few moments, her slight moans reduced to uneven breathing. Nurse Penny's footsteps rushed back down the hallway. She entered the room holding a bottle, followed closely by Samuel. He saw me and paused slightly before approaching Mrs. Lincoln.

"She is in great pain," I said, then regretted it, for it wasn't my place to speak.

"This will stop it," Nurse Penny said and unstoppered the bottle.

"Wait." Samuel pressed his hand against Mrs. Lincoln's forehead, felt her pulse, and brushed the hair off her face. Once he straightened, her breath slowed to normal. "Look at her."

"She's sleeping," I whispered.

Samuel nodded. "Perhaps all she needed was a cool cloth and darkness. Nurse Penny, please see the compress remains in place today and keep the room dark. Keep her hydrated and avoid giving her any red meat. I will check on her again this afternoon. Let us leave her alone, Isabelle." He gestured for me to leave with him.

I was flooded with the feeling of selfish disappointment as I realized what Samuel's orders meant. Mrs. Lincoln would not be taking me driving after all.

"Don't worry. She'll be all right," Samuel said, patting my back.

I shook my head. "We were to go in search of Gregory's driver today. I suspected he heard all we said to one another. Perhaps Gregory said more once I fell that would implicate him."

In the narrow hallway, Samuel's body was close to mine. Without a corset or any proper clothing I felt exposed, but I didn't back away.

"That could be dangerous," he said. I could feel the heat of his breath on my cheek. He needn't stand so close, but neither of us moved for more space.

"I have to see him. He is the one person who can prove my story to Dr. Patterson."

"I, too, would like to see you released. You don't belong here."

"Where do I belong then?" I held my breath waiting for his answer.

Despite myself, I shifted my feet. The floor creaking made both of us jump, and he dropped my hand. The moment was ruined.

"I have some free time this afternoon. I was going to catch up on paperwork, but perhaps I could take you for a ride instead? We could search out this driver," Samuel said, careful to keep a proper distance.

"Thank you," I said. "That would be appreciated."

"I'll come find you when it's time to leave."

I nodded.

He turned to leave, then looked back at me. "I hope you know I don't always agree with what Dr. Patterson chooses."

His words gave me pause. "You are a good friend, Samuel," I replied, for it felt the only proper thing to say.

His face betrayed the slightest disappointment. "Yes," he said. "A good friend."

Then he turned on his heel and left.

CHAPTER 28

While I waited for Samuel, I placated Dr. Patterson and tried to behave as if nothing had changed by joining that morning's sewing circle. Helping Mrs. Lincoln had delayed me, so I was the last to arrive. I stepped into the room and was greeted with a cold reception. Not a woman greeted me or even smiled as I entered. Instead, I felt as if I'd walked into a hungry wolves' den, but couldn't imagine why. My hopeful demeanor slipped, but I refused to lose it entirely and sat beside Marilla as I had all summer.

"Good morning." My words made the room even quieter. When no one replied, I added, "I missed breakfast. Was it tasty?"

Marilla adjusted her posture so she was facing me, but didn't look up. The bones in her cheeks looked more pronounced than normal. The pillowcase she worked on sat in her lap; her hands shook too much to hold it.

"Please don't pretend to be my friend," she whispered. Her eyes rose to meet mine, and she continued, "We all know your story. We know that you were only pretending to be one of us."

"We heard you quarreling with your mother," said Mrs. Allan.

"Yelling," Marilla pointed out. "You always could speak!"

I sat back in my chair and rubbed my forehead. It never occurred to me to think of how my actions would impact the other patients. From their perspective I must seem heartless. I pulled at the slip I was mending while I tried to decide how to defend my actions without telling them the whole story.

"Yes," I began. "I chose to keep my silence, and I ask you to understand that I had my reasons. But I never intended to hurt any of you."

None of them responded. Luckily I was spared when Samuel appeared.

"I finished early. The carriage is ready," he said.

"I'm coming," I replied as I stood up and placed my sewing back in the basket. The moment I left the room the conversation resumed. I would need to find a way to right their perception of me, but it would have to wait until later.

Samuel offered me his arm, and together we walked out the front door and to the wooden carriage that was waiting for us. As we approached it, he gave me his hand for assistance, and I took it just to feel my hand in his. It wasn't until I was standing in the buggy that I saw a small box on the seat.

"What's this?" I asked.

Samuel's face nearly matched his plum vest. "Oh, just something I saw and thought of you."

I opened the box and inhaled sharply as my stomach flipped. Nestled in the small box was a folded cream shawl with embroidered roses and lilies all over it. I immediately put it around my shoulders.

"Thank you," I said. "This is beautiful."

Samuel beamed. "I noticed yours was missing." I wondered when he'd slipped out to purchase it. Not knowing made it more special somehow.

He jumped into the seat beside me and clicked his tongue. The horses began to trot, pulling the buggy with them. I hugged the shawl around me and let my shoulder bounce against Samuel's.

"Which carriage company did Gregory rent from?" Samuel asked as we turned onto the main road.

Panic gripped my chest. "There's more than one?"

Samuel nodded. "There are the Simstock Brothers and Wayne's. Do you remember what the carriage looked like?"

How could I forget? "It was white with a red stripe around it and a velvet interior. I believe the horse was white, and the driver wore a top hat with a green ribbon."

Samuel nodded. "The Simstock Brothers have a carriage like that. Let's go there first."

The Simstock Brothers Carriage Company was little more than a barn and storefront at the end of a narrow side road. It smelled strongly of animals and manure, but had a clean look about the yard.

Samuel helped me out of the wagon and followed me into the storefront. The man behind the counter was well past forty with a round stomach and even rounder cheeks. He stood up as we entered.

"What can I do you for, sir?" he asked.

"We've come to speak with a driver of yours," Samuel said. I kept my arm through his and placed my other on the counter. The man may respond better to Samuel's inquiry, but I'd not be brushed aside.

"No trouble, I hope," the man said, raising an eyebrow.

"No, no. My sister here went driving with a friend and left her gloves behind."

The man shifted some papers on the desk. "I don't have any notes of forgotten items from the last week or so."

"They were a special gift," I explained, playing along with Samuel's story. "Surely it would be acceptable for me to speak with the driver. If nothing else he might remember where we drove so I could go back and look for them."

The man sighed and flipped through his record book. "When did you say you went out?"

"Sunday," I said. "It was in a red and white carriage."

"A Mr. Gallagher hired it," Samuel added.

I could've kicked Samuel. For all his education, he didn't really know much. Gregory would never leave a paper trail, not when one of his hired men could just as easily do the arranging.

"I'm sorry," the man said. "But the only carriage I let out Sunday was to a Mr. Pendleman."

Samuel looked crestfallen, but my heart raced. Could it be he'd given us the name of Gregory's spy? I leaned forward to get a good look at his book. Then, just to be sure, I pressed him further. "The driver I seek was a dark-skinned Negro who wore a green ribbon around his top hat." I smiled, hoping to win more information.

"Oh, that would be Alfred." He shrugged his shoulders and pointed to the barn. "He's with the horses."

"Do you mind if we speak with him? It would ease our minds to find those gloves," Samuel said.

The man laughed. "They must be special. Go see him if you like." He gestured toward the stables and went back to his work.

Samuel and I didn't waste time with pleasantries, but left the small room and headed straight for the barn. Dirt billowed around my skirt as I rushed through the yard.

"Don't be too friendly, Samuel. If Gregory's man hired him he could be a spy as well."

Samuel shuddered. "I'm glad I'm with you instead of Mrs. Lincoln."

"Mary Lincoln has more gumption than you credit her with." I stepped around a small puddle.

"Perhaps," Samuel mused. "It can be hard to view patients as more than their illness."

I placed my hand on the metal handle of the barn door. "And yet, it is doctors more than anyone who need to be able to see past those labels."

The door creaked as I pulled it open and we stepped into the dark barn. It smelled like manure. I held a glove to my face until I adjusted to the stench. There were horses' tack, brushes, and saddles adhered to one wall and horse stalls along the other, but no men. Then, from the far stall, someone coughed.

I proceeded to the back of the barn with Samuel following after me. My cream gown swept over hay and puddles of water. "Sir?" I said once I reached the horse stall. The driver was there, picking dirt out of a horse's hoof.

The driver turned around, and his jaw dropped. "That you, miss? You the one who jumped from my carriage?" His voice was raspy. The smell of cigar smoke clung to him.

I nodded. "That was I."

"I was worried you hurt yourself tumblin' like you did." He didn't mention that he'd rushed the carriage away from me and hadn't bothered to return.

"I'm fine as you can see," I assured him. Now that I was looking at him I realized what I was asking of the man. A Negro could be beaten for speaking against his employer.

Samuel cleared his throat. "I believe we have a favor to ask." He nudged me forward a bit.

Alfred's eyes were wide, and he put the grooming brush aside. I smiled shakily to steady myself and asked, "Do you remember that carriage ride?"

Alfred dropped his eyes so quickly that I knew he had heard everything. In that slight movement I felt how wrong this was. I couldn't be sure if anyone would believe this Negro over Gregory, or if he'd even get a chance to speak. I was sure he'd lose his job at the very least. I couldn't regain my life by stealing someone else's.

Alfred turned his hat in his hands. "I remember the argument. It isn't every day someone jumps from my carriage to avoid a man. That was brave."

I fought a smile.

"Do you remember the particulars of what they discussed?" Samuel pressed. "Anything could help us. I mean, this woman—"

"Stop, Samuel," I interrupted.

"But—"

"Look at him. We can't ask this of him. Think of what we are asking."

Alfred stood up. "Miss, I'm afraid I wouldn't be much help. It's all confusing. It wasn't until you started jostling with the handle of the coach that I started paying attention. And when you jumped, I just knew I shouldn't turn 'round to get you, but he didn't ask me to neither. I brought him back here and the whole time he kept sayin', 'An accident. It was an accident.' He was right upset. I felt plum sorry for the gentleman."

"An accident?" I repeated the phrase trying to make it fit my picture, but it was wrong.

Samuel clucked his tongue. "Paints a different picture. Is that really all he said?"

Alfred paused. "He tipped me well and left. I don't know what else to tell you, sir."

I took his hand. "Thank you, Alfred. You drove off when I needed solace from him and have spoken with honor now. I can't ask for more."

Samuel stood as if to contradict me, but I put my hand up, stopping him.

Alfred looked at Samuel. "There is one more thing I will say. I didn't know Mr. Gallagher, but the man who hired the coach for the day is a regular client. I don't recall the exact name, but I see him here at least twice a month arranging rentals."

That affirmed what I already suspected.

"Thank you, Alfred," I repeated. Then I turned and left the way we entered.

The bright sunshine caught me off guard and I stopped walking for my eyes to adjust. Samuel caught up to me and we quickly found our carriage. One of Simstock's men helped me to my seat. Samuel settled beside me and started the horses down the road.

"What now?" he asked. "We still have no proof. Why didn't you ask him to provide testimony to the sheriff?"

I crossed my arms. "He's a Negro. To help me he'd lose his job and possibly have to move. I can't ask that of him. Besides, you heard what he said, he didn't have much proof to offer." I relaxed and pulled the shawl around my shoulders. "There is still Mr. Pendleman. Do you have the ability to continue today?"

Samuel clenched his jaw. "We shall see this to the end. Dr. Patterson can spare me for a bit longer."

CHAPTER 29

Samuel let the horses amble down Batavia's streets for a short time. Once we found ourselves clip-clopping down Main Street, Samuel turned to me and asked, "Where shall we go?"

"Well, we could try Mr. Pendleman's address," I offered. When Samuel gave me a quizzical look I explained, "His address was in that clerk's record book. I doubt he'd make one up. Perhaps we'll find him there?"

"You are a clever woman, Isabelle." He gave me an unreadable look.

Not knowing how to reply to that, I told him the address and he guided the horses to turn left and onto a brick walkway.

Off the main thoroughfare and in a residential area, there were far fewer people. Tall trees spread their branches over the street creating a shade from the blazing summer sun. The few people who were sitting on their porches didn't bother with us. It dawned on me that Samuel and I were alone without even the chaperone of the public to guide us. The thought gave me goose bumps. I wondered if Samuel would think less of me for not insisting on a chaperone.

As if reading my thoughts Samuel cleared his throat. "If you'd like to delay our search until Mrs. Lincoln is well enough to join us, I would understand. I didn't foresee how improper this would be."

For a moment I nearly nodded, but forced myself to shake my head. "No, I want to be done with this and with Bellevue. I've wasted too much time already."

Samuel nodded. "You know," he whispered. "I never believed you to be insane. The first day you arrived, Dr. Patterson gave me your folder to read as he couldn't make heads or tails of what ailed you. All I saw was a scared woman, not some lunatic who had no other option than to be locked away from her family and friends. And then, when I met you and saw the anger and fear that lay just beneath the surface, I knew with even more clarity that you were special."

I tried to smile. "You gained my trust through your respect of my silence, and I needed someone to trust. I needed to know all men aren't monsters. And you, Samuel, are the kindest and most decent man I've ever known." My shawl fell off my shoulders and exposed my neck to the beams of sunlight that flickered between the tree branches.

The horses were clopping slower, for Samuel had all but dropped the reins while he gave me his complete attention. "Your trust is an honor I treasure," he said in a hushed voice. Then he blinked and took my hands in his.

My heart thudded in my ears from the closeness of his breath and the softness of his hands. He brushed a loose piece of hair off my cheek and tucked it behind my ear, letting his finger graze my cheek as he did so. The reins fell between us and the horses slowed to an easy pace. I leaned in toward his touch.

Samuel didn't wait a moment longer. He pressed his lips against mine and held my hand to his heart. His lips were soft and gentle and his chest firm. He held me close for an instant before pulling away with a sheepish smile on his face.

He rested his forehead against mine. "Sorry, but you have no idea how long I've wanted to kiss you."

I grinned and laced my fingers through his. "No, I didn't know, but I'm glad you did."

Samuel laughed and then glanced around as if remembering we were, in fact, in public. He bent down and retrieved the reins from atop his shoes and nodded. "Right, let's find this Mr. Pendleman and soon we will be done with Gregory Gallagher forever."

Mr. Pendleman's home was in the middle of a residential block and looked like every other house around it, with a wide porch, whitewashed siding, and dainty lace curtains peeking through the windows. Never would I imagine a scoundrel living here. Yet, that is where Samuel drew our horses in, locked them in place, and escorted me to the front door.

There was no reason to be afraid, yet my hand still shook as I rapped on the door. The knocks seemed to echo through the house. After a moment, someone in a swishing skirt rushed down the hallway and began unlocking nearly half a dozen locks on the other side of the door. When she was done, she opened the door a crack and peered out at us.

"What do you want?" she asked.

"We'd like to speak with Mr. Pendleman," I explained.

The woman, barely older than a girl, opened the door a bit wider as she picked up a toddler from the floor behind her. "He is away on business," she explained. "Can I give him your card?"

"Well, it is rather important that I speak with him today," I said.

"What is this regarding?" The woman bit at the corner of her mouth and glanced over her shoulder back into the room behind her. The baby shoved his fist in his mouth as a string of drool slid down his chin.

218 / *Sarah Barthel*

"Just some business we need clarification on," Samuel said, waving his hand as if it were nothing she'd understand. His manner was condescending, until I realized he was using the same games Dr. Patterson used to get what he wanted.

After nodding, I added, "I am willing to pay extra for the time. Do you know where he went?"

The woman, who had stood straighter at the mention of money, bounced her child, who was beginning to fuss. "Yes, he went to Joliet yesterday for the week to do some business with an associate."

Samuel nodded, but showed no emotion. "Thank you for your time, ma'am. I'll find him there."

The woman closed the door, leaving us on the doorstep alone.

CHAPTER 30

"What do you mean we can't go to Joliet?" I demanded. We'd been discussing this the whole drive back to Bellevue. Now that the building was in view it seemed imperative I make my point. "Katerina said that's where she knew Gregory from . . . it's too much to be a coincidence! I feel in my bones that we should follow him."

Samuel rubbed his eyes. "Isabelle, Joliet is no mere day trip. We are talking about spending at least a night away from Bellevue, which Dr. Patterson will not allow. And even if he did, there is no one to chaperone you. I cannot take you alone, and there isn't anyone else to be spared."

"But, Katerina mentioned she grew up in Joliet. Surely the work Mr. Pendleman is doing is for Gregory. Perhaps he's destroying evidence. Whatever the reason, I have to go. Now. Tomorrow at the latest."

Samuel rubbed his forehead. "I know you want to go," he admitted. "I just don't know how to make it happen. I don't want to ruin your reputation."

"Samuel, I've spent the last month as an inmate in a sanitarium. I think my reputation is pretty much ruined, especially if Gregory makes good on his threat and spreads the news of where I've been living. I have to discover why he killed Katerina, clear my name, and get out of here."

The horses pulled up to the brick building and stopped dutifully. They knew they were home and were ready for their feed sacks.

The moment I stepped out of the carriage Agatha burst out the front door.

"Dr. Deston, you are wanted straightaway." She had his doctor bag in her hands. "I've never seen Jesminda like this. Dr. Patterson had me give her a sedative, but she is still pulling on her hair and muttering over and over."

"Where is Dr. Patterson?" Samuel took his jacket off the back of the buggy's bench and put it on.

"He's with Mrs. Allan right now. Somehow she found some drink and has taken quite a spell. Mrs. Patterson is working with Marilla to get food in her. Her weight seems to have plummeted below the required level. It's been a strange day." Agatha held out his doctor bag to him. Then she noticed me. "Oh, Isabelle. Pardon me. There is a young woman come to visit you. She's waiting in the back parlor. I'm sure you'll find her." She rushed into the house after Samuel.

Who did I know who'd visit me here? I pulled Samuel's shawl around my shoulders and walked into the house. It was dark and still on the first floor. From upstairs I could hear footsteps and muffled conversation. I walked to the back parlor and opened the door.

Someone had lit the main lamp so she had not been left in the dark. Lucy paced back and forth in front of the fireplace while wringing her hands around a pink handkerchief. A flowered hat sat tilted upon her head. I rushed to her side and embraced my friend.

"Lucy," I whispered, pulling back. "But . . . how?"

Wringing a glove around her finger, Lucy stuttered. "I know. But. I-I had to come. You are in an asylum, Izzy."

I looked around me and shrugged. "Yes, I am. And you left home to marry Patrick. We've both had an eventful summer."

Lucy turned toward the fireplace. "We are not yet wed."

"What?" I grabbed her hand. "Lucy, why not?"

"Because, I came here." She spoke simply and met my gaze as if she were daring me to yell at her.

"But . . . the minister . . . you explained it all. I'm fine."

"Isabelle Larkin, look at yourself. You are living in a sanitarium, your former fiancé is a murderer, and your gown is covered in mud. You are *not* fine."

Despite myself I smiled. Lucy was the balm my torn heart needed. "I'm doing my best. What did Patrick say?"

"I didn't tell him." Lucy's ears reddened. "Don't look at me like that. The train was there, and I had to choose. I left a note with the ticket master. We'll be married when you are safe and by my side. Someone who loves me should give me away."

Brushing all my arguments to one side, I chose to accept Lucy's choice. It was done, and I was glad to have her near.

"Gregory visited last Sunday," I said, sitting on the chaise longue.

"What?" Lucy dropped beside me. "How did that happen? Who let him come?"

"Mother pulled me out for the morning. We went to church, and he took me for a carriage ride. I told him all I knew." I rubbed moisture into my eyes. "By now he's told everyone where I am and ruined me for proper society."

"Isabelle, no one will believe him."

"No, it's all right," I interrupted. "Oddly, I don't care anymore. There is more to life than those snooty society ladies. And Lucy, we both know they'll believe him. He's handsome and well admired. There's nothing they like more than spreading gossip."

Lucy slumped against the cushions. "I suppose I'm ruined as well."

"You followed your man west and returned unmarried. I think we're both in the same boat."

"Yes, I guess so." Lucy sighed. "But I'd rather this than do my family's bidding."

That was the first time I'd heard Lucy speak ill of her family, and it felt good. Our lives were just starting, and we were making decisions for ourselves.

"Enough of this." Lucy resumed proper posture. "How do we get you out of here?"

"I've already begun working on that. I believe the key may be in Joliet." I explained all that had happened that day. "I have to go. Soon."

"Let's go." Lucy stood up and reached for her traveling bag.

"Now?" I asked. "There are things to do first, papers to get signed and Samuel—"

Lucy stomped her foot. "Forget all of that. You said yourself we are both lost causes. Now, I believe there is a train leaving in an hour, the doctors and everyone are busy, so now is the time to go. I've been here for a while and have been listening. They aren't going to just let you go have a holiday with me, right?"

I smiled, caught up in Lucy's energy. "I've missed you, Lucy."

Within moments we were in my room packing any necessities and the few valuable jewels I had with me in case we needed funds.

"I have some money in my bags, but not much," I said, tossing the small purse into the carpet bag we were packing. "It should cover our train fare."

Lucy nodded as she pulled a tan gown from my wardrobe. "I just can't travel with you looking like that."

I laughed. She hadn't lost all her properness out West.

As she unlaced the back of my day dress she asked, "Can I ask one question?"

"You can ask anything."

"Why didn't you tell me back in Oak Park? It isn't as if I didn't see you before you left. Perhaps if you'd said something, I could have helped. Maybe we could have prevented this." She gestured around the room.

"He is dangerous. I didn't want to put you in harm's way and, well, I . . . I wasn't positive you'd believe me."

"Not believe you?" Lucy pulled the laces free. "You are my best friend. I'd have thought you had more faith in me."

"And even if you had, how could I expose you to such danger? It seemed like Gregory was already following me."

Lucy grasped my hands. "You are so stubborn, Isabelle Larkin. You don't have to face everything alone."

"Well, it is certainly easier with friends," I said, trying to show my gratitude.

"That it is." Lucy squeezed my hand. She threw the tan gown over my head and helped me button the bodice.

"That's about it." I locked my bag.

"Time to go," Lucy agreed. Her voice wavered. "Will the doors be locked?"

I shook my head. "Only at night. They are busy with the patients and dinner. If we are going to go, it needs to be now."

A wave of unexpected guilt hit me. Samuel. He'd know where we went the moment he saw we were gone. Did I owe him an explanation?

"Come on, Isabelle," Lucy insisted.

She opened my door and jumped back. Mrs. Lincoln stood in the hallway, glaring at us. "What on earth are you girls doing?"

Her hair was disheveled and her eyes were swollen. She clung to the wall for support, but her very presence demanded an answer.

Lucy was shocked into silence. I forgot to tell her about my neighbor. There wasn't time now to elaborate.

"Mrs. Lincoln, Mary, you have to go back to bed." I took her arm and started the short walk back to her room.

"If you don't tell me what you are doing, I will call the doctor." Her voice held all the vigor her body had lost.

"Very well, but it is of the utmost secret nature." Once she nodded her understanding, I spoke quietly. "We are going after Gregory."

"Oh!" she gasped. "So your day today was productive."

I nodded.

"Is Samuel going with you?"

"No, I am." Lucy stepped forward, finally finding her tongue.

"Oh, I see." Mrs. Lincoln sat back on her bed. "You leave me no choice, Isabelle."

"What?"

"Give me my jewelry box." She pointed at the box on her dresser.

Lucy brought it over to us on the bed. In her other hand she clasped both our bags in case we had to run quickly. Mrs. Lincoln opened the box and lifted out the insert. With a quick gesture she pulled out a stack of bills. She handed them to me.

"Robert doesn't know about this," she said. "I couldn't prevent him visiting or anything that followed, but I can give you the means to do what you have to do." She shook the money in her hand. "Take it. Please."

"We shouldn't," Lucy said at the same moment I took the money and said, "Thank you."

"Get going then. I'll do what I can to conceal your escape." She deflated with fatigue. We had worn her out.

I helped her lie down and covered her with a blanket. "If you see Samuel, explain for me?"

She nodded and waved us away.

With that Lucy and I ran down the stairs and out of the house.

CHAPTER 31

Two young women with little luggage was hardly something to gawk at, yet I continually felt as if someone should recognize me. Batavia was not a large town; someone could be on the train who was on the river walk and heard Gregory's shouts about my well-being. They could see Lucy and me and demand to have us sent back to Bellevue Place.

"Excuse me?" Lucy said to the ticket agent. "When is the next train to Joliet?"

The man looked up at us and then checked a large schedule on the wall beside him. "You'll have to change trains in Chicago. Train for Joliet doesn't leave Chicago until tomorrow morning."

"Is there a train to Chicago tonight?" I asked.

The man nodded. "In about twenty minutes." He paused and looked at us carefully. "You ladies have accommodations in Chicago?"

Lucy bristled at his question. "We can take care of ourselves. Thank you, sir." She handed over the money and we waited for the train to arrive.

There were few people around the station, but I clung to Lucy's arm. Any moment Mrs. Patterson would discover that we were gone and send someone out after us. It wasn't until we were seated by ourselves and the train lurched into motion that I actually relaxed. The car was full enough that we spoke little on the trip to Chicago. And we were careful to be in the middle of the group to disembark once we arrived in Chicago.

"Well, now what do we do? The train for Joliet doesn't leave for another twelve hours." Lucy looked around us.

"I don't know," I admitted. "I don't know if we dare spend money on a hotel room. We may need it later."

"Agreed." Lucy's voice was firm, but she looked overwhelmed in the crowded station.

An elderly man jostled past us.

"What did you do when you went to Patrick?"

An instant blush rose on Lucy's cheeks. "It isn't proper, but I slept in the station waiting room when I had to wait for a train. Well, slept might be an overstatement."

"I never would've guessed you had that in you." I gasped in surprise. "That sounds so scandalous."

Lucy snorted. "You'd think so, but sitting up all night in an empty room is hardly the Grecian romance."

"Well, let's find the waiting room and settle in for the night."

On our way through the station we found a sandwich vendor and bought dinner. Just as Lucy described, the waiting room was basically empty. A pair of older women had taken seats at the far corner from us.

"Do you think anyone will remember us?" I asked.

"And do what? Send a telegram to Batavia? I doubt we are very interesting to look at." Lucy unwrapped her sandwich and took a bite.

"True." I tried to get comfortable on the wooden bench. "I don't want anyone to jeopardize what we are doing. Samuel will know where we went the moment he notices we are gone. I

just don't know if he'll worry enough to divulge that information to Dr. Patterson."

Lucy raised an eyebrow. "I have to ask. Is there something
between you and Samuel?"

Despite myself, I felt my face flush. It was the one topic
I'd avoided when I'd explained what had happened. "There
shouldn't be, but the more I spend time with him, the more I
like him."

"Well, he clearly cares for you. Helping you clear your name
and everything. That is not a doctor's job." She wiped a piece of
ham off her cheek.

I refused to meet Lucy's eyes. "Perhaps he does care for me,
but that doesn't mean it's smart for me to allow him to pursue
his affections."

"If you have feelings for him, what's holding you back?"

I paused as I tried to find a way to explain my hesitation.
"He's studying to be a doctor. He has plans to build a house
and make a life for himself." Lucy shrugged her shoulders at
my explanation so I went on. "Forevermore I'm going to be
known as the inmate of an asylum—a lunatic. I can't put that
on him. It would ruin him."

Lucy bumped her shoulder against mine. "You love him. You
do—you're in love with him."

"That's impossible. He's a good friend. That's all it is. I can't
be in love with him." As I spoke, I remembered how my body
responded to his kiss, and my lips tingled.

"Say whatever you like, but I know you too well, Isabelle.
You'll see I'm right soon enough." She smiled. "The way you
talk about him. I never heard that warmness in your voice when
you spoke of Gregory."

His name put a dark cloud over us. "I never loved him, you
know. I told you I did, but I really loved the life he promised
me."

"I know. I always knew." Lucy patted my hand.

* * *

Lucy and I linked arms as we pushed through the crowds at the Joliet train platform. It was early in the morning and on the walkway in front of us men walked to work and buggies jostled as they carried gentlemen to their destinations. They all had someplace to go. We'd made it to Joliet, but neither of us had been here, nor had we much more to base our search on than Gregory's name.

"What now?" Lucy asked me.

"I don't know," I admitted. "I hadn't thought this far."

"We will figure it out," Lucy said as she adjusted her grip on her bag.

I let the crowd continue to move around us for a moment while I thought of how to proceed. Then I shook my head and said, "That blue carriage over there. Let's hire it to take us through town."

Lucy nodded. The driver was sitting on the front bench reading the paper.

"Pardon us, but could we hire you to take us to town?" Lucy asked.

The man jumped and looked down at us. "Of course, ma'am. That's why I am here."

He climbed down and assisted us in getting into the back of the buggy.

"Where to?" he asked.

"Can you just take us through town?" I asked.

Lucy raised an eyebrow at me. I explained, "I know Katerina grew up here. She said she knew Gregory as a child, but I never thought to press for more details. I was so sure she was mistaken."

Lucy nodded. Then she crossed her arms and exclaimed, "That stupid Gregory Gallagher. What a mess."

The driver cleared his voice. "Are you looking for Gregory Gallagher? If you like, I can take you to the Gallagher estate."

"What?" Lucy and I said at the same time.

Gregory had claimed to be from Kentucky. He insisted upon it and had a whole story to back him up. But this was too much a coincidence to ignore.

"Yes," I said, my voice shaking. "Please take us there."

For as long as I'd known Gregory, he'd claimed to be from a Kentucky horse-breeding family. His father and brothers had died during the war fighting for the South and his mother passed five years later during the influenza epidemic. Because his family was gone and he was so charming, few questioned his story further. Even I didn't know much else about his past. I never even thought to ask what happened to his estate or his horses. Could he really have invented everything? Even worse, was it possible no one saw though the lies?

The driver tugged on the horses and we turned down a long, curved drive. The brick house was easily four times as large as Bellevue and twice as tall, but showed signs of much needed repair. The paint on the porch was chipped and the flowers were overcome with weeds. My stomach lurched. Something was wrong here. No house this grand should be left unattended.

"Do the Gallaghers still live here?" I asked.

The driver shrugged. "I don't know much about that."

"Of course," Lucy said, soothing my prying question. "Thank you for the smooth ride." She passed some money to the man and motioned to be let out of the carriage.

Once we climbed from the carriage, we all stared up at the building. Tall, dark stone cast its shadow over us. The windows were cloudy with dust, and most of the curtains were closed.

"Shall I wait for you ladies?" the driver asked.

Lucy and I exchanged looks and then I replied, "No, thank you." He nodded his good-bye and moved on down the road.

"All right then." Lucy removed a hair from her face and adjusted her soft pink gloves. I could hear the slight trepidation in her voice as she asked, "Do you really think this is Gregory's estate?"

"I know it seems strange. But I think it must be. I mean,

Katerina says she knows him from here and now there is a Gallagher estate? He must have lied about his past. The question is why."

Lucy nodded. "Why would you change your entire family history?"

"There is nothing he wouldn't do to secure the future he desires." I winced at how alike I had been to Gregory. After all, I was the one who had been prepared to marry a man I didn't love—and clearly didn't know—for a certain lifestyle. I had been a fool.

Arm in arm we climbed the steps and paused on the porch landing. The front door was ajar.

"Do we ring?" Lucy asked.

I'd come too far to be deterred now. Whatever the danger, this was going to end. The story would be concluded, even if I was hurt in the process.

"No, we are going to go in."

I pushed the door open far enough to allow our gowns through and we walked into the circular entryway. Morning light poured through the white curtains, giving a misty light to the house. Upon the walls were portraits of elegant men and women with Gregory's blond hair and penetrating eyes. The pictures continued up a wide marble staircase. There was no doubt this was his family's house. The furniture was covered in white drapes and gave off a barren mood. Sunbeams came in through the cracks in the curtains and illuminated the dust floating in the air. I winced at how loud my footsteps sounded in the dead space.

We walked toward the staircase and gasped at the same time. There were handprints in the dust all the way up the stairs. I could feel Lucy tighten beside me.

"We are going to go up, Lucy," I whispered.

She nodded as her breath quickened. "All right."

"Try not to touch anything. If someone else comes, I don't want them to see we've been here."

Lucy tightened her grip on my arm and nodded again. Then we ascended the staircase. When we reached the top, a vibration, like a chair being moved across the floor, came from the farthest room to the right. My heart caught in my chest; someone was here. I wanted to flee, but I forced myself down the hall toward the sound. The hallway was dark and only became more so as my pulse pounded in my ears. Lucy inhaled sharply. I reached forward and pushed the door open.

CHAPTER 32

On one side of the fireplace, there were two oversized leather chairs. On the other side was a large oak desk and a man methodically sorting through stacks of papers. Two tall windows flooded the room with light. When the door butted against the wall, he startled and looked up.

"Miss Larkin?" He shoved the remaining papers into one large pile. He winced at his mistake. He shouldn't have known who I was.

"Mr. Pendleman," I guessed. I hoped I sounded more confident than I felt. "What brings you to the Gallagher estate?"

Lucy dropped her grip on my arm and took a slight step toward a side table where an assortment of letter openers lay. I was sure she'd be able to defend me if it came to that.

"What brings *you* here?" He frantically stuffed a stack of papers into his leather satchel.

"I came to find you." I spoke as simply as I could to avoid giving anything away.

He crossed to the front of the desk, mere feet from me, and held the briefcase in front of his chest. "Sanitarium or not, you are an interesting woman, Miss Larkin. I can see why Gregory was so intent to find you."

"Thank you," I said. "You are an interesting man as well. Interesting that you discovered me at Bellevue and hired a carriage last Sunday. Interesting the type of men you choose to do business with."

Mr. Pendleman startled. "You know I tracked you down, eh?"

I coughed to stifle my surprise. "It wasn't hard to uncover when I heard you and your associate outside my window."

His face reddened, and he turned into the light. He was young, hardly a handful of years older than I. Gregory usually only used the most experienced men. What had caused him to hire this young man instead?

"You have no idea what kind of man Gregory is," I whispered. "If you did, you wouldn't take his money."

"I think I have a better grasp than an escaped inmate does." Mr. Pendleman fingered his collar nervously. I wondered if he was one of those who believed mental illness was contagious.

Placing the satchel on the desk, he untied his necktie to free his throat. Lucy pinched my arm and glanced from the satchel to me. I nodded my understanding. I'd keep Mr. Pendleman busy as long as I could.

"If you'd done your job, you'd know I'm not a lunatic or even affected. Perhaps you have gotten a chance to read my file. I *chose* Bellevue over marriage to Gregory. Have a seat, Mr. Pendleman, and I shall tell you why."

I gestured to the chairs before the fire and to my surprise Mr. Pendleman came across the room, not giving mind to the satchel he'd left open on the desk. Lucy inched toward the desk slowly, but Mr. Pendleman didn't notice her as he sat in the tall leather chair. Taking advantage of this distraction, Lucy grasped the satchel and began looking through the papers. Hoping I kept my façade of confidence, I lowered myself into the chair across from Mr. Pendleman. I jumped as the house settled, but relaxed when no other sound came. I prayed Lucy would find something. I met Mr. Pendleman's gaze and set my shoulders as Mother always taught me. She said it exuded power.

The high-backed chair nearly engulfed Mr. Pendleman's small frame. His suit looked navy against the black leather, and the bushy mustache seemed unkempt. Something in his look felt off for this situation. After a few moments it occurred to me. There was no skepticism or distaste in his gaze. He looked hopeful. As if I may have the key to some question he needed answered.

As I explained the truth of Gregory and Katerina, Lucy pulled the papers out one at a time and examined each. "So you see that is why I entered Bellevue," I explained. "That is why Gregory had you seek me out, Mr. Pendleman, to silence me, not to save me." Once the words were said, I wondered if I'd given him too much of my story to be safe, but also knew the worst he'd do was take me back to Bellevue and commit me for insane ramblings.

Mr. Pendleman held up a hand to pause my story. "Lawrence, please. My name is Lawrence. I was hired to find his beloved fiancée. Had my service concluded there, I would never have believed a word you've said. However, given what I have found here today, I believe it is possible you might be speaking the truth." He adjusted his cuff links so he could avoid any eye contact.

Lucy's speed with the papers picked up until she pulled a faded and torn one out and read it. Her eyes widened. As she skimmed the words, her hand rose to cover her mouth. I jumped to my feet and went to her side.

Lawrence turned over the side of the chair to follow me. "Ah," he whispered. "I see your friend found it."

I took the letter from Lucy's hands and read the words for myself. In scrawled writing lay a letter to Gregory.

Dear Gregory,

This may not be for me to tell you and it certainly is not something you will want to hear, but I believe everyone deserves to know where they come from.

I love your mother like a sister. Therefore you know I'd never say something about her that was not true. Please do not hate me for what I'm about to tell you.

The year before you were born your mother went on an extended vacation to Paris, or so your father deemed it. In truth, she ran away to live with an impoverished artist with whom she fell in love. It didn't last. When she returned, no one made much fuss about it. Your father covered her tracks well.

It was when you were born eight months later that many neighbors raised their eyebrows. In truth, the only thing that saved her reputation was how fervently your father claimed you as his own, not only giving you his name, but declaring you the heir to the Gallagher estate on the day you were birthed.

And yet, when your mother died, the name she whispered was Pierre, not your father's. I don't know what drew her to Pierre, nor why she returned. I only know he existed, and your mother loved him.

Perhaps it is mean of me to tell you this, but I cannot go to my grave without knowing that you have heard the truth.

Many Blessings,
Catherine Smarkal

The letter's creases were worn, as if someone had opened it many times. The top corners were crinkled into rounded edges. It took me a moment to absorb what this letter implied. Gregory was a bastard, the product of an affair. I knew what men like Uncle Walter would say of him behind closed doors. If word of this leaked out, his career in politics would be over. The scandal would do him in.

Lucy took the paper from my hands and reread it for herself. "Who is Catherine Smarkal?" she asked.

I paced in front of the fireplace between Lawrence and Lucy. My mind flew through all my encounters with Katerina when I remembered why she had come to Oak Park in the first place. Her mother had told her to look up Gregory if she ever needed anything, but he wouldn't see her. In fact, the mere mention of her terrified him. I gasped.

"That's Katerina's mother," I exclaimed. "She must be. Gregory thought Katerina was coming to blackmail him. That was why she frightened him so deeply. He thought she knew all of this and would hold it against him to get what she wanted. That's why he killed her."

"You're sure?" Lucy asked. "I don't remember much about Katerina."

I thought for a moment. "I'm sure. It read S . . . M . . . something on her post box." I shivered at the thought. If I had walked away then and not followed the sound of the shouts, my life would be as I'd planned. I'd be married to Gregory. My stomach reeled at the thought.

Lucy gave a sudden scream of surprise and Lawrence jumped to his feet. Both stared at the doorway. I spun around to see what had startled them and I froze. Gregory's tall frame filled the doorway.

"So, you finally found out." He almost sounded relieved, as if something he long dreaded had finally happened. He crossed his arms over his chest, but didn't pass through the threshold.

"Yes, now I know," I said.

Behind my back, I folded the letter and motioned to Lucy to take it. Before she could react, Gregory held out his hand. "I'll take the letter back."

Lucy came to stand beside me. "It's over. We know what happened."

"Accident or not, Gregory. It's time to go to the police," Lawrence agreed.

Gregory ran a hand over his face and pinched the bridge of his nose. "I knew better than to hire you, Lawrence. Since school, you've always been so damn honest. But I also knew your reputation was yet unproved so I could accuse you of slander if things became too involved."

Lawrence jumped in surprise. "You told me you loved her, that you missed her and needed to know where she'd run off to. Was all that a lie?" His eyes darted from Gregory to me in confusion.

Gregory slumped against the doorframe as his voice broke. "No. That's the saddest part. I really do love her. Isabelle, you knew I didn't love you when I first proposed, but your absence has made me see how much I truly care for you. I can't imagine what you must think of me." He pulled his eyes away from mine and blinked. "I must have that letter."

Lawrence jumped in front of me. "Just turn yourself in. Tell the truth about what you did and clear the name of the woman you love."

In a swift, almost casual movement, Gregory shoved Lawrence against the fireplace. Lawrence's head smacked the brick mantle with a wet sound and he slumped to the floor.

Gregory looked down at his schoolmate for a moment before returning his attention to Lucy and me. "Just give me the letter, and I'll leave." His mustache twitched as he spoke. It was a movement I'd never seen. That alone put me more on guard than I was already.

"Gregory, this is foolish. How much damage do you think you can do before you are caught?" I asked. Lucy grasped the letter from my hand and slid it into her pocket.

Gregory glared at me. "Please, Isabelle. All I want is the letter."

Lucy snorted. "No, first you want the letter. Then you'll want us to stay silent. I know how you obtained Katerina's silence. I'd like not to meet her fate."

It was my turn to tense up. Lucy didn't know Gregory the way I did. Directness only aggravated him.

"I've always respected you, Lucy. Don't force my hand." Gregory's hands trembled at his sides.

Lucy looked pointedly at Lawrence on the floor. "Did you respect him?"

Her hand slid into her pocket. She pulled out a letter opener. I blinked, surprised she'd actually taken one from the table. I wasn't sure she even knew what to do with such a weapon.

"Lucy," I whispered, trying to warn her.

"No, this is getting out of hand. He is getting out of hand." She raised the letter opener and glared at Gregory. "For someone who says he is in love with you, he has an awfully violent way of showing it."

Smack! Gregory's hand slapped Lucy's cheek. The force was such that she fell to one side, the letter opener flung from her hand across the room, far away from us. She landed on the floor with a thud. She turned and looked up at us, and a trickle of blood began to slide out of her nose. She scooted away from Gregory, nursing her face and shaking her head. I was on my own.

Lucy was right, this was getting out of control. I looked around for something that might qualify as a weapon. The table of letter openers was too far away for me to get to without Gregory stopping me. The only other things nearby were a few small vases on a table.

Gregory set his gaze to me and sighed. "I'm not a monster."

"Yes, you are." I stepped back from him.

"Isabelle." His voice was stung, like a boy's.

"You killed Katerina! You murdered her. And for what? A secret?"

Gregory's face turned crimson. "How dare you speak so!

You have no idea what my life has been like. The sneers that followed me whenever Father was not by my side. The pity from other children. And then, when Father died, to get that horrible revelation from that woman. No, you are not strong enough to live with the consequences of my life. Now, give me that letter."

"No, it's too late for that," I said.

I tried to move toward the desk, but Gregory darted and blocked my movements. He was too smart to let me get my hands on anything useful. I was going to have to think of something else.

"It's never too late, Isabelle," Gregory said.

Lucy cleared her voice and stood up shakily. Her hand still covered her nose with a handkerchief. "It's over. Can't you see that, Gregory? Too many people know. It's time to turn yourself in to the authorities."

Gregory's eyes bulged, and his breath quickened. "Not yet. It has not come to that. It hasn't. It was an accident. I never meant to hurt her, only scare her. I'm no criminal." Gregory balled his hands into fists. "Can you see that, Isabelle? Surely if you ever cared for me you'd know I'm no criminal. I'd never mean to harm anyone. Didn't you care for me, even a little?"

It was strange. Here we were demanding incarceration and all he wanted to know was if I cared for him. I glanced at Lucy. She motioned with her eyes to the tall, heavy velvet curtains that were mere feet behind her. They were tied back with large rope ties. I hoped I understood her plan.

I turned back to Gregory and stepped toward him. "You killed that innocent girl just to cover up your secret, and all you want to discuss is the honesty of my affection? Gregory, you are a murderer!"

His torso constricted, and he retreated to the wall as if hit. "No, perhaps my actions were wrong, but hers were worse. She tried to blackmail me. I'd have been ruined; we'd have been ruined."

"No." My voice was firm. "Do not lump me in with your villainy. There is no 'we' anymore."

Gregory hunched over. "But you said you saw everything. You must have seen that I didn't intend what happened. You must know I'm not a monster!" He reached out and grasped my wrist. It was the same one he had hurt before, and the old bruises burned under his pressure. "Please, I did not plan any of it."

I could scarcely hear Lucy move behind me, but I knew she was doing something. All I had to do was keep Gregory's attention solely upon me. "Planned or not, her life is over because of you." He tenderly brushed one finger down my cheek. I shuddered at his touch, but could not let myself flee.

"I really do love you, Isabelle." He pulled me against him and kissed me. It was all I could do not to shove him away. Lucy had a plan and I trusted her strength. "We could still be happy."

The light changed slightly in the room and I knew Lucy had at least one set of the ropes. Gregory continued to look down at me, pleading with his eyes. I had to play along.

"Could we be happy? After all that's happened?" I batted my eyes like I had when we first started dating. From the corner of my eye, I searched for something to use against him. Just to the side of us was a small table with a glass lamp.

"Of course." Gregory's eyes lit with hope. "Put this all in the past and start over. Our wedding is a mere month away. Do you think you could?"

I hesitated and edged toward the table. "Could what?"

Gregory seemed to think that I was moving closer to him, and he rested a hand on my waist.

"Could you forget all that's happened?" Gregory pulled a loose hair from my cheek and tucked it behind my ear.

I stepped to the side again. "Forget? That would be asking a lot."

Gregory nodded. "I realize that. If it helps, I didn't mean for it to happen."

Again I adjusted myself so the lamp was mere inches behind me. "Perhaps in time I could learn to forget it. We could start over even stronger than before . . . without lies."

Gregory propped my chin up with his finger. "Think of all we could be."

"We could be spectacular." I pulled him toward me. Pressing my lips to his, I grabbed the lamp and smashed it against his head with all my strength. Shards of glass flew past my cheeks.

Immediately, Gregory fell to the floor in a pile of broken glass and cuts. Moaning, he shook his head and tried to sit up, but couldn't and fell back down. It didn't seem as if he remembered I was in the room with him. He wasn't unconscious as I'd hoped, but he was truly stunned. That was good enough.

Lucy was at my side in a moment, making quick work of tying the ropes into knots around Gregory's arms and legs. All I had to do was hold him still while she did all the work.

"Where did you learn to do that?" I asked.

Lucy smiled. "Patrick taught me."

Gregory growled as he came to and tried to move his arms. His eyes flashed to me, and I jumped away from him. Gregory kicked and rolled, trying to get to his feet. His effort was in vain. All he managed was to put his body in an even more ludicrous position with his neck against the wall and his hands between his knees.

"Don't do this, Isabelle." He shuffled so that he lay on the ground, his head tilted in my direction. "Your reputation is already precarious because of where you've been living. If my past comes out, you'll be ruined. Who will want to marry a deranged girl who spent time in an asylum and is connected to a bastard? Be reasonable. Save yourself and me."

My hands clenched into fists as I turned back to Gregory. "This is how I save myself. I don't care what others say about me anymore. I'd rather have half the state think exactly what you said than allow you one more moment of freedom. You said you loved me. Prove it. Turn yourself in."

Gregory looked dumbfounded. "You've changed," he whispered.

"I'll take that as a compliment."

"And she isn't alone. She has me." Lucy linked her arm through mine and glared down at Gregory.

Just then Lawrence groaned. Without thinking Lucy and I both rushed to his side and tried to help him sit up. There was a large lump on his head, but beyond that, no visible injuries.

"What's this?" Lawrence rubbed his eyes. Then he saw Gregory a few yards away from him. "This is highly irregular."

"For once I agree," Gregory growled.

Lawrence sat up and put his spectacles back on. "What happened?"

CHAPTER 33

The next day, Lucy and I sat on my bed at Bellevue Place, the late edition of the paper sprawled out between us. Dr. Patterson had given her a compress to reduce the swelling in her cheek, but she wasn't using it. Wisely, no one tried to send Lucy to a hotel. Instead, Samuel made up another bed in my room for her.

"I can't believe it!" Lucy smacked the paper and shook her head. "You let him take all the credit?"

I smiled. "I didn't stop him, if that's what you mean."

Lawrence had turned Gregory in to the sheriff and stayed with them while they questioned Gregory. I was glad to be excused and done with the whole affair. What I had not anticipated were the local reporters picking up the story. Even more shocking was when the Chicago papers ran the story the following morning. Samuel had sneaked the front pages in for Lucy and me to examine. Of course, Lawrence's version had me on the floor unconscious and himself fighting Gregory and saving the day. The important thing was that everyone finally knew of Gregory's crimes; I didn't care who got the credit for exposing him.

"Let Lawrence have the notoriety," I said.

"You really don't care?" Lucy leaned on her elbow and raised an eyebrow.

I smiled. "I have all I want. Besides, it never hurts to have a private investigator in your debt."

Lucy laughed.

A hesitant knock made us both turn toward the door. Samuel stood in the doorway, his bag under one arm.

"I came up to check on Mrs. Lincoln and thought I'd make sure Lucy was applying that compress to her face." He looked to my vanity where the compress had been discarded long ago.

"It smells," Lucy said.

"If you go to Dr. Patterson's office he will make you a new application. Tell him the problem and ask him to add lavender to soften the stench."

Samuel stepped inside the room so Lucy could pass. After a sly smile at me, Lucy grabbed the old towel and left us alone.

Silence filled my room as neither of us spoke for a moment. Then, as if the conversation had never paused, he stated, "I would've found a way to take you to Joliet."

"Oh." Did he think I was disappointed in him? "I know you would have done your best, but I found my own way there. It was easier with fewer people involved. And now, well, Dr. Patterson has no reason to fire you for getting involved in my problems." I got up from the bed and put the papers on the side table.

"But your arm is bandaged again. He could have really hurt you." Samuel took my wrist gently and checked Dr. Patterson's wrapping.

When he finished I pulled my hand away. "I'm stronger than I look."

"You are full of surprises, Isabelle." Samuel looked down at me and smiled.

"How is Mrs. Lincoln?"

"She is still under sedation. I can't explain much more." Samuel shifted uneasily.

I nodded my understanding. "Her ailments are her business. I just wanted to talk to her."

"Once the sedation wears off I'll be sure to let you know."

"Thank you." I smiled at him, and the next moment he had my hand in his and kissed my fingers before dashing out of my room.

Once Samuel was gone, I sneaked across the hall to see how ill she was myself. To my surprise she was sitting at her desk with a pile of correspondence in front of her. Her pen scratched against the paper hurriedly. I paused to watch her. Her hair was pulled back in a loose braid and her back was straight as she worked. She was still in her nightgown, but given the sedation, that wasn't surprising.

"Mary?" I stepped into her room and shut the door behind me.

She turned from the little table and a huge smile spread across her face. "Isabelle, my dear. I hoped you'd visit. They've been keeping the world away from me." I went to her side and put my arms around her. She grasped my face and pressed her forehead to mine. "Your ordeal is over. You saved yourself. How proud you must be."

I grinned and pulled away from her embrace. I *was* proud of myself. "Yes, it seems to be over. How are you?"

She rubbed the side of her head. "Sometimes I feel almost normal and then the tomahawk begins to beat against me once again and I can barely breathe for the pain."

I assumed she was referring to her chronic headaches and simply nodded in sympathy.

"I received a letter from Myra Bradwell," she continued. "I had written her in regard to your situation, but now that it is resolved I may see if she can help better *my* situation." She set her pen down. "I do not want to die in this place."

"No one does," I agreed.

"Oh!" She clutched her head and sighed. "That blasted pounding."

I put my arm around her and helped guide her back to bed. There was a washcloth in a basin of water and I put the cool cloth over her eyes.

"Thank you, Isabelle," Mrs. Lincoln said.

The door opened and Agatha sashayed inside. "Oh no. Pain back again?"

"Pounding," Mrs. Lincoln said.

"I didn't think sitting up would do you any good, but what do I know." Agatha glared at the letter-strewn desk. "Well, I came up to give you this." She held out a letter.

Mrs. Lincoln removed the washcloth, sat up a bit and took the paper from Agatha. After she scanned the contents a true smile formed on her face.

"Oh my," she whispered. "My sister has offered me her spare room, provided Robert will allow it."

"That is wonderful news," Agatha exclaimed.

"Surely Robert will consent," I agreed, hugging my friend.

Mrs. Lincoln nodded absentmindedly. "Yes, I must reply straightaway." She tried to sit up and then lay back down. "But perhaps it can wait until later. The mail won't go out until to-morrow."

I glanced at Agatha, who nodded for me to leave them alone. "I'll take over, dear. Go see your family."

"Family?" I asked, confused.

"Didn't Mrs. Patterson tell you? Your aunt is coming to see you shortly."

Mrs. Lincoln snapped her fingers at me and I gave her my attention. In short breaths she said, "No matter what. They are family. Don't turn away family."

I nodded and left her room before she could impose more restrictions upon me.

Just as Agatha said, I was called down to visit with Aunt Clara about an hour later. Lucy's compress filled my room with a medicinal lavender smell that made both of us rather sleepy. She curled up on my bed and nodded her good-byes.

"You won't come with me?" I asked.

She shook her head. "Aunt Clara won't harm you. But she could drag me home to Mother. I'll not invite trouble. Patrick is waiting for me and once I am better, I'll go back to him."

I hadn't changed my dress or put any of the extra touches to my appearance I normally did for my aunt's behalf, but I decided it didn't matter. If she had read the papers, she wouldn't expect me to look perfect today.

I reached the bottom of the stairs and found her waiting outside the parlor doors. Before I could ask any questions she held up her hand.

"You and I will have much to discuss later. For now, someone else needs to speak with you."

I glanced from her to the closed doors and my stomach plummeted. "Please, no." I didn't have the energy to fight anymore.

"Now, give her a chance, Isabelle. You may not be ready to forgive her, but she's your mother." Then she opened the doors and nudged me forward into the small room.

My back stiffened as I saw Mother standing by the window. She wore the light green day gown I once called my favorite. The stern expression that had hardened her face for the last three months was gone, replaced with puffy eyes and pale cheeks.

"Isabelle." Her voice cracked. "I'm so sorry. I should've believed you. I see that now."

Those words that I'd longed for did not summon the relief I craved. Instead, they repelled me. Of course she wanted forgiveness now that everything was proven and those who mattered believed me. What she never understood was that it was her confidence in *me* that really mattered.

"Why did you come?" My mouth was dry, and I worked hard to maintain my calm demeanor.

Mother blinked. "You are my daughter."

"That didn't matter when you left me here." I leaned against Mrs. Patterson's rocking chair for support.

Blanching at my words, Mother sighed. "I was angry. I thought you were behaving that way to anger me."

"Anger you?" I nearly squeaked with shock. "You thought all of this was to solve some kind of vendetta? Are you insane?" I took another step backward.

"I said I was sorry. We were all taken in by that man's charms, and I couldn't see past them." Her hands shook.

"I'm glad you see all that now." I blinked slowly. Then I thought of Mrs. Allan and her grief when her daughter chose to exclude her from her wedding. Did I want to be that cold and unfeeling?

I turned my eyes to Mother once more and tried this time to truly see her and not be colored by my anger. The skirt of her gown was wrinkled and marked with dust. It wasn't made for traveling. She must've read Lawrence's interview and come straight here without collecting herself first. I glanced about the room and found her small traveling bag in the corner to support my conclusion. Her face showed little sign of deceit or contempt; rather, she appeared remorseful and defeated.

"Mother, I don't know if I will ever forgive you for not believing me, but I do not want our relationship to die because of it. I cannot offer you more than that." I gripped the back of the rocking chair until my knuckles were white.

"It is more than I expected." Mother nodded, but did not make any movement to hug or even touch me. I suspected she knew that would be too much.

"Dr. Patterson will discharge me to Aunt Clara's care, but I would rather your signature on the paper." I swallowed. Mother rarely admitted she was wrong, and a large part of me didn't really believe she'd put it on paper.

"I already have spoken with the doctor. He is drawing up the paperwork now." Her words made me dizzy with relief. "You are free to leave when you wish, and as soon as Lucy's swelling subsides, we'll return to Oak Park."

"Oak Park?" I repeated like a dullard. "I'm not sure I wish to return there, and I know Lucy doesn't."

At that, Mother's face hardened. "Oh, I know all about Lucy. I promised her mother that were I to find her, I'd bring her home. Her parents are worried beyond all belief. I'll not let them go through what I went through."

I closed my eyes and laughed. "When will you learn that you cannot control everyone? Lucy loves Patrick and is going to marry him no matter what. And I . . ." I paused, unsure how to continue. Samuel and I had shared only one kiss, but I knew I wanted to keep him in my life. "I have my own reasons for staying in Batavia."

Mother's eyes grew round, but she nodded. "All right. Perhaps allowing Lucy to continue with her choices will convince you that I've changed my views."

Despite myself, I smiled. "Perhaps it will. Thank you, Mother."

With deliberate steps, I walked across the room and kissed her cheek. When I pulled back, her eyes were glassy. Instead of speaking, or allowing herself to cry, she took my hand and squeezed it. All was not mended, but there was hope that it might be someday.

Aunt Clara must've been listening at the doors, for the next moment she flung them open and gushed, "Thank goodness for small miracles!"

CHAPTER 34

At that moment the front door burst open.

"LUCY!" a man's voice exclaimed. "Lucy D'Havland?"

It was Patrick!

I rushed to him, blocking his way to the stairs. "Patrick, she's here. It's all right."

If I hadn't known him so well, I don't think I would've recognized him. In a three-piece suit and a bowler hat, he looked much older than before. He was thriving, and it made my heart swell with pride for him and Lucy.

He rubbed his face and glanced about the entryway. "She's here? Thank God. I've read the papers. What an ordeal! Is Lucy well?"

I led him into the sitting room, where Mother gave up her seat for him. "Her cheek is swollen, as is her nose. She'll be fine."

"Thank goodness." Patrick sat down and put his face in his hands.

Mother, clearly displeased with Patrick's arrival, sulked in front of the window. However, I couldn't worry about her misconceptions.

"Dr. Patterson has given her a compress to help reduce the swelling. She's sleeping right now, or she was before you started yelling." I poured a cup of water from the side table and handed it to him.

"When she left before our wedding, I was sure she'd run home. I was sure she'd gone to marry another."

Mother's feet pounded upon the floor as she grabbed Patrick's arm. "You're not married?" she exclaimed. "That girl gave up everything, and you didn't marry her?"

"Stop, Mother," I insisted.

Patrick pulled his arm back. "I tried, but she left. The minister is only in town every two or three weeks, and I wanted to do it right, in a church. She deserves at least that."

"They had a minister and the church reserved, but Lucy chose to come here instead and help me," I explained. "She risked everything for me. It isn't Patrick's fault."

Mother looked down at Patrick and tilted her head, considering. "He really loves her?" she asked.

I nodded.

"And her him?"

"More than anything," Patrick said.

"Then I shall call upon the church and make the arrangements," Mother said briskly. "Isabelle, do you think Lucy will be well enough by week's end?" She stood and put her gloves on.

I couldn't believe my ears, but said, "To be wed? I believe she'd be ready today."

Patrick rose. "Mrs. Larkin, I don't know what to say. Are you certain?"

Mother straightened her shoulders. "Recently I have learned that sometimes daughters know what's best for themselves. Perhaps assisting you will heal some of the pain I've caused Isabelle. Besides, you must marry, and sooner rather than later."

Emotions battled for attention within me. I still wasn't ready to forgive Mother, but was grateful that she saw a way to help Lucy and Patrick.

The floor creaked behind us. "I heard shouting," Samuel explained as he slipped into the room.

"Samuel, this is Patrick, and I'm sure you remember Mother."

"Pleased to meet you, Patrick. Lucy speaks often of you." Samuel reached out and shook Patrick's hand.

Stepping back, Samuel stood beside me and rested a hand on my back. He whispered in my ear, "I've missed you." His breath was warm, and I smiled.

"Isabelle, why don't you take Patrick to see Lucy. She's awake, I believe."

Mother cleared her throat. "We have not yet finished our conversation, daughter."

I hesitated, but Patrick was already in the hallway waiting for me.

"It will do Lucy good to see Patrick, and I owe her that," I explained.

"Very well," she said reluctantly. "But have him wait for her on the veranda at least. It's unseemly for a man to visit his lady's bedroom."

Patrick grinned. "Nothing I do shall ever tarnish Lucy's reputation. Isabelle, I'll wait for you and Lucy in the back gardens."

Tilting her head appraisingly, Mother tapped her lips. "Lucy may have chosen better than Mrs. D'Havland ever imagined. We'll speak more later, Isabelle."

Before she could take back her words, I slipped out of the room and rushed upstairs to tell Lucy all the good news.

True to form, Lucy insisted on being presentable before she saw Patrick. She was awake when I found her, but her hair, normally in perfect ringlets, had hardly been brushed through since we'd returned.

"Izzy, he can't see me like this. I'm horrid!" She plopped herself on my vanity stool.

I laughed. "Oh, Lucy. You could have the plague, and Patrick would think you the most beautiful woman. He loves you."

Lucy unstoppered a vial of rose-scented perfume. "Please, Izzy, help me."

"As if you even have to ask," I assured her.

I dampened a washcloth and began to clean her cheek.

"While you were gone, I got to thinking, Izzy," Lucy began as I untied her bandage to work on her hair. "Without a fiancé, there is little holding you here. I know you and Samuel are close, but just in case you aren't ready for another man in your life, I wanted to offer you a home. There are so many opportunities out West. The towns are just forming and much work is needed. I doubt anyone would blink at your time here, and your skills with organization and politics would be of great use."

I pulled the brush through her hair. "I think I'm done with politics. It was Papa's dream, not mine . . . not really. I just want to be useful at something."

Lucy nodded. "You could be useful out West. And if you moved, I wouldn't have to miss you."

In the silence, I brushed the snarls from her curls and piled her hair back off her face. Moving didn't sound as awful as it once had. Actually, the idea of it felt freeing, to be in a place where no one knew me, or my history. I smiled at Lucy in the mirror.

"I think that would make me happy," I admitted.

Lucy beamed. "I can't wait to tell Patrick!"

I looked her over once more before sending her off to find her beloved. Once she was gone I sat down and tried to figure out how to explain my decision to Samuel.

CHAPTER 35

The next day Mrs. Lincoln was taking an afternoon carriage ride when I found her son Robert waiting for her in her room. He sat at her desk thumbing through her letters. I left Lucy to pack my gowns and walked across the room.

The clacking of my shoes upon the floor alerted him to my presence, and he turned toward the door. "Isabelle, what can I do for you?"

"Robert." I walked into the room and shut the door behind me. His eyes widened at the impropriety, but I didn't care. "Your mother is suffering here. She needs to be released, and I believe she has found a compromise which will be amenable to you both."

Robert glanced from me to the door again before asking, "When did you start speaking?"

I thought Dr. Patterson had promised to explain that fib. "I always could. The day we first met, I was angry with your mother and didn't want to cooperate. I know it caused some further conflict between the two of you and for that I am sorry."

The room was still as Robert considered my words. Lucy

dropped something across the hall. I shifted from foot to foot and waited. Finally, Robert stood from his desk, crossed the room, and opened the door.

"Thank you for clarifying that misunderstanding. However, my relationship with my mother is none of your affair. I'd thank you to please leave." His voice left little room for argument.

Defeated, I walked back into the hallway. Then I spun back to face him. "Just let me say this—no matter what has happened between the two of you, she is your mother, and that is more important than anything. Trust that I know it is hard to forgive, but your mother is heartbroken and desires only to be loved."

Robert squinted and his grip on the doorframe tightened. "You are too bold. Now, leave me."

I nodded and swallowed the rest of all I wanted to say on behalf of Mrs. Lincoln.

"Thank you for listening, Mr. Lincoln." With that, I retreated to my room.

When Mother is determined, nothing stands in her way. In just three days she hired the church and arranged a ceremony at which Queen Victoria herself would marvel. Perhaps the only thing missing was an overdesigned wedding gown. Personally, I thought the white dress Lucy chose to wear was beautiful because of its simplicity. I had pulled her hair up and pinned small roses in between her curls. Yet, nothing could compare with the glorious smile on her face as she held Patrick's hands and promised to love him forever.

After the ceremony, our small group gathered on the front lawn of the church as Patrick and Lucy climbed into their carriage. I ran over and grasped Lucy's hand.

"You are the bride of my dreams."

Lucy reached down from her seat and kissed my cheek. "We'll see you soon?" she asked, her eyes searching mine.

"Once things are settled with Mrs. Lincoln and Mother, I'll come."

After blowing everyone a kiss, Lucy beamed at Patrick and the carriage lurched into motion.

Once they passed the church gate, most of the crowd dispersed, but I stayed until they turned a corner and I could no longer see them. After a moment, Samuel sauntered up beside me.

"She's the happiest I've seen her," I said.

Samuel gazed off to where they'd disappeared. "They make a handsome pair." He paused. "Are you still thinking of moving out West?"

"I'll have to live somewhere, and returning to Oak Park doesn't feel right. The stigma of Bellevue will always shadow me there. And Lucy says there are a lot of opportunities for women out West."

Samuel turned to face me. "You know, Patrick mentioned that there aren't many licensed doctors in his area. A man with my training could make a good life for himself." He smiled.

His words were everything I wished to hear, but I couldn't let him give up his blue house or any of his other dreams. Not for me. I began to step away, but he grasped my wrist tightly and gently kissed my lips.

"Isabelle," he whispered into my ear. "You know how I feel about you. If you care for me even a fraction of that amount, I know we'd be happy."

"But your plans . . . your house."

Samuel laughed. "I want you. The rest is simply geography."

A small fluttering started in my toes and crawled up my body. Could this really be happening? Was Samuel really willing to uproot himself and move hundreds of miles away just for me?

He took my hand and got down on one knee. "Isabelle, will you be my wife?"

I paused and thought of all he was giving up. Then I forced myself to stop. If my reputation were sound, I'd follow him anywhere. A warm feeling spread throughout me, ending in a smile. I never thought I could care about someone so much.

I knelt down so our faces were level and ignored the wet grass beneath us. "Yes, I'll marry you, Samuel."

Samuel pressed his forehead to mine. "My strong, smart, and beautiful Isabelle. Forever shall not be long enough, but it is a start."

His hands wrapped around my waist. When his lips met mine, his passion swept me away.

Opening my eyes, I saw Mother standing at the edge of my vision. For a moment, I thought she was frowning, but as I focused on her, she smiled and tipped her hat to us. Leaning my cheek against Samuel's, I smiled back at her.

Mere months before, I'd promised myself to a man I felt little for and a life that held little for me. And now, I was planning a new life out West where my life would matter and I'd have Samuel by my side. This was a life I'd never envisioned . . . one I never could have imagined. And I had created it on my own.

I never thought I'd feel so alive.

AUTHOR'S NOTE

One of the first places I visited when I moved to the Fox Valley area was Bellevue Sanitarium. I was driving through Batavia and saw a sign that read, "Bellevue Sanitarium, Home to Mary Todd Lincoln in 1875." Having nursed an interest in the Lincolns for most of my life, I turned off the main road and drove up to the two-story yellow brick building. It is now a set of condos, but the exterior is much the same. I sat in my car imagining what life was like when Mary Todd Lincoln stayed there, and what had caused her to be admitted.

I tried to approach this story from many different angles before Isabelle's character came to me. One of the constraints my research presented was the stigma that was placed on sanitariums and how it could ruin a young woman's life. Knowing that stigma existed, I wondered if there was any reason a woman would choose to live there. From that one thought, Isabelle's story began to take shape.

Bellevue Place was a home for upper-class troubled women. In May of 1875 there were about twenty women living there with a wide variety of ailments. At least one woman suffered from eating disorders, as Marilla does in this story. Another woman had to keep her hair very short because she pulled it out otherwise. And others were simply in need of a break from their lives. Some women lived their entire lives there, but others were genuinely cured by the Pattersons' care.

Dr. Patterson was the director of the sanitarium. His wife was in charge of the day-to-day staff duties. Some sources state that Dr. Patterson's son was his assistant. In my research I wasn't able to confirm the fact that he had children. Some sources supported the son, others claimed there was a daughter who possibly had severe autism. Due to the lack of consistent information, I chose not to include children for them.

Dr. Patterson believed in a regimen of a good diet, outside activity, regular bathing, and mental stimulation. He said in an ad for Bellevue that they would not use drugs on patients unless absolutely necessary. The only exception I found in my research was the use of sedatives that were administered to some patients at bedtime to aid in sleep and to others when they got out of hand.

Much of Mrs. Lincoln's story was omitted from this book, as it is Isabelle's story. Mary Lincoln's life was filled with sadness. After the death of her third son, Tad Lincoln, Mary Lincoln's behavior became erratic. She sent telegrams to her eldest and only surviving son, Robert, claiming visions of him on his deathbed. She also insisted that he was trying to murder her. She wrote letters complaining of an Indian spirit who would rip off her scalp and replace it with another one, stick pins in her eyes, and beat her head with a tomahawk. Eventually, Robert feared for his mother's health and made the tough decision to have her declared legally insane. The process for this involved taking his mother to trial.

There have been numerous debates as to the reasons behind Robert's decision. Some claim he was worried about the amount of money she was spending. Others say he was justly worried for her mental health. Others point to the laundry list of embarrassing events she caused and say that Robert needed to put her away. I chose to take the view that Robert was both worried for his mother and embarrassed with her behavior.

Like Isabelle, Mary Lincoln obtained her own freedom from the sanitarium. With the help of a lawyer friend, Myra

Bradwell (and Myra's husband), Mrs. Lincoln gained enough interest in her case to get Robert to sign her release papers. A year later, in June 1876, the courts declared her sane. Her sister offered her a room in her house in Springfield. Mrs. Lincoln didn't stay there long, however, due to too many painful memories of her life with Abraham before the war. She died July 16, 1882.

ACKNOWLEDGMENTS

There are many people who helped bring Isabelle's story to life. I'd like to thank my agent, Steven Chudney, for championing Isabelle's story and finding it a home, Martin Biro and the whole Kensington family for bringing her to life, and my wonderful critique partners for listening to endless versions of these pages. Jennifer, Jenny, Natalie, Jenn—this book would not be here without you. And last (but never least), I have to thank my wonderful husband, who has listened to me fret over Isabelle for years. Thanks to all for the love and support.

Connect with Us

Visit us online at
KensingtonBooks.com
to read more from your favorite authors, see books
by series, view reading group guides, and more.

Join us on social media

for sneak peeks, chances to win books and prize packs,
and to share your thoughts with other readers.

facebook.com/kensingtonpublishing
twitter.com/kensingtonbooks

Tell us what you think!

To share your thoughts, submit a review,
or sign up for our eNewsletters, please visit:
KensingtonBooks.com/TellUs.